LETTERS
TO OMAR

LETTERS
TO OMAR

RACHEL WYATT

COTEAU BOOKS

© Rachel Wyatt, 2010

Edited by Jack Hodgins
Designed by Tania Craan
Printed and bound in Canada at Friesens

LIBRARY AND ARCHIVES CANADA CATALOGUING IN PUBLICATION

Wyatt, Rachel, 1929-
    Letters to Omar / Rachel Wyatt.

ISBN 978-1-55050-448-4

    I. Title.

PS8595.Y3L48 2010   C813'.54   C2010-903842-8
10 9 8 7 6 5 4 3 2 1

2517 Victoria Avenue
Regina, Saskatchewan
Canada   S4P 0T2

AVAILABLE IN CANADA FROM:
Publishers Group Canada
9050 Shaughnessy Street
Vancouver, BC, Canada   V6P 6E5

Coteau Books gratefully acknowledges the financial support of its publishing program by: the Saskatchewan Arts Board, the Canada Council for the Arts, the Government of Canada through the Canada Book Fund, the Government of Saskatchewan through the Creative Economy Entrepreneurial Fund, the Association for the Export of Canadian Books and the City of Regina Arts Commission.

In memory of P.K. Page; a perfect friend.

Let us... linger in the beautiful foolishness of things.
Okakura-Kakuzo, *The Cup of Humanity*

Chapter 1

JAKE WAS A LOVELY BOY. Dorothy didn't tell him that. She gave him a bottle of beer and watched him snap the top off.

"Thanks, Great Aunt D."

"Now that you're over twenty how about just calling me Dorothy."

"You behave like an aunt."

"Being your granny's cousin only makes me something twice removed. Though I suppose we do share a little blood, a gene or two."

He was sipping beer from the bottle as if he had all the time in the world and would be back tomorrow, as if he weren't about to set off to Afghanistan, as if she hadn't put the idea into his head.

"I'd love to go myself, you know."

"You'd frighten them – Dorothy."

"Perhaps they need a few old women out there to shake some sense into them."

"You'd get shot."

"That's something you must avoid at all costs. Your mother would never forgive me."

"I'd be pretty upset myself."

She turned away and rinsed her hands under the tap, wishing she could wash away the words she'd said to him only a month ago. Who would believe that anything in this bureaucrat-infested world could happen so quickly?

"I went to see the guy of my own accord," he said, reading her thoughts. "Truly. And even now I can turn around and say no if I want. I don't have to go. But I'm dying to get over there. It will be an 'awfully big adventure.'"

"Don't quote that. I should have read better stories to you when you were little. About birds and flowers and talking kittens."

He had his grandmother Kate's crooked smile and his mother's green eyes. They said he inherited his reddish hair from Jonathan Brooks, the father he'd never seen.

"You'll go back to university next year?"

"Depends. I guess. Right now I don't want to go on with engineering."

He looked at the clock and stood up.

"Plane to catch," he said. "Got to pick up Mom and my stuff."

"Emails. You'll send emails?"

"Of course."

Of course! Messages could bounce off satellites but he would still need an earthly connection. He walked down the path. He had kissed her. He had gone. The chocolate Easter Bunny she'd bought him for the journey was still lying on the table. She rinsed out the beer bottle and put it on the table by the door for recycling.

∽

Her middle finger was painful again so she tapped at the computer keyboard with her thumb to open the file and read what she'd written that morning. *Dear Mr. Sharif,* (he wasn't a duke or a prince of the church so that sounded right and not over-familiar) *It's your birthday today so I thought I would write. You're seventy-four. I'm two years younger, born in 1934. Funny thing, age. A few weeks ago, I was sitting here saying to myself that I have most of my own teeth, my hair hasn't fallen out yet and I can keep arthritis at bay with pills, and that, therefore, I should do something useful.*

The phone rang as if her words had provoked it.

"Happy Easter, Elvira," she said in response to the girl's greeting.

Elvira was likely hoping Jake was still there but didn't ask, trusting to be told or maybe to hear his voice one last time. She only said politely, "How are you, Aunt Dorothy?" Elsie's granddaughter was even less of a relation than the boy but time and birthday gifts made strong bonds.

"I'm fine. The lights are flickering. A thunderstorm? An imminent power cut? The crook Gervais hacking away at the cable to my house? One more ploy to make me move. They think I'll go quietly into a retirement complex, three meals a day, medical help on call, Tuesday and Thursdays we go to the mall. At any rate, I'll keep on writing till the computer dies. Or I do. Are you doing anything special this weekend?"

Elvira murmured something about the snow up north being too poor for skiing.

Dorothy said, "This is a bad line. Come and see me when you can, dear," and hung up feeling that she should have been more pleasant. The china on the tray was not the girl's fault.

At least her ex-colleagues hadn't given her a two-thousand-piece jigsaw puzzle with a picture of a country cottage on it. Two years since the farewell party, April 3rd, 2004 to be exact, and a mite of anger was still stuck in her gut like a furball. We'll miss you around here, her co-workers had said insincerely. They'd long been muttering about her being kept on way past retirement, hinting at blackmail or sexual ties from decades ago when she might possibly have been young. *I was the boss's right-hand woman.* Someone else was in the corner office now, checking market prices, dealing with accounts, setting up meetings and arranging special events. It was a position of power. The parting gift, delicate blue and white teacups and saucers with plates to match, represented the staff's delight that old Dot would no longer be there to set them straight or to suggest to jelly-faced Melissa that she might eat fewer donuts and wear clothes that covered more of her skin.

Microwave and dishwasher-safe, the gift of china implied that she would have nothing more to do than make tea for her friends and wait for death. They would be surprised when she and Kate and Elsie were called to Rideau Hall to pick up a medal from the Governor General for their services to mankind and their pictures appeared in the paper and their names were passed to the Nobel committee in Stockholm for consideration. They had yet to do anything to earn a hint of that glory but Harvey Lent, the first stepping stone on the route to recognition for services rendered, was due to arrive in half an hour. She hoped the other two would be on time. As a group they had to look businesslike, viable, able.

The phone rang again. Elvira hadn't finished what she intended to say. Dorothy listened. She had, after all, put her name on a list of volunteer readers never expecting that Elvira's school would be the lucky winner. "I'll be there," she said, and marked the date down in her diary. It would be a chance to recruit the girl to help with the so far unplanned fundraising effort.

As for the boy, Mr. S., it was in fact only a suggestion but his mother sees it as persuasion. Was it a cop-out, a substitute for not being able to go there myself? It's not as if he'll really be in harm's way. Not for a time anyway. And it was not, absolutely not, anything to do with Kate and my father. I got over that a very long time ago.

There has to be a long training period, hasn't there? Besides, if people don't have adventures when they're young, they tend to take risks when they're old and that can be a disaster.

I read a piece about you in the paper this morning, an interview in which you said you'd given up drink and gambling and that you are leading a quiet life. I want you to know how glad I am. I feel we have known each other for forty years, ever since I first saw you tramping through the snow to be with your love. You were a modest hero then and I'm pleased that, in your old age, you have opted for dignity. I didn't want to see you going off debauched into that good night.

Had she remembered milk? Did Harvey Lent take sugar? She'd bought peanut butter cookies. Was he allergic to nuts? She'd switch the kettle on as soon as she heard the doorbell. They'd moved the meeting from Tuesday to this afternoon because Elsie had the Red Cross event to attend. Elsie and Richard led a life a bit closer to Mr. Sharif's than hers or Kate's, and allowances had to be made for the burden of wealth.

We share the same zodiac sign but my life has been very different from yours. I mean, for instance, you live free in a fancy hotel while I live in this little house where I can't afford to have the bathroom fixed or new tiles laid on the roof even if there was time. Toronto, my city, isn't Paris but it has gracious old buildings, a Great Lake, and trees that glow red and gold in the fall. Anyway, despite our different backgrounds, we've been tied together by a thread that may be invisible to you but is there all the same. I've always been able to see from your eyes that we are on the same wavelength so to speak.

Perhaps they'd manage to stick to the agenda today instead of wandering off into gossip and the latest tennis scores and what had happened to the Williams sisters, who seemed to have peaked too young. Cousin Kate had a way of tuning out when she disagreed with what was going on instead of addressing the issue. In fact she tuned out a good deal of the time these days. If Kate did arrive first, Dorothy would say in a subtle way that it really was time she got over Robert the swine's departure. And what was this WorldAidNow project all about if not to help her do that? But Kate had regressed and liked to talk about their early days in Canada as if they'd been pioneers. She would hark back to the barely remembered years in Yorkshire as if they'd been a happier time. As if Dorothy's dad, Dennis, had done harm when he persuaded his brother's widow, Kathleen, to bring her daughter Kate to Canada too and share a house in Niagara Falls.

It had made sense for the two single parents to live together with their girls. And there had been plenty of good times. Right now though, the past hung around Kate's neck like the proverbial bird, and no amount of telling her to move on made a scrap of difference. She retreated into those early years as to a safe place. But the past was a creaky structure and didn't offer firm support. Last week Kate had even mentioned the third child again, a phantom they'd created out of flimsy evidence when they were teenagers and for whom they had occasionally searched.

The Mozart symphony she had been half-hearing on CBC radio had been replaced by the Vivaldi piece that always made her feel impelled to jump up and down. She used her new remote to switch it off.

If Elsie arrived first, she would straighten the furniture, add more cookies to the plate, avoid questions. Getting involved in the tragedies of the wider world might help her to see that Alice had simply made a choice and that it wasn't her parents' fault. She should be thankful that one of her daughters lived nearby and still spoke to her, even if it was only Isabel the Disillusioned.

So there you were, tramping through the snow in your shabby coat while I was doing exactly the same here in

*Toronto. Our climates were similar. Our worlds were differ-
ent. I was going quietly every day to the office where I
worked for Mr. Big Money, while all around you people were
invading the homes of the very rich and committing bloody
deeds in the name, as usual, of freedom. You suffered bravely
as you trudged towards Lara across a million cinema screens.*

No sense in telling the old actor that she also had enjoyed
an affair or two. It was none of his business. She'd googled
his name but there was too much information and she preferred her own version of the facts.

All the print on the screen suddenly became miniscule.
For the hundredth time, she cursed Bill Gates, his company
and all who worked therein. She tapped every key she could
think of. Went to the useless 'help' file. Nothing worked.
And then, of its own accord, the type returned to normal. It
had occurred to her more than once that if her first husband,
Graham J. Graham, had owned a computer, he might not
have died in the way he did. Though, in moments like these,
she could picture him ripping the monitor from its moorings
and angrily heading down to the lake with it clutched to his
chest and throwing it into the water, this time letting go. No
one knew and no one would ever know whether he had simply meant to throw his typewriter into the torrent that
evening and then return home. She still thought of him fondly and hoped he knew in his last moments that his death was
not her fault: Her final words to him had not been meant as
a command.

The phone rang again. Politely she apologized to Aretha
Jones for backing out of Meals on Wheels. She had simply,
she said, in the months after her retirement, taken on too
much. It was time to focus her energies and commit to one
thing in a serious way. A slight bitterness in Aretha's voice
told her not to expect food brought to her door a year or
two hence when she was too weak to open a can of soup.

A few weeks ago, when she'd told Kate and Elsie that it simply wasn't enough to sit around drinking coffee and saying, did you see the news last night, isn't it terrible, the world's in a mess, people are starving/dying/homeless, they'd raised their eyebrows in a here-she-goes-again way and Elsie remarked that she did her share, thank you. But they'd come around, and, after surveying all the charitable organisations that were reputable, the ones that spent less on administration than they disbursed, they'd picked WorldAidNow&Tomorrow and laid out a plan. Now they were three elderly women with a purpose. Acronym:TEWP. Website: Not yet and maybe never.

You first became truly exotic to me, Mr. Sharif, when I saw you in the desert. Deserts are rare here though I believe there is a small one in British Columbia – without the camels. But there you were all in white, and with that headdress; a sheikh to your toenails. If I'd been there, I would have leapt – can you leap onto a camel? – onto the saddle with you. It would have been easier perhaps if you'd made the animal kneel down the way they do. In your tent, we would have drunk coffee out of tiny cups and eaten delicate sweet cakes and succulent dates, the sort we used to have at Christmas that came in those barge-shaped boxes. And then as the sun set suddenly as I believe it does in the Sahara because there are no trees or hills for it to sink slowly behind, we might have lain down on your couch.

My first husband, perhaps knowing that he would come to an untimely and sad end, was not great in bed. Sex of the joyful kind was of little interest to him. So you won't mind me telling you that our relationship, yours and mine, has been more intimate than you might have imagined. I haven't mentioned your accent in case you are embarrassed by it, but I love it; it has always made my heart flutter.

When Harvey Lent, WANT's Ontario director, arrived he would thank them for choosing his charity upon which to expend their efforts. That would be the way he talked, *expend your efforts, ladies,* as he metaphorically patted their heads, hers grey with fading brown streaks, Kate's white, and Elsie's costly chestnut, and told them that the need had diminished; all was right with the world and they could go back to their tatting. Or would he see them as a promising group with a prospect at least of large bequests in case of death? Death was certain and, given their ages, perhaps not far off. What Lent wouldn't see was their potential and, in her case, a need to make up for past sins.

I was sorry a few years ago when I learned that you were spending all your nights playing bridge or hanging around casinos. It cooled our friendship for a while. Though I suppose you might have said the same thing about me watching the same movie over and over or staying up nights writing to people I don't know. I gather that you get to spend time with your grandsons and I'm happy for you. I have no children.

Three-fifteen. Better get a move on. She'd printed out the agenda, short though it was, and also made a list of possible projects. At the meeting, Elsie would add class, Kate would add seriousness and she herself would sit there and try to look like a prime mover. Whatever that was. In any case, it was up to the director to impress them. Their effort might be small at the moment but it could grow, it could spread. Standing on the podium in Stockholm, modestly but becomingly dressed, listening to the official saying, *We honour these women for raising one billion dollars to help in our fight against world poverty,* they would be famous at last. Of course they would have to donate the money to the cause but surely she could keep a little bit back to have the bathroom done over and maybe take a trip to Bilbao to visit the new museum.

I'd like to tell you something about the room I'm sitting in as I write this. The two armchairs face the window and are covered in blue leather and are extremely comfortable. This table is marked with stains from hot coffee cups. My last husband was from Russia and had no use for coasters. There are two of my paintings on the wall and two brass candlesticks on the mantel. Six family photographs stand on top of the television: Pictures of my parents on their wedding day, and of my 'niece' and 'nephew' and my 'great-nephew,' Jake. Delphine and her brother Brian are my cousin Kate's children so they're really second cousins. Delphine's son, Jake, therefore is perhaps a third cousin, but we won't climb up the family tree right now.

Delphine hadn't yet got around to blaming her for Jake's departure but if anything were to happen to the boy, God forbid, there would be no forgiveness. Not ever. The affection of years would be cast at once into the furnace of hate.

She picked up the wedding photograph and stared at her mother's face. If she'd lived, would she have been loving and kind? "Would we," she asked the pretty face, "have argued as I grew older about my clothes, my friends, my decisions? I wish... I have often wished..."

I wonder whose photographs you keep in your hotel room in Paris. I imagine there to be several large pieces of black and white furniture with acres of space between. Someone makes sure there are always fresh flowers. There are fine oriental rugs on the floor. And I bet it smells ever so slightly of incense.

She inhaled. Her sense of smell was no longer acute. She got up to light the candle. In moments its piney scent would cover stale odours of cooking, unclean corners and just plain daily neglect.

On my bedroom wall, there is a picture of you, a poster really, from the movie. It's you dressed in your uniform, looking bewildered and somehow lost. (I called my last cat Zhivago, by the way.) The poster is curling at the edges and keeps slipping off the wall. Zhivago died of old age last spring. My friend, Matt, says he can get me a new poster by ordering it on the Internet. I just feel that's very impersonal.

So I have a request, no, not for money, Mr. Sharif, though, being rich, I expect you get a lot of letters asking for help with granny's expenses in the Home or to finance an amateur movie or to send young Dwayne to India to find his soul. Money would spoil what you and I have between us.

"Though I must say a few thousand would come in handy," she said aloud. "But let's not get into the unequal distribution of wealth right now." She began to type more quickly; the errors could be corrected later. The director had to be presented with women who were in all senses *with it.* She came to the point.

Mr. Sharif, though, if you'll pardon the liberty, I've always called you Omar in private, what I would really like is a photograph, a black and white picture of you as you are now. I don't want one of you as you were then. In a sense we have grown old together and I would like a picture that reflects our age.

I've been too shy to ask before but like you said in the interview, life is for living, not for wasting time. In return, I'll send you a picture of myself taken at the company's Christmas dance four years ago. The dress isn't something I would ever wear to have dinner with you in your Paris hotel but it was right for that particular occasion.

She looked out the window hoping to see her cousin, but it wasn't Kate who was walking up the path, it was him, the director, Harvey Lent himself, arriving early, damn him. Early people were the spies of the world, the overeager, the ones who were always there first. Whenever you had an appointment with them, even if you got there on time, you were already late. And here he was, blue down jacket, sweater, briefcase, taut expression. She cast a quick glance around to make sure there were no signs of degeneracy lying about, pushed her hand through her hair and straightened her collar to create an impression of elderly competence. She opened the door wide in a welcoming way and said, "Do come in, Mr. Sharif."

∽

They would have been on time if Kate hadn't wanted to stop in at the post office.

And then it was embarrassing. International postage? The same price? England, Afghanistan, China? Regardless of distance. It makes no difference, madam. The clerk handed over the stamps with a shake of her head, and then Elsie reminded Kate that she might just as well give the letter to Mr. Lent to send over in whatever kind of system WorldAidNow used for its own mail. And she felt sad that her friend's mind had deteriorated so much that buying stamps was a difficulty. In any case, Jake hadn't left the country yet. Why was she writing so soon? Nothing had happened that he didn't know.

As they were leaving the store, and it was a store, its shelves full of artifacts for sale – crafts, cards, toys – and not a place simply dedicated to incoming and outgoing mail, Kate said, "I'm not crazy. I was thinking about the distance and the odds of getting shot or blown up. Delivering mail here in Toronto. Delivering mail in Baghdad or Kandahar. There is a difference, Elsie."

"No there isn't."

"OK!"

"Sorry, Kate. The Boreks' dog woke me up at five. I complain and it's quiet for a few days. But then they let it stay out again. Richard bought me some earplugs but I'm afraid to wear them in case I miss something. I want to move to a place in the middle of a hundred acres with no neighbours."

"And no social life. You'd die."

"What do you mean? I'm not some hare-brained idiot flitting about from party to party. I work. It's all for charity. You know that."

There was a silence. The light turned red as Elsie drove through the intersection. She could feel Kate putting her own foot on an imaginary brake.

"I don't know how Delphine's going to cope now that Jake's gone," Kate said.

"Look how she coped when she got pregnant." Elsie said.

"Your Alice was a big help, then."

"Yes."

"Isabel and Mike are back home?"

"Before she went to Paris I told her. Isabel, I said, be content with the books. Or if you must go, take in Chartres, go to Rheims. She was letting herself in for disenchantment. The man's been dead for fifty years. Stories are bound to come out. Saints always fall off their pedestals sooner or later. Most of them."

"I'd like to go to France one more time," Kate said.

"Before!"

Kate laughed. "It's got to be before we're eighty now."

"We didn't write down what we wished for 'before seventy.'"

"It didn't seem worthwhile, and yet here we still are. We didn't expect to have expectations, I guess."

"You got what you wanted before you turned forty."

"What I said I wanted: children and tenure."

"What more could you have asked for?"

"Things I didn't know were available to me. Dorothy kept the lists?"

"Yes," Elsie answered, "she has."

"We haven't had a 'girls' outing' since you sold the cottage."

"Richard sold the cottage! Isabel still moans about it and it's been four years." "Do you miss it?"

"I don't miss the driving."

"Those Labour Day weekends were great."

They had laughed and splashed around in the lake and drunk too much wine and then driven back from Muskoka on the Sunday so that Elsie and Kate could get their kids ready for school. And once every decade they'd written out their desires and ambitions: things they wanted to achieve and acquire before they were thirty, forty, fifty, sixty.

"Before I'm eighty," Kate said, "I think I'd like to die."

Elsie didn't allow herself to feel guilty about Kate's remark. Sorry, yes, that Kate was the first of them to lose a grip on life. In their youth, she'd been the leader, the bright young woman who played the tunes they danced to and got them into trouble and out of it. Then for years she'd been the busy academic, writing, talking, involved. But she hung back from life now. She'd allowed herself to become a sorrowing widow and the man wasn't even dead, only absconded. And today she was fretting because Delphine's boy, her grandson, was flying towards danger. It was partly to rouse Kate into action that Dorothy had set up this charitable venture. Elsie looked at her friend and wanted to shake her. Her coat was a sandy beige. No coloured scarf enlivened her appearance. No touch of lipstick enhanced her mouth. With her high cheekbones and wide-set eyes she could, even at this age, have looked beautiful. There must have been some Viking blood in her Yorkshire forebears. But she was pale, drab. In fact, she sagged. And her new hearing aids were visible beneath strands of hair.

"I'm going to take you to my spa, next week," Elsie told her.

"It's too expensive."

"My treat."

"I mean, generally. We shouldn't be spending money like that."

"Then the spa will go out of business and seven nice young people will lose their jobs and go home to live off their parents. Not to mention the ones who make those aromatic oils and all the equipment. In India and Brazil where they gather the coconuts and beans for oil, poor peasants will..."

"Shut up, Elsie."

Elsie knew that one of Kate's sorrows, if sorrows could be counted like birds on a wire, was her loss of scholarly advantage. She'd retired ten years ago, at sixty-two, and now others were publishing papers on the frequency with which Peter Walsh fingered his penknife while he thought of Clarissa Dalloway and on the true effect of sub-zero temperatures on the Canadian novel. Young postgrads were writing books about the spread of information technology and the consequent decline of literature and Kate's name no longer appeared in highbrow journals.

For years, because she was absorbed in a departmental row at the time, Kate had blamed herself for her daughter's 'mistake.' But Delphine, as Elsie could have told her then, was a sexy little teenager and her mother didn't know the half of it. She stifled the thought that was approaching, *Alice would never*, because the reason why Alice 'would never' had become obvious over time. In any case, the 'mistake' had turned out to be a joy – till today.

She parked the BMW outside one of the handsome brick homes at the top end of the street. The two empty frame houses on either side of Dorothy's at the end of the cul-de-sac gave the crescent a dangerous appearance; all kinds of squatters, druggies and criminals could move in any day, start fires, shoot each other. At the very least it was a prime location for rats.

Kate peered in the window.

"He's not much to look at," she murmured.

Elsie recognized another of her friend's regrets and said, "We're here to back up Dorothy in this new scheme of hers. What he's like is unimportant."

She could see the man leaning backwards to avoid a torrent of words and possibly spit.

"Delphine will never forgive her if anything happens," Kate said, thinking of Jake.

"They protect them well," Elsie said, not at all sure that 'they' did or even if 'they' existed. It was a mere comforting lie, a few words that meant, *let's go in and do what we're here to do.*

Dorothy had set out fine cups and saucers instead of her usual mugs and arranged cookies on a plate with unaccustomed elegance. There were even small cloth napkins. She welcomed them and introduced them to the slight, worried-looking man on the sofa. He did make an effort to stand but Elsie held out a commanding hand and he sat down again.

"Well, Mr. Lent," she said. "To begin with, we'd like to plan an event that will bring in several thousand dollars."

"What I've been trying to explain to your friend," he said in a defensive way, "is that the money doesn't always get to the places where it's most needed."

"And I've been saying," Dorothy said, " that it's a sin and a crime and the money damn well should get to those who need it."

"You do see," Mr. Lent replied, "that we're not in control of the circumstances. It's a difficult environment. That's why we need young people."

Kate looked at the man. He might have been a curate from a Victorian novel hoping, perhaps, to marry one of the daughters of the house except that here there were no daughters. What he truly was, this harmless-looking man, was a pander for a modern minotaur. Need young people indeed! And he was here because Dorothy had woken up one morning with an excess of charity in her mind, a dangerous feeling that something must be done and that she and her friend and her cousin were the ones to do it.

Elsie said, "We were only suggesting, Mr. Lent, that if our first effort works as well as we expect it to, we could do more. I have contacts. We have ideas."

"It's a matter," the man said, "of sending the right message."

Dorothy half rose from her chair and then said, "We are not stupid, Mr. Lent."

Perhaps we are, Kate thought, and then put herself into the foreground and made her statement.

"What we have in mind is an approach to people who are able to donate large sums. We might put together a mixed-media show to let them see what is at stake here. By the end of May, we'll have something to demonstrate what we mean to do. We'll start with a small event. Even spreading the word surely makes a difference."

The man nodded and smiled, half-believing, but Kate knew that what he really wanted was to get away from these three elderly harpies as fast as he could.

"There's still the matter of getting the money to the right place," he said.

"That's your job, surely," Elsie replied.

"Ah, not exactly. There's an office in Ottawa. They dispense the funds. See where the most need is. And so on."

"So what's the problem?"

"Warlords, Mrs. Graham. AK-47s. Opium."

Kate said, "What we need to know, Mr. Lent, is whether it's worthwhile doing anything. If we're simply making money for thieves, why should we bother?"

There she had him. Dorothy was pleased with her. She watched the man backtrack, cookie crumbs dropping down his jacket. Yes, well, it was just that – and, of course, every effort would be made and they would do their best to get the money to the school or the hospital and hope that the right kind of people had control of the village wherever it was. And even the widow's mite...

Dorothy saw him out, feeling the pent-up thoughts of her friends aimed at her back like arrows.

"He thinks we're three crazy old women," Elsie said.

"Let's show him we're not."

"Or prove that we are," Kate said. "He wasn't in the least pleased. He wants donations from rich people. He sees us as bake-sale material. Girl Guide cookie sellers. Bottle collectors."

Elsie said, "It's all a matter of planning."

"I'll get us a drink."

"Not for me," Elsie said. "I've got Richard's sister and family coming for dinner tomorrow and I have to pick up a few things. I wanted them to come on Monday but no. It has to be what suits her. I'm not doing the whole Easter feast thing. It's a casserole I just have to reheat, but there's the salad and the table."

Dorothy brought Elsie a glass of cranberry juice and herself and Kate a glass of the new organic Merlot she wanted to try.

"Here's to TEWP!"

"Do you still have the 'before' lists?" Kate asked.

"You want to look at them now?"

"No she doesn't," Elsie said. "She thinks we should write down what we want before we turn eighty. Just staying alive and healthy will do for me, thank you."

Dorothy thought of Jake and wished for him to stay alive till he was thirty, forty and decades beyond.

"You have to admit," Kate said, "that looking at us from Lent's point of view, we are three old women. Past it."

"Speak for yourself, Kate," Dorothy answered. "Drink up both of you and go home and think of brilliant ideas. I have a letter to write."

Before she touched the keyboard, she thought for a while about inequality. And this was a letter she would send. After all, there was a shared secret here.

Dear Mr. Ericsson. (He would note the formality and be pleased)

My friends and I are involved in raising money to help with the tragic civilian situation in Afghanistan. We have thought about Iraq but that disaster is beyond any slight help we might give. Or anyone perhaps. I thought that given the years we spent working together (Discreet, Dorothy. Very good. Avoid any hint of blackmail.), *you might be happy to make a contribution. A cheque made out to me will go towards the arrangements for our first event. And you will certainly be invited to whatever it turns out to be.* (Not very businesslike.) *Of course you will be named as a sponsor.*

Best wishes,

Dorothy

After she'd mailed the letter, she wondered whether he would expect a tax receipt. Too late she realized that she should have asked him to make out the cheque to WANT.

∽

Kate chopped the parsley fine. She loved its old-fashioned mellow flavour. The board shook as she banged the knife down hard. The grated breadcrumbs and lemon peel were already in the bowl. She'd cleaned the capon inside and out and would put the dressing into it at the last minute. Delphine's first Easter without Jake. Perhaps it would be smart to rent a video tomorrow and avoid too much reminiscence. It might be smarter still to go to church, but neither of them had been inside a holy place for years. It was Dorothy's fault. There she was at her age stirring things up almost as if – almost as if, having no kids of her own, she was jealous of other people's. Jake should have been at university instead of heading off to a country so bleak and so violent.

That line from the hymn they'd sung at school, *Time like an ever-rolling stream bears all our sons away,* was dismal and prophetic. Time didn't have to take her grandson. Of course she'd have lost Jake long before if the family hadn't been religious then and Robert a pillar of the church. What if, all those years ago, someone had used the words *abort or adopt*? It didn't bear thinking about. She was grateful to the god they'd sung and prayed to for keeping the surprise baby safe. In that world no one went around altering *sons to persons*, or adding *daughters* and changing the rhythm of old poetic lines.

How the teachers at Graydon High had discovered that Delphine was pregnant before her own mother had noticed was a mystery.

"We can't tolerate this kind of thing in our school." There they were like two bad children, mother and daughter, called into the principal's office on that cold March morning twenty-three years ago. In some schools there would have been compassion and help, but here there was chilly accusation.

The day came back to her with astounding clarity. Roualt's painting behind Mr. Marston's chair never lost its colour. The voices from the schoolyard below were as shrill as today's crows. The edges of the wooden desk remained sharp to the touch. No details of that scene had faded the way memories are meant to do over time. And then Delphine leant forward and threw up over Mr. Marston's desk. Kate was never sure which of them screamed. But they left the mess for him to clear up and walked out without, as she happily recalled, an apology.

The scream that began that day was continuous: A long loud wail that came from the mouths, serially, of her mother, her friend and, seven and a half months later, the baby. The baby had been a huge surprise to Brian, who had not been let in on the secret and was too busy playing hockey and preparing for university to notice that his sister was growing larger. Or at least he had pretended not to know. He was a sly boy and surely couldn't have ignored all the whispering, the visits of older women and the fact that Delphine no longer went to school.

Robert had blamed Kate as if she'd told their daughter to go and have sex with the Brooks' boy and get herself into 'that condition.' Sullenness festooned the house. But after a couple of weeks' deliberation, he had given Delphine a cheque for two thousand dollars and then stayed out of the way. He was about to be promoted and from then on, entering into his new role as if he had been born to it, Judge Charbonneau became a man of balanced opinion. He could have continued to be a distinguished member of the community, and they could still have been living in the house she'd hated to leave if only... I can't help myself, Kate, he'd said on Easter Sunday three years ago, looking at her as if he expected sympathy.

But way back then, barely heard amid the yelling and the cries of who's going to look after it and what were you thinking, a quiet voice had said gently, We will take care of it. That was Elsie's girl, Alice, Delphine's best friend. She'd talked to Delphine as if they were still twelve years old and not eighteen, conjuring up pictures of a playhouse in the backyard and dolls that could be left out all night in the rain without coming to harm. The next weeks and months were a blur, an expanding blur. And that summer, wearing a large hat and a long skirt, dragged down by both, Delphine had tried to work at the poetry they'd been studying in school before 'the fall,' because that was what they said. *She fell.* Into temptation, into a vat of boiling oil, into the arms of the rapidly disappearing Jonathan Brook. He had faded out of sight, out of the province. Too young to be a father, his mother said, which had led to strong words from Kate. And the poetry was dreary stuff: *Deep in the shady sadness of a vale, Far sunken...* So Delphine had given up on it and read Jane Austen to her unborn child instead. At least she'd read *Pride and Prejudice*, but most of the time she leafed through magazines, movie magazines, home care magazines, parent magazines, picking out advice, recipes, ads for everything that could be eaten, worn, sat in, slept on, visited.

Kate smiled as she recalled the day in the office and the ensuing turmoil and the deep pleasure of buying clothes for the doll who couldn't be left out in the backyard overnight. Her own mother's prognostications of a long descent into poverty without work, without qualifications, without a man because who would want her granddaughter now, hadn't removed the smile from Delphine's face as her belly swelled and all the older women she knew looked at her more fondly the larger she grew. *Have another piece of cake, Delphy, you're eating for two now.* And Alice kept on saying, *We will look after it.* Some friends hinted at dire consequences, a single mother, too young for motherhood, but none of those depressing sibyls had prophesied that her beloved grandson would head off to a country where he might be killed or badly injured.

Kate suggested calling the baby Helena if it was a girl, William if it was a boy. But when the baby arrived Delphine, holding him, looking up from the bed, said, "His name is

Jacob Chance Charbonneau." And any thought the Brooks
had of being grandparents to the child went out the window
along with any support they might have been about to offer.

"Jacob is a solid name," Delphine had said then. "And I
like hearing Johnny Mathis singing that song, and my
Chance is a 'fine thing.'" Rocking the baby gently, she
crooned, "'Chances are, your chances are awfully good.'"

Kate saw in that moment that the young mother was a
child herself. A child with a child. And she had wept.

Delphine had refused to put "father unknown" on the
birth certificate and persuaded Mrs. Brook and Jonathan to
come with her to the registrar's office. Looking like a
stunned deer, the boy had signed his name with a shaky
hand and allowed his photograph to be taken. *A child needs
to know who his parents are.* He'd fled back to university
in New Brunswick, married young and had four children.
The Brooks, sure that their son had been cunningly seduced,
never spoke to the Charbonneaus again. Their loss!

Delphine poured more green tea into the little cup and
rejoiced that she'd managed to suppress the impulse to shout
at Jake there in the airport, *After all I've done for you.* She
had instead put on a show of pride as he turned to wave one
last time before he disappeared through the entrance to
another universe. And he had not returned quickly through
the security gate to say, *I can't go, mother dear, how can I
leave you?* which, for five minutes, standing there like a
dumb statue, she'd half expected him to do.

So when she got back to the city after driving through
heavy holiday traffic, she'd come to *The Pink Wok* on Dundas,
Jake's favourite restaurant. Three tables away, the only other

customer was eating very slowly and staring around as if he wanted to make time pass. He was good-looking in a solid way, sad. Perhaps he was one of the recently unemployed. At her usual table near the back the old woman was deftly eating noodles with her chopsticks. Jake had figured she was the owner's mother because she was always there and possibly had been up since dawn chopping vegetables in the kitchen. However hard her current or past life, at least *her* son had not gone off to Afghanistan.

The place needed a better-written menu and a more enticing line on the window than "Our food will not disappoint." With the right ads in a few travel magazines and theatre programs and the offer of unique foods from a remote Chinese province, customers could be lured from as far away as Niagara and perhaps Buffalo too. Add in a picture of the Chinese grandmother wearing a cheongsam and smiling, and there'd be a queue to the corner. Maybe.

The waiter brought the packaged food to her table. Chow mein. Black bean chicken. Egg foo yung. He handed her a fortune cookie.

She sipped more tea and broke the crust open. The little slip of paper read, *You will meet your fate outside the door.* She and Jake had laughed over those predictions many times and never believed a word of them though she had kept several favourable ones in her wallet as if they were charms and might come true. This one sounded dire. Was she going to slip on the icy sidewalk and break her leg? As she lay in hospital, the limb suspended in traction, friends would murmur that the "accident" was due to her unhappiness at Jake's leaving. Or maybe her future in the shape of a handsome man was even now approaching, slowing down his steps so that he would be outside at exactly the right moment. And how was she to know which moment that was? If she went out of the restaurant too soon, he would still be two blocks back and she could hardly stand there waiting for him. If she went out too late, he'd be crossing the road, out of sight, never to be met in this lifetime.

She caught the waiter's eye to let him know she wanted the check. She would allow fate to take its course as it always did in any case. Fate could have held back the letter confirming Jake's position with the aid organization. The post office was not always efficient. Thousands of letters got lost every year, delivered to the wrong address or mangled in the machinery. But this one with its call to the war zone had arrived at the right place, neither stolen nor chewed by the dog next door. She herself had carried it to her son like a butler in a movie except that she had no silver tray. While he opened it she had, in a fair imitation of nonchalance, gone to stack the breakfast dishes. Then she allowed him to tell her the news, managing a taut smile and, "That's great, Jake," in response. And now he had gone. At this very moment the plane was probably skimming down the runway.

She wanted to spend the entire weekend taking stock of the gap in her life. There was a sudden deficit. From that morning in the principal's office to this, her son had been there. His life had been part of her life and the beat of his music had throbbed through the house. In all of his days so far, even when he was away at Western, there had been considerations, plans to make, clothes to buy.

You're still a good-looking woman, Delphine, her friends had begun to say after Bert's accident, some of them insensitively soon after, as if with all her advertising skills, she should go out and market herself. Now they would renew the attack. She pictured the ad: Woman, 42, a little on the plump side, round face, brown hair not grey yet, green eyes, seeks male for sex and other purposes. Job: Assistant Creative Director for Hunt and Berdak Advertising. Hobbies: reading, watching TV, avoiding strenuous exercise.

She walked out of the restaurant gingerly. City workmen had cleared the ice and salted the sidewalk. Falling wasn't an option here. She looked right and left. There was no one coming in either direction. Her car was in its parking spot across the road. She smiled at her own silliness and looked up at the sky. Fate in any shape was not apparent. She moved away from the building in case a chunk of masonry decided to fall on her head. There were footsteps behind her. The man from the other table had come out of the restaurant. She turned to look at him. He stood still and appeared to be waiting for her to speak.

"Jonathan?" she said.

"Marilyn?" he replied, laughing.

"I'm sorry. I thought you were someone I once knew."

"Well, I could say I remember you from somewhere but it wouldn't be true."

"'Marilyn?'"

"Someone I once knew."

"My fortune cookie."

"Mine too."

She had to go home. Standing there waiting for her fate to be delivered to her like a pizza-hold-the-anchovies, was ridiculous. And besides it was cold and snowflakes were beginning to drift down. A late storm was threatened, the last bite of winter.

"Goodbye, 'Jonathan,'" she said.

"See you around, 'Marilyn.'"

He strode towards the art gallery and for a moment she watched him. He was wearing a smart navy topcoat, no hat, pulling on gloves. Well, you let that one get away, she told herself. And then remembered her reason for being in the restaurant. Chance, the fine thing, had set out on his adventure. She came back to grief. It was no time to be looking for fate in the shape of a man.

Bert, her partner for ten good years, Jake's loving stepfather, had driven off an icy road into a tree when the boy was thirteen and there had been no live-in lovers since then. She and Jake had mourned together and survived together, cheering each other along in the dark moments. And now he was gone. *I'll email. I'll send pictures.* He would meet a sensuous veiled woman who spoke only Afghan, they would have six children, he would forget his own language and never return. *Be careful, my child.*

She drove home with care, had driven with care ever since that awful night when the cop had appeared on the doorstep with his black news. The radio announcer said, "As of tomorrow, the Don Valley Parkway North will be down to one lane." She switched stations and found Diana Krall singing, "Love me. Love you, baby." Humming along, she parked the car alongside the curb outside her house and saw a man standing at the door. Waiting. Waiting for her. She'd won the lottery and the bag in his hand was full of money? Or tickets for a trip to Vegas? Or was he going to jump at her, force her to open the door and let him inside and steal the picture her mother thought was a Braque? She reached for her cellphone.

"Don't do that," the man shouted. "It's all right."

"Jonathan?" she said for the second time in an hour, feeling foolish and wondering why she expected to see him of all people. What did she want after all this time for Chrissake? An apology!

The person was half turned towards her. He was wearing a leather jacket and gloves and holding a large bag.

"I don't need anything today," she said as she got closer to him.

"I'm not selling," he said.

She saw that besides his soft bag, he was carrying a long narrow instrument case, the kind that mafia hit men use as a cover for their machine guns.

I should turn and go back to the car and drive around till he's gone.

The man reached for her. Delphine bashed him with the bag from the restaurant. Noodles and vegetables burst out of it and sprayed onto his jacket.

"Hey! Don't you remember our promise, Delphine?"

Delphine looked at the features, the short blonde hair, the smooth cheeks, and saw familiarity but recalled no promise.

The stranger laughed. "We always said that wherever we were, whatever we were doing, we'd meet up again when we were forty. And here I am. Only two years late." He set his instrument case down on the step and brushed Chinese food off his shoulders. "I've come to see the doll who couldn't be left out in the rain."

Kate prodded the fattest part of the capon and watched the juice trickle out. Was that a slight tinge of pink? She poked the fork into the skin by the leg and the leg came loose. It was cooked. Was it overcooked? The potatoes mashed with parsnips and butter were ready and the beans were strained. The others had offered to help but this was the cook's private mad moment. Stirring the gravy with one hand, she shook the jar of dressing over the salad with the other. She'd torn the recipe out of a magazine in the dentist's waiting room. It was such a weird mixture that she felt it had to be good: Equal parts vinegar, oil and marmalade. The gravy was a fat-free chicken stock, white wine and herb concoction. Grey as it looked, it tasted delicious.

The guinea pigs in the other room were talking quietly.

"I really thought he was some kind of saint." That was Isabel.

Then Mike's deep voice. "And what saint were you out with till 9 o'clock that night? That's what I'd like to know."

"I got lost."

It was unlike Mike to be aggressive. In all the six years he and Isabel had been together, Kate had never heard him speak sharply to her. Why here and why now?

Delphine said, "It's easy to get lost in a foreign city."

As Kate poured the gravy into its boat, she heard Dorothy comment, "It's a sad thing when someone you've admired loses their gloss."

"What is stupid," Mike went on, "is to go about having illusions about people you never knew in the first place."

"You're not likely to have illusions about someone you know," Dorothy said. "Once you get to know them."

"Isabel," Kate called. "Could you give me a hand, please."

Isabel was near tears. "Mike never said anything till now," she whispered to Kate. "It was the man in the Barron house, the one who told me the story. I went to a bar and had a glass of wine with him and then another. I couldn't help it."

"Perhaps Mike's hungry. Take the veggies in, please. It's all ready. Delphine!"

For the table, Kate had taken out the fine linen cloth and napkins that had been part of her mother's trousseau. The delicate drawn threadwork around the edges was torn here and there and all of it had to be washed by hand. But this was her first major feast in three years and she'd aimed for elegance. Beside each place, there was a small gift. And in the centre was a ceramic horseshoe filled with yellow and purple flowers, the colours of Easter. Sorrow and joy. The rarely used silver cutlery shone – she'd polished it yesterday. And she had actually gone out and bought six matching long-stemmed wineglasses. She was only sorry that Elsie wasn't here to admire her effort.

Delphine came into the kitchen and picked up the heavy dish with the capon on it and carried it into the other room. She set it down in front of Mike. Any of them were capable of slicing the beast, but it had always been a man's task. He picked up the carving knife and fork and began to cut into the breast with slow precision. Kate wanted to snatch the knife from him and take over but had to watch, fretting that he was giving everyone too little. But the plates were soon filled with vegetables, cranberry sauce, gravy.

She sat back and sighed and enjoyed the murmurs of praise and all the words that were a cover for the absence of Jake. She wished that Brian and Megan and their children lived nearer. Then it would have been a real family gathering, although Delphine and her brother had an edgy relationship and might have quarrelled.

Dorothy said, "Why do we have to have a feast at Easter? I doubt if they did that in the first years on the Third Day."

"Need to eat after Lent."

"It's just another excuse to pig out."

"Primitive," Mike said. "It's another day when the lonely and depressed get to feel lonelier and sadder."

Mike carried the troubles of the city on his back as if, all around him, here at the table, sat starving street people waiting to be fed. There was something about the man, in spite of his gentle face, that induced guilt. To forestall Dorothy who was taking a deep breath prior to weighing in with her own view of the matter, Kate said, "There is a beauty to Easter. The idea of renewal, of life after death, of redemption in a way."

"But what an awful way to die," Isabel said.

And for a moment Kate felt a shiver of dread and noticed that Delphine had stopped eating.

"The question is," Dorothy said, "was it necessary?"

"The real question is, was it true?"

"If so many people have believed over so many centuries, then perhaps that makes it true whether it happened or not."

"That sounds like Peter Pan and Tinker Bell, Mike," Isabel said. "Clap your hands if you believe in Jesus."

"Many do just that and so he lives on."

"Cut some more capon, please, Mike," Kate said. She could sense a downward spiral. None of them exactly believed in the Christian story now, but for her and Dorothy and even for Delphine, there were remnants of faith, pricks of conscience that made them uncomfortable to hear words of denial. They were in fact superstitious. She poured more wine into their glasses and waited for an upturn in the conversation.

"I made a blueberry pie, "Delphine put in. "Jake's favourite. Do you think they're having a celebration there?"

"Unless they're in some enclosed place, it might not be wise," Dorothy said. "Why are we sitting around the table enjoying this fine food when we should be weeping about the state of the world?"

Kate looked at the carving knife and then at her friend.

Isabel said, "You're a laugh a minute, Aunt Dorothy."

"I haven't finished. I was going to say that it's important to do what we've always done. Continue in our traditions. It makes a framework for us to live in. And in that way... in that way –"

Dorothy had lost herself in a web of ideas. Kate smiled. Her friend's mind had always been a crowded place and now that she was older her thoughts were sometimes hard to keep hold of – like slippery fish.

Isabel and Mike cleared the dishes while Delphine got strips of paper and pencils out of the sideboard drawer.

"They sell this game in a box now," Dorothy said. "Twenty-five dollars at least."

"I suppose it's cheaper than buying a dictionary if you haven't already got one," Kate answered.

Mike was the first to choose a word. "'Hexamerous,'" he read out and spelt it. Kate thought she knew what it meant and wrote her answer. When everyone had put down their own definitions of the word, they handed the slips to Mike who smiled as he read them out. "'The ability to satisfy six lovers at once.' 'A plague on all things American.' 'The curse of love.' Interesting, guys, but this is the right one. 'Having six parts.'"

"Six parts of what?" Dorothy asked.

"It doesn't say. Of anything, I guess."

A point for Kate.

Isabel gave them "hirple" and none of them came close to its true meaning. Dorothy picked "interjacency."

In the end, amid cries of unfair because she knew more Latin than they did and could figure out the roots of words, Kate won the chocolate egg.

Delphine left early saying she had a project to finish, taking a plate full of leftovers with her as if she planned to work through the night.

"We've filled the dishwasher," Isabel said. She went out of the door hand in hand with Mike. Reconciliation had taken place in the kitchen.

Dorothy was the last to leave. "If you can do this for a few, dear," she said, "think what you could do for a crowd."

Alone, Kate sat down and ate the last piece of pie. We eat for comfort, she thought. We eat for love.

Chapter 2

THE FIGURES ADDED UP ALL TOO WELL. Dorothy tried again. There was no hidden treasure. There would be no refund from a grasping government. Why don't you get an accountant? Elsie kept asking. But why pay a large fee when all her working life she had dealt with amounts much larger than these? She could still add and subtract and was proud of her ability to send the form electronically to the tax office. If there were errors, she would hear about them soon enough.

Not sure whether her indigestion was due to yesterday's capon and pie or the stress of Jake being in danger or worry about the promised fundraiser, she made a mug full of chicken bouillon from a cube and then sat down to calculate possible savings from income. There would be enough for a cheap flight to Paris and a train ticket from the airport to the Gare du Nord. But there it stopped. A hotel was out of the question and even a little *pension* if there still were such things would be too expensive. She pictured herself sitting in an all-night café near Sharif's hotel, ordering coffee and croissants till the money ran out, waiting and watching.

You would have thought that after three husbands I would have a decent amount of money to spend. But since Graham's death appeared to be suicide, the insurance company wouldn't pay up. Some people thought I'd driven him to it. In fact, he took the bus to the Falls that night. Sorry. I couldn't resist that. Don't you find that a little black humour helps sometimes? Anyway, it was partly Kate's fault that he went off carrying the typewriter.(My Smith Corona portable.) If she'd been more positive about his manuscript

he might have been living now on the proceeds of his thir-
teenth novel. As for the other two men I married, one was
well – a mistake, and the other was an exotic. Like you. And
a gambler. He is probably still gambling. But I loved them
all in the beginning and could have loved the "mistake"
longer if only.

It was still just light enough for her to take her drink into
the yard to look for signs of life. A few snowdrops stood
bravely upright. Crocuses had dared to thrust their green
tips above the soil. And there were buds on the forsythia.
Promising green shoots. She picked up the damp election
poster that had been buried under the snow. The wrong
party had been returned to Parliament again. Her candidate
hadn't stood much chance and now the country had shifted
further to the right. She looked at the leafless maple trees
along the sidewalk and then at the battered, empty houses
on either side of her. Kate and Elsie both advised her to
accept the developers' offer, sell and move on. Be mature
about it. They meant, act your age. Get an apartment. Be
free. Be confined. Fit into a smaller space. After all, she was
only defending a piece of earth approximately 200 by 150
metres. But she was going to defend it till they brought the
bulldozer and knocked her and the house down together.
This space, this piece of ground, was her island. A haven, a
place of her own. Privacy and peace existed here. She knew
her rights. Be reasonable, the crook Gervais told her, smiling
villain that he was. Think about it. Think! And think that,
with the money from the sale, she could travel. There was a
world out there.

At university she'd taken a course in rational thinking
but none of it remained except the notion of steps and logical progression. All she recalled with any clarity of that
term was the blond hair and desirability of the guy she sat
beside whom she had illogically decided to marry. And he,

although he had achieved an A in that class, had never understood her quest for answers.

Their fifth anniversary: They were in Vancouver where Graham J. was giving a paper at a conference on the declining whale population. That evening, they'd walked along the seawall in Stanley Park and for some reason or unreason, the conversation from all those years ago had remained in her mind like a script.

Why is that man wearing a ski jacket on a day like this?

You ask too many questions.

I'm supposed to go through life ignorant?

You're meant to know things or find them out quietly.

So why is that man wearing a ski jacket on a day like this?

I don't care, Dorothy.

He could be ill and unable to keep warm. On the other hand, he might be crazy. And I'd have to speak to him differently according to which it was.

That's ridiculous.

It was at that moment, before she could explain that saying "Lovely day" to the man in the jacket would in the first case seem sarcastic, and in the second condescending, that Graham had walked towards the water and to all intents not returned. True, he'd been a physical presence for another month. He'd eaten dinner with her that evening in the hotel. He returned to Toronto with her on the plane, waded through the weeks like a man walking through molasses and then, on a sunny morning, he'd said goodbye, taken her typewriter and promised to return for his clothes later. At least she'd been smart enough not to ask why he was leaving her on a Sunday.

She had missed him, cried for him, blamed herself, been angry, found an unsatisfactory man, in that order. And continued against her will to carry the guilt.

"Hello there."

"Hello?"

"I'm here to canvass the area about the plans for the site."

Dorothy looked at the face peering over the privet hedge from the abandoned yard next door. It was a deceitful face with narrow eyes and a sharp nose. Brown hair cut short. Man? Or woman with stubbly chin? About thirty-five, the aggressive age.

"You're the developers' spy," she said. "Get away or I'll call the police."

"I'm not on your property, Mrs. Graham."

"You will be if I pull you through the hedge."

"I'm really on your side."

"You are on the other side."

"You don't know that till I talk to you."

"It's nearly dark. It's Easter weekend. You've no business bothering me. Haven't you got a turkey to stuff?"

"If you would just hear what I have to say."

Dorothy picked up the rake and moved towards the hedge. The speaker threw some leaflets into the garden and moved away. The first folder was headed, "Luxury Retirement Living at Economy Prices. Three meals a day, lots of activities, companionship and..." Why not sex and debauchery as well? An orgy of sagging bodies and evil breath and clicking artificial joints. *Danse Macabre*. The second one was a travel brochure outlining trips for groups of fun-loving older people.

Her moment for logical thinking was ruined. She went inside and put the papers on the kitchen counter. Whenever she began to waver and to consider the developers' offer, she would only have to look at them to be able to say firmly, Mr. Gervais and Mr. Robinson, you will have to carry me out of here in a box.

A little later she heard a sound outside and opened the

front door to make sure that the person had gone. "Go lovely rose"! There were no fewer than fifteen on the doorstep. Had they been left there by the mean-faced interloper? Had Omar in some telepathic way read her unsent letter? There were five white ones, five yellow and five red. She looked at them for significance. What did they mean? The two extant ex-husbands had not been romantic. Friends and relatives; none were in the habit of sending flowers except on rare anniversaries. The card read, 'To Dottie. Happy Easter!' Only Graham had called her "Dottie" and he was dead. Most definitely dead. A bouquet from a ghost? More likely delivered to the wrong address. Somewhere in town a 'Dottie' was looking out for a gift from a lover who had forgotten to add his name to the card. She would have to call the florist. It would be a good idea to call the florist. Nice to call the florist. A really nice person would call the florist. Wouldn't they?

She took the perfect flowers inside to protect them and before she knew it was flattening the stem ends and finding two vases to hold them. There was no bomb attached. R. and G. had not embarked on a campaign of terrorism – yet. And the flowers would still be fresh on Wednesday for the next meeting of TEWP. Kate and Elsie would be curious but she would say nothing, only smile enigmatically. She practised for a moment. Lips almost closed. Eyes glancing sideways. Mysterious? Sexy? The mirror answered, *sinister*.

The computer was having an off day, moving arthritically from file to file. Finally she got into her email and found two offers of a wonder drug to enlarge her penis and the promise of a degree with no research involved, no reading, just send money. There was no mention of roses.

Dear Mr. Sharif, If you ever send me roses what colour will you choose? I suspect a dusky pink: three dozen old-fashioned roses with a scent that fills the house.

Have you been the kind of man who sent gifts and bou-quets to women, or did they fall into your arms gladly, expecting nothing but sex? Were they simply, foolishly, GRATEFUL!

Women still fell over themselves to sleep with football players or tall men whose only skill was to put a ball into a high basket, movie stars, billionaires young and old. You could only despair about feminism, self-respect, and the demise of real, true and lasting love which she herself had known three times, or rather four if she counted the poet. Leon was in a category all his own.

Thanks for the lovely bouquet, Omar.

She had to thank somebody.

Email to Xkate@redwood.ca
cc: Elsed@global.com

Before we meet Lent again, there should be some research into Afghanistan, the conditions, the people, the current government. We know the recent history. Kate, check other sources of aid. Elsie, think how we can raise most amount of money for least effort. Dorothy

Why not go to the source for information? She picked up her pen and drafted a letter.

Dear Mr. Karzai,

I picture you in a room hung with oriental rugs. I picture you spinning like a top as you wonder whom to appease next, who will give you most help, where the next attack might come from. Do you have any moments of peace or any time to make love to your wife? So I hesitate to bother you. (That only applies if I mail this letter. And I might.)

What I really want to say is that many people are think-ing about you and your benighted country and want to help.

A young friend of mine, Jake Charbonneau, is on his way there. He'll be working for a Canadian NGO called WorldAidNow&Tomorrow and hopes to deliver aid to the needy.

My friend and my cousin and I are planning a dinner...

Kate walked down the street trying not to tread on the cracks. It wasn't Friday but it was the thirteenth, and Tuesday was a yellow day. All precautions must be taken against malevolent fates. It was a day when harpies and demons came out in daylight. They lurked. She would give them no chance. If she'd had a four-year-old child with her, they could have jumped over the cracks together – a game. Being alone, she tried to walk in a normal way, measuring the distance and planting her feet squarely in the centre of each paving stone. By the time she reached the crossing at Bloor and Avenue Road, she was safe. She stepped out into the traffic and heard the awful screech of brakes suddenly applied and a man shouting, "Look where you're going, stupid bitch."

She stepped back to the sidewalk breathing deeply and forgave the departing driver. She had almost ruined both their mornings. She leaned against a window to steady herself. For goodness sake! When she'd said she wanted to die before she was eighty, she hadn't meant today or even tomorrow. Certainly not before Jake came back and perhaps got married and had children. Maybe there was a Someone listening up there, a Being who answered random prayers and who didn't know the difference between a prayer and a passing thought.

The window she was leaning against was filled with bright posters offering bargain trips to Cuba, to Hawaii, to London. The image of an elderly woman with untidy white hair was reflected back at her.

She went inside the shop and sat down.

"You nearly came to harm," said the woman behind the desk, whose name according to the little nameplate in front of her computer was Sheena. "The traffic out there is murder. You need eyes in the back of your head."

"It's the thirteenth," Kate replied.

The woman looked at her as if she was out of her mind and didn't bother to reply.

"Are you planning a trip?"

"If I wanted to go to Afghanistan?"

Sheena appeared sceptical and still kept silent though she did make tapping motions on her keyboard as if she were writing, *This woman is an idiot*, or, *It's only half an hour to my lunch break.*

"Why?"

"For my work."

"We don't get many requests for that destination. What kind of work?"

"Anthropology," Kate replied. All travel was, in a way, anthropology. And even though it was obvious that she was past retirement age, writers and academics were known to keep on working until they dropped dead or lost their minds. "I'm working on a book." Even sitting here, wondering how Sheena spent her spare time and whether she liked her job and what sort of man or woman she had sex with was a study of humankind.

"You're one of those," Sheena said, tapping on and perhaps writing a novel or a play. After a few moments, she looked across at Kate and asked, "You do know that it's difficult to get into that country and that it's very dangerous there."

"I know," Kate shuddered for Jake. "I know very well."

"What route?"

Fantasy! This was sheer fantasy. She was making her way

across the desert on a camel, swaying from side to side, woman and animal thirsty and tired. "The cheapest."

"You could go through Russia. Take the train."

And the train rattled on through wasteland, past ex-gulags, the ghosts of exiles trekking to Siberia holding out their arms for alms, for acknowledgement. *We were human too.*

"I need to know the comparative prices."

"It'll take time."

"I'll be back," Kate said as she left.

She had really come downtown to go to the bookstore but enjoyed letting her mind wander where her body was unlikely to follow. She wouldn't be back tomorrow and Sheena knew it. The woman had from the beginning written her off as old and incompetent and crazed from the shock of being nearly run over. Kate stood still on the sidewalk and watched the cars and trucks passing by then stopping and starting again, the drivers impatient when anything slowed them down. Then the idea that she'd been dismissed as an aging loony drove her back inside the travel agent's. She sat down opposite Sheena and said, "I've changed my mind. In fact, I want to go to the Kuril Islands via Hokkaido."

"Oh."

"In November."

"I don't think we have anything on that right now. "

"This is my number," Kate said. "Call me when you do have something." She stood beside the rack of coloured brochures and leafed through them as if she had plans to travel the entire world.

"Coral Islands," Sheena said. "Are they in the Bahamas?"

"Try K-U-R-I-L."

There was nothing of *The Lost World* about the Kuril Islands, Dr. Vorster, the ecologist, had said on the TV program. No remains of ancient monsters lay hidden beneath the grass. They were beautiful, gentle places with an astounding array of flora and fauna and he was fortunate enough to have a grant to study there. The butterfly he displayed was a wonder of colour. He spoke about it with reverence and love, pointing out the spots on either wing, the delicate head.

She'd admired the man for having as the focus of his life something so small, a little crushable creature that was here one day and gone the next. It had made her think of all the strivers in the city who talked about the "next big thing," "third generation" and who worshipped the ability to build larger, taller, stronger, or simply strove to get more and more money.

While Henry Vorster talked of the earthquake fault, cool winters, misty summers, volcanic eruptions, Kate had seen an emerald jewel in a cold blue sea. There was very little traffic on the Islands, there were no paved roads and it probably never felt like Friday.

"I'll be in next week. Give me the figures then," she said and walked out of the place feeling years younger than when she'd set out that morning.

She could make her way from there to Sakhalin. She kept a copy of *The Island* on her bedside table. But it was a changed place now, inhabited by oil workers and tourists instead of prisoners and lost souls. "I arrived at Nikolayevsk... it is a majestic and beautiful place." Thus wrote Chekhov who'd travelled slowly and harshly across Russia to get there, his tuberculosis worsening day by day. And he found men and women living a degrading, degraded life. Now strangers visited the old penal settlement to sigh over the horrors of its past and the cruelty of a government that could treat human beings as garbage; a problem of waste management.

At the independent bookstore, she asked what they had

on Afghanistan.

"Flavour of the month, professor. Not much except a novel. We've got a brand new account of the last fifty years coming in next week. *Blood on your hands*. Great reviews. And we'll get the history one for you. Are you working on something?"

"Not my field," Kate replied, though in a way it was. "A matter of current affairs."

"We'll call you when it comes in."

She walked along Bloor Street, past the Plaza and the ice cream shop Jake loved and through the alley to Cumberland. Only a few hardy smokers were standing around near the rocks in the little park behind the stores. April was a mean month in Toronto. There was a promise of flowers but the chilling damp of a day like today went straight to the marrow.

When she got home, she sat down to write a letter. Handwriting didn't allow for easy correction of mistakes but it did add sincerity.

Dear Dr. Vorster, Watching your documentary last week has made me feel that. (Oh right! Nobody wants that kind of responsibility.) *Dear Henry, I hope you don't mind...* (Too humble.) *Dear Henry Vorster, I shall be making a trip to Japan in the near future and am thinking of going to the Kuril Islands.* (Lie number one.) *You won't remember but we met at the Learneds in Montreal several years ago.* Lie number two. She signed herself Kate Charbonneau, Ph.D. adding weight to her words.

She wouldn't mail the letter till Thursday, because Thursday, the colour of oranges, was a good day for sending out signals to the wider world. Of course, she didn't really believe in all that, but days did have their own distinct colours and that had to mean something.

Her mind was so filled with images of a rare landscape,

a different light, a place so remote from her apartment and the routine of life that she almost believed that she might make the journey and began to think of the clothes she would take if she did.

She went into the bedroom and saw that the poltergeist had been up to mischief again. This time it was the old photograph that was her family history, the roots of her life. It had not simply fallen from the wall but lay several feet away, face up, glass unbroken. Like her graduation picture a month before, it appeared to have been willfully yet carefully thrown down. Why this picture? What message was the spirit trying to convey?

Kate picked up the old photo and looked at it. She'd had it tinted and enlarged. Her father looking into the mirror appeared to see himself as a cog, a cipher whose life was in the hands of others. He was no longer free. He had accepted the 'king's shilling,' and must report to camp by evening. Or else? Or what? Or life would be a chase: Him the hare with the dogs of war snapping and yelping behind him till they caught him and brought him down.

Her mother, Kathleen, looking over her husband's shoulder, seemed to see all around him and in him and beside him the aura of adventure; a compound of fear and bravado, loss and surrender. The scent of blood and sweat and smoke had settled into that room. A moment later, she must have turned away and put his folded shirts into the bag that lay open on the bed. She had written on the back, "We both died the day this picture was taken." But John and Kathleen Bowles hadn't died that day. Not in the real sense of death. Only in the sense of a parting that might be forever. And was.

It was Dorothy's father, Dennis, who had snapped the picture in that particular, private moment. He was waiting to go back to the airfield with his older brother, John, to the airfield from which fewer than twenty per cent returned.

Dennis had taken six other photographs that day with his new camera. To come back alive required a huge amount of luck and making that record was itself a talisman. What else had those young men done to appease the terrible gods of the time? Tucked a rabbit's foot or a four-leaf clover into their uniform pockets? Or a prayer book that would stop the named bullet?

John had died a few weeks afterwards, shot down over France. And Dennis returned four years later to live on, shadowed by guilt. Was it guilt that had made him move with John's widow and child, Kathleen and Kate, to Canada, to care for them along with his own daughter? And maybe to ignore the stricture about sleeping with your brother's wife?

The picture brought tears to Kate's eyes. So many thousands, millions of young men and women whose lives ended before they'd barely begun, killed for what? That war and the one before it had been fought in the name of saving civilization. What, in the name of various gods, were young men and women dying for now? She pulled herself together. The odds of Jake coming safely home were ninety-nine to one. He was an aid worker, a helper, a bringer of good and not a warrior. Uncle Dennis's bequest of the photographs and the old camera were not meant as some black reminder of death. He had said to her once when she was about ten, "We all build memorials in our own way to what we think is important, to people we admire. I've kept these to honour all those brave men, your dad and myself included." Kate had remembered this in various offices where men and women covered the walls with certificates of their own academic achievements and pictures of themselves standing beside the great and the good. *We honour those whom we admire.*

The two little girls who were playing downstairs when those old photos were taken had grown up in the shadow of war and of sorrow. Kate knew that her father had been a shy, withdrawn man who died as much from horror of killing as from his wounds. Dorothy, motherless from birth, had been left as a little refugee in their household when the men went off to fly their planes. They were three abandoned females who stopped to listen for bombs and gunfire in the night and, in the daytime, for the footsteps of men returning home.

But Jake was fine. He would be fine. And many weeks and months had to go by before she could expect to hear his voice calling up, "Hi, Gran" from the intercom in the lobby.

∿

Elsie was watching Richard watching the Maple Leafs play Dallas. The fact that hockey went on well into early summer was a joy to him. He was wearing his old high school football sweater. Number 72. His age now. He'd become a distinguished-looking elderly man, medium height, ruddy complexion, a full head of grey hair.

"Look at that," he shouted as the puck crashed into the boards two feet wide of the net. "No score. End of the second. Some of those guys need glasses."

The players skated off, clumsy in their heavy gear, to drink juice, to be exhorted by the coach, or, if they were benchwarmers, to demand ice time.

Elsie asked, "What do you want for your birthday?"

"Anything that requires too much thought is bound to be expensive," Richard said. "Don't go crazy now." But the look on his face was one of anticipation.

Last year he'd been delighted by the two-volume set of books on ancient pottery. Perhaps he should have been an archeologist instead of spending his days looking at charts, company books, advertising campaigns. His had been a life of bottom lines. Elsie blamed his family.

They were scavengers, the Edwards. Tiny bars of soap,

packets of sauce, little sugar sachets were treasure to them. Towels on the bathroom rails bore hotel monograms. She'd hated Christmas at their house. His parents and siblings dismissed it as a commercial plot that destroyed the true meaning of the season. The gifts they gave each other were handcrafted mysteries or boringly practical. For all that, they were not churchgoers and the Nativity story held no magic for them.

When, later, she could afford to buy real gifts, Elsie had been touched by Richard's gratitude, his childlike wonder as he gradually became accustomed to what she and her family thought of as a real celebration. She kissed him and went to the kitchen.

Celina was standing by the stove stirring a mixture of chili peppers and horseradish and tomatoes and garlic, and singing a birdlike tune. Elsie sighed. The sauce would be far too spicy for Richard and she would have to scrape it off the fish. She had tried to explain that sauces made without peppers were still tasty, but Celina closed her ears to such heresy. If it hadn't been for all the years she'd worked for them. All the years! Celina was older than Richard and should have been at home, retired, at rest. But any suggestion that she should quit provoked a hysterical scene that often grew into a threat. *I've been in your house for thirty years. I know you. I know him. I stay home, I die.* And as she aged, she doggedly made the meals she had learned to cook as a girl in Mexico.

She only came now three days a week, and on Tuesdays and Thursdays Elsie could make the kind of food that she and Richard preferred. At least she thought it was what he preferred. He ate whatever was put before him with words of more or less appreciation.

She wondered sometimes whether having two close women friends all her adult life had diminished her relationship with her husband, had diminished him.

Because they did discuss men. They had talked of their men. Laughed about them: Dorothy's three, Kate's delinquent judge and Richard, the only one who remained. He was a good man. A loving man. Perhaps, all these years, he had deserved better. Was it a credit to her that they had stayed together? Or to him? But then, she thought, a marriage could run for decades fuelled by those early years of romance, of rushing one to one, and memories of fine sex. The pressed yellow rose in the cookbook had faded to dark gold but hadn't fallen apart. Not yet.

"How's Carlo, Celina?"

"The same as always. A donkey. He tells me I go home. Cook only for him."

Elsie got the silver cutlery and the Audubon placemats out of the sideboard drawer. The flowers in the centre of the table were beginning to droop but would last one more day. And it was an evening for candles, not dark yet but cloudy. She stopped, matches in hand. She and Kate and Dorothy would arrange a dinner. That's what they would do. A large charity dinner. Celina could cook the food and afterwards, Elsie could tell her that it was her swan song and give her a large cheque for severance pay. The event needn't be grand, but the people who came would admire their effort and it could become one of a series. Dinners for Afghanistan aid. They could pick out a village, a very poor village, to be the beneficiary. Later, they might go there and be photographed with the grateful chief or leader.

She poured a glass of wine for herself and a whisky for Richard and went to watch the final period with him.

Kate couldn't get the Kuril Islands out of her mind. She'd told Elsie she wanted to die before she was eighty, but now what she wanted was to go to that rarely visited place on her own. The idea had entered her mind and now stuck there like a burr. She decided to call Delphine, who had hurried away after dinner on Sunday and hadn't been in touch since. There hadn't in fact been a thank-you email from any of the guests. But such courtesies were rare these days.

She hadn't meant to say, "There you are, dear," like a neglected mother. But she did.

"Hi Mom."

"You've heard of *ignis fatuus*?"

"Spirits that lead people to their death in swamps? "

"Sometimes it's a butterfly," Kate said. "And it's not always death. Not a swamp either."

"I wish you wouldn't ask hard questions when I'm half asleep. My brain wakes up and it takes ages to settle down again."

"But haven't you ever felt a need to do something out of the ordinary, something way different from your usual life?"

"Good night, Mom."

"Before you're fifty perhaps?"

"Since you've woken me up, give me a line for a sport shoe company. You've got a literary mind."

"Run, rabbit, run?"

"This isn't for a magazine that's going to end up unread in a doctor's office. It's TV. OK it isn't prime time but a lot of lonely people watch geo-docs."

"Like me."

"The message they want is; we're green, we're active, we're eco-pure."

"Our boots do not crush tiny orchids."

"Something more classical."

Were Jake's boots trampling at this moment on poppies?
"'Stumbling on melons.'"

"Mom?"

"Marvell."

"Marvel at these boots?"

"Andrew Marvell, Delphine."

"Good night and thanks. Come and have coffee in the morning."

Kate had a sense that someone was in the room with Delphine. Had she, as soon as her son left, taken a lover? And why should she not? Because and because. There were all kinds of infidelity and none of them were good.

She woke up tired. She'd dreamt of struggling across an icy waste and then being in a guest house, looking out the window and seeing sheep on the street. She threw a muffin at one of the sheep and it glared up at her. Its face was green. After that she was trying to catch a bus home. Home was a place she thought she knew called Sourby Bridge.

She called Dorothy and Dorothy said, "Of course. Sowerby Bridge. It was close to where we lived in Yorkshire. In the great Before. Before we knew anything. Before we were here. It's not far from Halifax."

BC. Before the widow and the widower emigrated with their daughters to Canada. Before Confusion. Dennis and Kathleen had tried to be parents to both girls, turning up in support at school events and interviews. Teachers and friends alike had required an explanation: My father died in the war. Dorothy's mother died when she was born. Dorothy's dad is my uncle. My mother is Dorothy's aunt. In that small town, the family had been marked as odd if not worse.

∽

I suppose if you were to involve yourself in a charitable enterprise, Mr. Sharif, you would begin by setting up a trust. And perhaps you have. The kind of people you know could donate enough money to keep a Third World country in clean water forever. My friends and I will start small but we have large ideas.

The second meeting with Harold Lent hadn't begun well. Elsie, not noticing the man's car parked down the street, had come in yelling, "Isabel is pregnant and won't admit it." Kate, behind her, had said in a lower tone, "She's forty and you have a grandchild already if you'd only give her some of your goddam time."

Lost ground was recovered when Elsie made her social standing clear to Mr. Lent. After that he spoke almost exclusively to her, leaving Kate and Dorothy in the positions of tea-pourer and cookie-passer. Mr. Lent could see money in Elsie. Dorothy's shabby house offered nothing unless she was an eccentric who gave her money to the poor and preferred to live a lean life. That had perhaps crossed his mind as he was leaving because he'd turned to her and said, "I'm sure you ladies can make this work."

"'I'm sure you ladies can make this work!'" Elsie said. "Patronizing creep."

Dorothy said, "All we need is a venue, a menu and a list of guests."

They were sitting at the kitchen table with paper and pen.

Kate said. "Let's make lists again. What we want before we get to eighty."

"No," Elsie insisted. "This is serious. If we fail here, Harvey Lent's lack of faith will be justified. It has to work. It has to raise significant money. Celina will do all the cooking. All we have to do is be the gracious hostesses."

"These bought cookies are probably full of saturated fats."

51

"We've been eating saturated fats since we were born and not worrying about it."

"Computers," Elsie said, "will make it easy. I know someone who'll design a simple invitation."

"Who's going to look for a room? Space. And for how many?"

"I called a few places but they're booked. Weddings. Graduations. It's the time of year," Kate replied. "And we don't want to pay much, if anything."

"I've got to go for my lesson, "Dorothy said.

"Look," Elsie said. "This won't do. Other things have to give way."

"Email me with what you've decided. Oh and lock the door when you leave. I don't trust the crook Gervais. Don't look at me like that. I'm going to ask Matt to paint an appropriate mural for us. It will be a point of interest."

"'Another fine mess she's gotten us into,'" she heard Kate say as she picked up her portfolio.

As she drove down the street, Dorothy wasn't sure why she'd spoken to the other two so abruptly unless it was because she wasn't telling the truth. They were her best friends in the world and it was wrong to deceive them, but sometimes they were just two old women with predictable attitudes. They were, though, the companions she'd been allotted in life. God-given, if she'd really believed in God. There had been periods as long as two years of falling out, of two against one. But the trinity had endured for a long time and they would go on, harnessed together, until there was no more 'before' and, in her view, no 'after' either.

The traffic was slower than usual, an accident up ahead maybe. At least it gave her time to think. It was her turn to begin the discussion today and she had no idea of what to say. The others would expect her to arrive with an idea and all she could think of was this charity dinner. Putting the plan into effect was going to take time. There were letters to write to potential donors, *We are planning an event to raise money for displaced families in Afghanistan*, contacts to make, daily news from Afghanistan to read, research to do into the more remote parts of that wrecked country, a guest list to arrange. And all that before it got down to knives and forks.

Matt's house was set back from the road in a wild garden. She'd offered to tame it and to plant bulbs in the fall, but he'd told her not to behave like a suburban housewife. On the way home she would stop by and ask him about the mural; there was no time now. The group despised lateness. Half a mile beyond one of those dingy strip malls that look particularly desolate on a damp, cold day and made her despair for the human race, she found the Centre again and narrowly missed crashing into the leader's pickup as she parked in the drive. Her talk, she decided as she walked up to the front door, would be about worldwide destruction. *And besides, they want to tear down my home.*

"Come in, Dorothy," Mervyn said, holding the door wide. "I'm glad you could make it."

She took off her boots and coat and walked into the dimly lit room. Five other people were already there sitting on two couches. They turned to her with welcoming smiles that made her want to back out at once, but she'd promised herself to give it three tries and this was only her second visit. Moving from her house was going to be a major traumatic event. She had come to this place partly for help in advance and partly to search for her soul. She sat on the wooden rocking chair and looked around. Even in the semi-darkness, there was colour and glitter in this room. Rugs on the furniture and the floor sparkled with shiny decorations, mirrors and silver thread. The effect was more harem than therapy.

"Hello," she said, recognizing two of the others from last time.

"I don't think we're expecting anyone else," Mervyn said. "Did you all have a good Easter? Not too much chocolate I hope. I thought we'd begin with expectations. I want you to think of two things that you hope for in the short term. After all we deal in the short term here. Day to day."

Dorothy, off the hook for the moment, tried to summon up two wishes that would involve no explanation. No way was she going to tell these strangers about her friends or about the planned dinner. Grand hopes for world peace and universal love would sound pretentious, not to say despairingly impossible.

"Hold those hopes in your left hand. Now pass them to your next-door neighbour."

I've driven halfway across the city for this, Dorothy thought, truly glad she hadn't mentioned the group to Kate and Elsie, who might have scoffed or felt hurt that she hadn't come to them for help. She "emptied" her left hand into the right of the man in the yellow shirt and felt soft fingers groping at her other hand.

"Now then, Dorothy, what have you given to Reg?"

"Why are we passing on to people hopes they might not share?"

"I thought we'd agreed last time that there weren't going to be questions at this stage. So Dorothy?"

"It was my turn to begin and I'd thought of talking about destruction."

"We'll come to that. Your hopes?"

"They're private."

"We'll move on and come back to you in a minute."

Reg had given his neighbour hopes for winning the lottery and for a cure for his wife's asthma.

"Asthma is a nervous condition," the recipient said. "You should check your own behaviour."

"No, Natalie," Mervyn said. "We don't go into that. Not yet."

Dorothy listened and learned. She'd read about the meetings on a piece of paper tacked to the notice board in the library. *Group empathy. Dispel your worries. Discuss your fears. Two sessions a month.* Elsie had spent years in therapy. Kate had gone to a psychologist for months after Robert left her but stopped because the woman was, she said, digging too deep. And who am I, Dorothy had thought, not to seek help? To assume I can get through life without ever having my mind investigated, without understanding my own motives and actions? And I do have fears: of death; of harm coming to Jake; of my friends dying first; of living too long; of dying in agony. That was really all. *Timor mortis*, Kate would have said. Absolutely! Dead on.

"So Dorothy?"

Natalie had given her the hopes of learning to swim and avoiding car accidents. She smiled her thanks. Fat chance to the first and yes to the second. They were nice people. There was no point in hurting their feelings. Some of them were obviously damaged. All of them were afraid. She had come to this place to shed some of her fears and appeared to be acquiring a new one; the dread of being engulfed in a tsunami of sympathy, a stifling group hug followed by a letting go of all her treasured inhibitions. She would shriek, howl and say, *I caused my cousin's grandson to go to Afghanistan and if he should come to harm, I will die.* She got up and said softly, "I don't feel very well. I'll go home and see you next time."

"We don't like people to leave during the session," Mervyn said. "I'll get you some mint tea."

There was something in his voice that made the tea sound

like a threat. She recognized it as the menace of insistent kindness.

"I don't think so. But thank you very much." She put on her boots and coat and ran out the door. And knew that her true fear was of being found out.

She looked at the dial; it was well over the speed limit as if the entire group was in pursuit. She slowed down as she imagined the headline: "Elderly woman drives into telegraph pole knocks out electricity brings city to standstill." An achievement of sorts but not on today's to-do list.

Matt wasn't home. She looked through the studio window and stepped quickly back. His latest canvas depicted an orgy of bodies and blood and inhuman acts. She wasn't naïve. She was aware of evil. In fact it was on account of evil that she and Kate and Elsie had made up their minds to take action. Depravity existed all around: Movies, TV, books, dispensed images of it in all its variations. But evil was other people, other places. She turned away from the picture and calmed down. As far as she knew, Matt had not committed murder or rape. He was simply expressing his view of a mad, violent world.

She stopped at the corner store and bought a carton of low-fat yogurt and a copy of *National Geographic*. The picture on the front cover of the magazine showed an enticing scene: Unbounded, rippling desert dotted with camels and nomads.

What was I thinking, Omar? Group "sharing." Me! It must have been a desperate moment when I signed up for that. After Graham's death, I tried talking to a counsellor and listened to her advice on how to grieve, but who makes those rules? It's something best done on your own, as I finally told her. All those questions were pure nosiness really. And to have her sitting there making notes! I did what any sensible person would do in a time of sorrow and stress. I ran away. Changed countries for a while. And fell in love again.

She turned to email to see if there were messages from the outer world but there was only one from the HelpLine asking if she had any free time. But those days were over. Alternate Fridays and every Sunday evening for fifteen years she'd sat in that cubicle waiting to respond to calls from the desperate. *You have a soothing voice, Dorothy.* But it was the words that mattered. Always the words. The wrong ones could be as destructive as gunfire.

Dear Marie,

It was July 5th, 1993. I pictured you as thirtyish, wearing a print blouse and a dark skirt. (I always liked to visualize the person at the other end of the line. They weren't all women, you know.) You began talking in a whisper and I had to ask you to speak up – something we'd been advised not to do as there could be someone threatening nearby.

Have you called 911? I asked. I only want advice, you said. Long pause. And then you told me about the dog and the bath and the shampoo and I laughed. I laughed very quietly because of the others. We did get hoax calls. And then I turned angry because you appeared to be tying up the line, you in your print blouse and dark skirt, chuckling to yourself while desperate people were trying to get through.

I read about you in the paper a few days later. Five to be exact. How did I know it was you, Marie? I recognised the details, that's how. You'd told me that the dog was a Schnauzer. But you didn't mention the heat of the water, or the man nearby. And I'd mistaken your hysteria for laughter.

Fortunately it turned out well in the end but I quit the next week and told the organizer it was because of stress in my own life. I send a donation every year. This is a mea culpa *just thirteen years late.*

~

On Delphine's screen, a pair of unoccupied hiking boots was walking slightly above the ground. She parachuted an occupant into the boots, a tall bearded man, smiling, enjoying the scenery and still a few inches off the earth. The boots were made of recycled rubber and paper and coconut fibre and were said to be light, waterproof and long-lasting. Jump in them, dance in them. What was the copyright on 'these boots are made for walkin''? She drew a mountain stream and set the man down in it. She called him Lou.

She hoped Alice, who now called herself Alec and was out with the car, was taking care. She'd been driving on the other side of the road for eight years and might easily forget where she was. All she'd asked for so far besides a loan of the wheels was a couple of weeks lodging. She needed to be in the city, she said. Reluctantly because she'd intended to spend a few hours moping in there before cleaning it out for his return, Delphine had shown her Jake's room the night she arrived. It had become foreign territory, and a different kind of music filtered down to the floor below. Jake's Room: The homemade sign on the door was curling at the edges. Pictures of animals she'd hung on the walls when he was little had long ago been replaced first by hockey idols and then by posters of groups: The RoadRats, Five and The Newly Dead.

Alec's other request was that her presence in Toronto be kept secret from her family. At least for now. The two of them hadn't settled back into the old easy companionship, and Delphine wasn't sure if this changed woman really was her old friend. She couldn't help feeling that there was another agenda and that this apparition from the past had come for a reason not yet told. The idea that Alec might be the fate predicted by the fortune cookie made her laugh out loud.

It had been years since Alice took off for England, and in the last three there'd been no letters, not even a Christmas card. Someone had said that Alec's new love, the woman for whom she had left her husband and child, had deserted her or moved on or died. But Delphine wasn't ready to ask, and Alice/Alec was saying nothing about the past.

They drank wine, talked of old times, talked of current times, looked at pictures of Jake together, but the conversation always ran above the true, like that kids' game of stepping around a room on the furniture, never touching the floor.

She heard the door and shouted, "Come in. You've got a key."

"I haven't. And you shouldn't leave your door open like that."

"Hello, Mom."

"Keep working. I'll get some coffee if that's okay."

"And bring me a cup, please."

When her mother came back, Delphine said, "I'm trying not to feel resentful."

"He'll be fine."

"I'm talking about the office! You know I should have had that job. Gillian's a dodo."

While she waited for her mother to tell her that life wasn't fair, she asked her what was wrong.

"It's this scheme of Dorothy's," her mother said.

"You don't have to go along, Mom."

"I feel compressed."

"Compressed?"

"As if I'm squeezed between them. Dorothy with her ideas and her energy and Elsie with that power of hers. Her money. And you know something, I think aside from the obvious good cause, that they're doing it partly for me. You know that awful phrase. To take her out of herself. As if, Delphie, I want to be out of myself. Where would I be if I wasn't in myself?"

Delphine looked at her mother's face. She'd always thought her beautiful and, when she was younger, wished she'd inherited the fine bone structure and gentle eyes, instead of her father's harder outline. But since her husband's defection, her mother's tendency to sorrow had turned her eyes downward and made her mouth tentative. She was the image of the woman in the TV ad before she found the right stain remover.

"They think I'm depressed for God's sake. I'm not depressed; I'm sad. Any sane person on this earth has to be sad. Cakes!"

Delphine waited for the connection she knew would come.

"My mother's Christmas cakes used to sag in the middle. Dip. There was a hollow. She filled it with icing. In Yorkshire, when a cake sagged like that, they'd say it was 'sad.' I think it describes me. And people keep trying to fill the hollow. They have some nerve."

"They're only trying to help."

"A sad cake was also slightly too moist. There were theories about what made them turn out like that. Too much butter. Too many eggs. Not enough attention paid to weights and measures."

"It's a good thing people don't bake much any more."

"Perhaps if they did, they'd know the difference between depressed and sad."

Delphine hoped that her mother was beginning to fight back. At least she'd stopped referring to her ex-husband as "your father, the late Judge Charbonneau." He was now referred to by the male pronoun as in, "*He* called and had the nerve to ask me to send the Shakespeare, as if the tart he's living with can read."

Delphine called her father occasionally but was tired of hearing a girlish voice say "Hello, is that you Delphine sweetie?" on the other end. "When are you going to come and see your Daddy?"

"A man doesn't come right out and say, 'I'm leaving you because you're old and your body sags and I want to have rampaging sex with this twenty-six-year-old,'" her mother said. "They use pious phrases. 'She understands me. You'll be better off without me. You'll have time for yourself. It will be best for both of us.'"

Delphine had heard it all many times in the three years since the judge had moved to Victoria with his love and wished that her mother could find other words, go back to quoting chunks of poetry, ancient and modern, refer to classical literary moments. After all, she was a woman who had read the great works and been nourished by them. Why could she not seek comfort there now? She reached for Kate's hand and began to talk to her about the marketing strategy campaign for the new hotel in Niagara Falls. It was a competition. A neat slogan was required, something with the weight of Plato behind it.

"If I can get their business, I can really set up on my own."

"The eighth natural wonder?"

"Used, Mom."

"Sleep here and you'll never sleep anywhere else?"

"Where luxury and economy go hand in hand?"

"I have it, Delphine. Close-up of the Falls. Someone going over in a barrel thinking, If only I could have got a room at the Ridgeway."

"If you come up with a good one send me an email."

"Whose backpack is that? Is Jake here? Is he back? Didn't he go?"

"No, Mom. Remember Alice? Isabel's sister."

"Elsie's Alice? She's here?"

"She's come back from the UK. Staying here for a few days."

"Well. Does Elvira know? Elsie?"

"She's not ready for that yet. Don't say anything."

"She was a lovely little girl. Wilful, maybe, but good really. Janie at the bakery said you had a man helping you with the groceries. And I wondered. You've been on your own a long time now. And with Jake gone. You have to be very, very careful. But if it's only Alice. I can't forgive the way she walked out on that child though, but I guess she'll talk to her parents when she's good and ready."

"She feels they cut her off."

"Well, she should get over it and go see them."

Alice came in carrying her instrument case.

"Hello, Alice," Kate said.

"Dr. Charbonneau. I didn't recognize you."

"I haven't been called that in a while." *Dr. Charbonneau* was a woman from the past; a confident teacher and mother who had no truck with superstition and coloured days. "Are you staying long?"

"I'm here for auditions. So it depends."

"You'll be calling your mom and Elvira."

"I'm not ready. In good time, okay."

There was a silence.

Kate drank her coffee quickly and said she had shopping to do. She'd wanted to make sure that her only daughter hadn't, in despair over her son's absence, taken up with some fellow who would destroy her regular life and take over the house and be abusive and drive her to drink and drugs so that she would lose her job and end up on the street. And all of that between Friday and Monday.

In the hall, Delphine whispered, "I'm fine, Mom. Alice will find a place soon."

"She used to have lovely hair. Does she have to dress like that?"

Delphine said yes and kissed her mother and told her that she looked great. She helped her into her raincoat and asked her if it was warm enough. Her mother, the sad cake, walked quickly down the path, carrying the burden of loneliness on her back.

"What are you working on?" Alec asked.

"An ad for these. They gave us each a pair."

"Let me see."

Delphine brought the soft black boots out of the bag and handed them across the table. "They're supposed to be waterproof and accident proof and will last forever."

Alec took her shoes off and put them on.

"I'm going to wear them," she said," to destruction. I think it's what's wrong with the world, all this advertising, sell at any price, beat down the competition. It's never true. It's all short-term." She danced around the room, kicking out her legs, kicking at the wall.

"Give them back to me."

"No. It's a matter of principle."

Delphine tried to get the boots off Alec's feet and fell on the floor, laughing.

"My mom was checking up."

"I make her feel uncomfortable. Like you."

"You have to allow me time."

"Say my name, go on. Say Alec. Alec. Alec."

"Alec. Alice. Alec."

"You'll get used to it."

"What I was actually planning to get used to," Delphine said still holding the heel of one boot, "was living alone."

"'I want to be alone,'" Alec whispered.

"My sixteenth birthday party," Delphine said and they laughed till they were gasping for breath recalling the kissing game they'd played and the boy who ran out of the room in terror.

"I'm going to keep the boots," Alec said when they were back at the table and Delphine had refilled their mugs.

"All right," she said. "But you'll be wearing them when you're seventy."

"So your mother really came to check up on you?"

"I think she follows me about or keeps an ear to the wall. She won't tell them you're here."

"Do you ever run into Isabel?"

Delphine said, "She and Mike were at my mom's for Easter dinner. And I saw her at a fundraiser for the new hospital wing. It was in that old house on the corner of Brexley."

"The monster's house. We used to run past it like hell when we were kids."

"She's your sister. Don't you talk to her?"

"We used to talk on the phone now and then. She sent me a couple of ridiculous gifts. In fact, just before I left England, I got a T-shirt from Paris. She seemed to have had a letdown of some kind there. So she thought of me. "

"Your mother thinks she's pregnant."

"She's left it a bit late."

"You'll be an aunt."

Alec slowly pulled the boots off, the left one and then the right.

"Last night on the way home from the club, I went to Rosedale and stood outside the house, my mom and dad's place. There weren't any lights. Your mom knows I'm here. They'll know I'm here. They could have got in touch with me any time when I was in Europe and they never did. I sent them birthday cards, Christmas letters. Nothing. Gifts for Elvira. Nothing. They didn't write back. I never thought they were so narrow-minded. What about love? I mean. I'm not making the first move if they're all going to slam doors in my face. I just don't need that."

Delphine picked up the saxophone case and pretended to play it as a violin. They began to laugh again but not easily.

~

Elsie was irritated. No wonder Dorothy had lost husbands the way others lost their house keys. Questions bounced off the walls of whatever room she was in. Why are you going out now? What's happened to all the white china? Why do you spend so much time in the library? Why are you reading *War and Peace*? At college they'd called her "Sherlock." And now she wanted to know why Elsie and Richard were still not in touch with their other daughter. It was not as if Alice had committed a crime, she said. And wasn't Elsie the first of them to "discover" k. d. lang? So why was Dorothy so interested now when the event, if it could be called an event, had taken place eight years ago? They hadn't driven Alice from them. She'd walked away. They had offered all the kinds of help money could buy if she would only agree to remain the same and return to her suitable marriage and take care of their only grandchild. And no, she'd shouted at Dorothy, it had nothing to do with "our standing in the community."

Dorothy's written wish had been to have three children before she was thirty. Instead, by the time she was thirty-seven, she'd had three husbands. In default, she'd watched Isabel and Alice and Delphine and her brother Brian grow up and had treated them all as if she were their aunt, an aggravating aunt. She'd spoilt them when they were little, offered dangerous advice in their teenage years, and now had this proprietary attitude when they were beyond need of help. Beyond the need of help! Did a person ever reach that state except when dead? That was a Dorothy question and Elsie shook it from her mind.

She was standing in front of the mirror holding up the dress she would wear to the May Fantasy Auction on Saturday. The dress was patterned diagonally, dark blue on lighter blue, and was supposed to make her look slimmer. She wasn't sure that it did. Perhaps it merely drew attention to her hips. No use asking Richard. He would want to know what it cost. And when she told him, he would be pleased that his wife could afford it while at the same time shaking his head and saying they weren't made of money. He suffered from financial ambivalence. But she had stuck with him. *I am stuck with him.*

Like Dorothy. Why was Dorothy sticking in her mind this morning like a matador's pic in a bull's backside? Ah Spain! Now there was a country. She and Richard had fallen in love all over again there while Dorothy back in Toronto had been busy getting rid of her third husband. The Russian she'd married on the rebound from Alfred Sparrow hadn't lasted beyond the second anniversary. None of her husbands had measured up to Dorothy's ideal. Which was? Elsie laughed aloud. A composite probably of Albert Einstein and Jack Nicholson and Justin Timberlake. Which parts of which guy she would put into the mix to make the whole man was another interesting question.

Clever Dorothy had arranged for them to meet that tired-looking guy who ran WorldAidNow, Ontario, knowing exactly how they would react. We can do better, world! It was a challenge. She smiled and put the dress down. Who cared what she looked like as long as she gave, gave, gave? I am a donor. I am a rich bitch. People kowtow. There will be wine and music and women will come up to me and kiss the space beside my ear and gush, *I love your dress*. Men will touch me and whisper, *You look ravishing*, and not mean it.

That very first day at the residence at Western when, a shy eighteen-year-old, she'd walked into the suite, two similar faces had turned towards her with that questioning look that Dorothy had retained and Kate had not. She'd felt instantly like a gatecrasher. She was moving in with two women who'd grown up together, who were cousins, who spoke in family shorthand, who wore nice clothes that they made themselves. When they went out in the evening, the other two treated her as a tag-along. After a few weeks, when they realized she was all right, laughed at the same things, loved the same music, hated the English professor, they stopped trying to get her to move out and became a happy trio with private jokes and shared outings. And she, being the poor one, had accepted their gifts. Lifelong friendship the best gift of all. Even if, as now, the other two were often irritating. Besides, she said to herself, I'm the only one who still has all her own teeth. She smiled at the mirror and pushed her hair back. No new wrinkles. And there was enough natural colour in her cheeks to keep her from looking like a ghost when the makeup was removed.

She took off her robe and put on her skirt and sweater. The blue dress hanging there didn't look too bad after all.

She went into Richard's study to tell him she'd be out all afternoon. He was watching a drama unfold on the screen of his new laptop, listening to the music on his headset, and reading the score at the same time. He'd come late to opera and, as is often the way with late loves, he was possessed by it.

"What?" he said, uncovering one ear.

"I'll be back in time for dinner."

"Okay." He replaced the headset and then said, *Valkyrie*.

He was preparing himself for *The Ring Cycle* that would open the grand new Four Season Centre in September. On a diagram, he'd shown her where their seats were in the third circle, "the best place in the House." But Elsie wasn't sure she had the endurance to sit through so many hours of greed and family strife and death. Passion, it's what opera is, he'd told her, sounding so desperate that Elsie wondered if there was another woman in his life. The figures on the screen soundlessly carried their dead heroes to Valhalla. She shivered and turned away.

Listening to the soundtrack from *Hair*, she drove to her friend's shabby house and waited in the car.

"I could show you a really neat condo," she said when Dorothy climbed into the passenger seat.

"Are you into real estate now, Elsie?"

"Okay. First things first. I've heard of a place on Queen that might do for the dinner. We have to go look at it. I think we can get it for next to nothing."

"Nothing would be best."

"Get real."

They were driving along Roncesvalles when Dorothy cried out, "Stop. Over there."

Elsie pulled up to the curb. "What! You nearly gave me a heart attack."

"Goats on sale."

"Are you mad!"

"You can put them in your big freezer."

"They have hairy skin."

"Come on. You eat cows and sheep and all sorts of hairy-skinned creatures."

Dorothy pushed Elsie into the shop. "And it's for a good cause."

"How many will we need?"

"They could be like geese. Not much left when they're cooked and all the fat's drained away."

"I imagine goats to be lean."

"Let's ask." She looked at the dark-skinned man who was sitting behind the counter reading a newspaper in an Arabic language and said, "How many goats do we need to feed fifty people, please?"

"That depends," he replied, "on whether they're very hungry people and if they like goat."

Dorothy said, "It's for a charity dinner. Can you give us a discount?"

The man looked at her with an expression in his dark eyes that could have been hatred. He stared at Elsie in her fine tweed skirt and plain brown jacket as if she had chosen the outfit specially to go trolling for goat, and picked up a fearsome-looking sharp knife.

"What I'll do for you ladies," he said, "is throw in an extra head."

They knew, they both said, when they'd put the plastic bags full of meat into the trunk, that he was making fun of them but they hadn't dared to laugh.

"We were intimidated by a butcher," Elsie said.

"We were held back by our own kind of racism," Dorothy answered. "We should have told him to keep the goddam heads. Just exactly what are you going to with them?"

"Celina can boil the flesh off and her husband will use the skulls in a collage."

"Sorry I asked."

"And the meat can go into the stew."

Dorothy was truly sorry she'd asked and sorrier that she'd drawn attention to the butcher's shop. She imagined sad eyes floating in gravy. There would be six eyes so the chance of one turning up on her plate was about one in eight. But Elsie was joking surely. She was, though, determinedly thrifty in some areas of her life.

The woman who showed them the vast empty room next to the bakery on Queen Street made light of the stains and the uneven floor. The building, she said, was to be reopened in the fall as a nightclub. The new owners planned to start renovating in July. Till then it was going for token rent.

"We'll let you know," Elsie said. If she'd been wearing a long skirt, she would have lifted it up around her ankles. As it was, she hardly liked to step on the floor and took long strides till she got back to the sidewalk.

"It might do," Dorothy said when they got back into the car. "As an absolute last resort."

To DelphChar@greenmail.ca
CC: Rubyslippers@tellu.net
Xkate@redwood.ca

Hello Mom, Aunt D, Gran.

Sorry about the multiple message but access is limited.

I'm sharing a tent with Ali. We've just eaten lunch, sand – wiches.

Kabul was amazing. You'd love the market, Mom. The mosques. You can see the Hindu Kush. Donkey carts and cars on the same roads. Soldiers everywhere. Occasional gunshots. We're far from Kabul now but I'm not to say where exactly. They treat us like part of the army. Same rules apply. And we're only here to help. The people need everything in this village. They have plenty of air and light and sand. The well off ones have a goat or two. The desert is unreal. I got here so fast because there was a vacancy. Hope you're all okay.

You can try replying to this but there's no guarantee I'll get it.

Ali knows a lot of the poetry you reel off, Aunt D. Says this village we're in now is forgotten because 'the captains and the kings' have left town. In other words, the media. I'll tell you about it next time. I know twenty-three words of the language. Ali wants to know the other lines of that poem. Love to all, Jake.

A vacancy. Dorothy knew very well what that implied. The worker in the field, the one sent out possibly only a few months ago, a young man doted on by his parents, engaged to be married, a bright future ahead of him, had been hacked to pieces or blown to smithereens. And so they had sent an untrained boy from Canada in his place. She shivered. The day had grown colder.

Long ago she had made bargains with the Fates: If you give me this, I will do that. But she couldn't recall that any one of them had worked. And what had she to offer now in exchange for the safety of one young person out of thousands?

To DelphChar@greenmail.ca
Hi there, Delphine,
   Don't worry when Jake talks about 'a vacancy.' It means someone has gone on leave.
   Come around for a drink after dinner tomorrow. Bring Alice. Aunt D.

To Xkate@redwood.ca
   Dear Mom,
   Good to hear from Jake. I do miss him. It's such a long way. And it's not just the distance. Love, Delph.

Delphine realized that her son had stepped onto a moving sidewalk and there was no way for him to get off it. In a year or two he would return to university and be older than the others because of what he had seen. In Kabul an ancient world greeted him, set back in time among modern towers. On some streets, men and women in long robes moved against an earth-toned backdrop of broken buildings.

They had walked into history. Richness and sensuality and incurable poverty. And in their tent two young men are talking.

How did you come to be part of this? Ali is asking in Pashtun or Urdu.

It was my Aunt Dorothy's idea, Jake replies in some kind of sign language.

To jcbw@afghan.gov.ca
Dear Jake,
    Lovely to hear from you. Keep in touch when you can. Everything's fine here. Even the weather. I'm busy at work with new clients and an ad for hiking boots, believe it or not. Change your socks as often as possible. I'm glad you have a local friend. Love, Mom.

To jcbw@afghan.gov.ca
Hi Jake,
    That poem goes like this, 'The tumult and the shouting dies,
    The captains and the kings depart,
    Still stands thine ancient sacrifice.' etc.
    It's a hymn really. Your mother and gran are well. Take care. Dorothy

To Xkate@redwood.ca
Good morning, Kate. Nice to hear from the boy. He sounds in good spirits. Remember the meeting. We really need to get it together. D

To jcbw@afghan.gov.ca
Dearest Jake,
    Do take care. Your mother misses you but is all right. At least she has some company now. I'll write to you by snail mail. Love, Gran.

    Kate pictured her grandson lying on the sand smiling, far from home, having an adventure, being young, quoting poetry. He had gone where she would never go and was seeing the little houses with white walls, the valleys, the trees, the distant mountains. He was travelling on roads that petered out to tracks, passing men with rocket launchers, people on horseback, hirsute warriors riding camels. His mission was to assess need and clear the way so that food and medicine could reach the desperate. He would pass through fields of "sleep-bearing poppies." God forbid he should become an addict. God forbid he should be hurt. Was it too late to go to church and put in a word? Kate thought it likely was. Especially if He was an all-seeing God and had read her paper on Christianity in nineteenth-century literature.

And there were women where he was. God protect him from the men if he dared to approach a pretty girl. You're not in Canada, she wanted to shout across the world to him. But surely, surely, there had been some kind of briefing. He had been propelled into the midst of that foreign chaos far too quickly. Goddam Dorothy, she almost said, but drew the words back into her mind and erased them.

Elsie was singing as she stirred the sauce. Onions, garlic, tomatoes, olives. When she had time she liked to make the Italian dish her grandmother had taught her. *Buy the best oil. The vegetables can be old but the oil must be fresh.* Isabel would come in looking as though she wanted a salad. Too bad. There were meatballs, there was foccacia bread and a mascarpone cheesecake.

When Isabel did come in, Elsie said, "You look pregnant," before she could stop herself.

"I'm not putting on weight, Mother."

"It's something about your face. I know that look."

"Nonsense. So how about, hello Isabel?"

"Hello honey, you look pregnant."

"Mother!"

"Now sit down and I'll get you a glass of lemonade. You won't be wanting wine."

"I do want wine. I want a big glass of red. I'll come and get it."

She followed her mother into the kitchen and was engulfed by the warmth and the odour and the homey sight of the bottles and jars her mother kept in rows along the back of the counter, and the photographs of Elvira at all ages on the fridge door.

"Mike called to say he'd be late," her mother said.

"Did he say why?" Isabel asked, regretting at once any hint of suspicion in her voice. Before her mother could build a castle of infidelity in the air, she said, "Oh yes. He mentioned a meeting. How long has this wine been open?"

"Only since you were here last week. How's work?"

"Boring at the moment."

"You'll be taking time off."

"There's a literary tour of Spain in the fall."

"Why there?"

"Lorca maybe."

"And suppose you find that another idol was only human after all?"

They wove a screen of words that meant nothing and Elsie let her daughter mix vinaigrette in the old wooden bowl while she arranged the table. She put new yellow candles into the wooden holders her adventurous grandfather had brought back from Australia in the days of sail, and set the vase of daffodils in the centre. The vase, imitation cut glass, had been given to her on Mothers' Day about thirty years ago. Alice had handed it to her with pride, and she had accepted it as if it were finest crystal from Tiffany's.

"Dad still in New York?"

"Till Wednesday."

When Alice had gone her way, she'd left her own house and this one full of tears and shredded feelings. No Thanksgiving gathering had ever quite managed to produce a sense of all being well again. Their father had replaced the only group photo of the four of them with a print of buffalo on the plains in bygone days. Even Alice's graduation picture had been moved to the far end of the upstairs landing. That was her mother's doing. As for the wedding photograph, it was possibly in the garbage. But Alice had lived her life at a distance. Someone had seen her, they said, in London. Others had sighted her in Paris. Like Elvis she was everywhere and nowhere but, unlike Elvis, now here. Her ex-husband had long ago recovered from her defection and, when he re-married, had chosen an older woman for security.

How many times had Alice asked herself if she was doing the right thing? How often had she held back and decided to keep on being Alice forever in spite of her desperate need to be Alec? To have a daughter who walked away, who kept on walking away was a stab in the heart. The wound never healed, only closed over for a time now and then.

"Seen Elvira lately, Mom?"

"I sometimes think she blames me."

"I don't see much of her either. I call her once in a while and then we have lunch, but it's never very close. I think she's wondering all the time if I'm going to talk about Alice."

Elsie said, "I could have done a lot for her. Taken her to some of the events, got her in on the junior charity circuit. She is our granddaughter after all. But she's not interested."

They were both silent, considering the child, the only family child, who obviously felt abandoned not only by her mother but by everyone who bore her surname, including her own father. Elvira probably suspected that her stepmother looked in the mirror every day to ask who was the fairest of them all and injected apples with cyanide for a hobby.

"How's work?"

"I don't think we're going to get the contract for the shopping mall. If we do get it the company is going to reward us all with a weekend at a spa near Guelph."

"That's nice."

"What would your ideal shopping mall be, Mom?"

"There's no such thing. But if there were, the shops would be boutiques. There'd be no sticky donut places and muffin outlets. Absolutely no kids' play area. The window displays would be works of art, and a string quartet might play or perhaps, at Christmas, a really good choir could sing. In fact, perhaps, a small podium for performances of classical music would be all right. Oh yes. And a man in a fine suit, striped trousers, black jacket, would be on hand to ask if he could help."

"Oh right! It's going to be built in a small town up north. And then there's the Emergency Room competition. Hospitals. Depressing places. Mom, have you ever wanted to do something different? What's that line of Aunt Dorothy's? To 'light out for the territory.'"

Elsie looked past her daughter through the window at the garden wall as if she could find the sliver of a door reflected there, a magic entrance to a new and different world. And then she said, "I hope Mike will be here soon. The sauce is ready."

"He won't be long."

"Get me a pie from the freezer, dear."

"Mother!" Isabel shrieked a moment later. "You've killed the Boreks' dog."

Elsie heard her daughter throwing up in the bathroom and smiled.

~

Standing on the doorstep waiting for her visitors, Dorothy looked around at the little square of garden. The harsh Ontario winters sucked life force out of plants and humans alike. She'd thought once of moving to Victoria, like Kate's ex, where it was never too cold and never searingly hot but felt that the place must lack challenge. The effect of weather on the human psyche. The effect of the human psyche on weather. *What effect am I having on the world around me? Unless I make some effort, nothing but solitary, broken old age looms ahead. What am I doing here?* The old existential record was playing in her head. She tuned it out and smiled at the two approaching figures. Delphine, for once looking really smart, was wearing a blue outfit and a pair of silvery earrings. Alice was wearing a dark grey suit and a pink shirt.

"I don't expect much from the daffodils this year," Dorothy said, pointing at the long stems with their hesitant buds. "Come in, Delphine. Nice to see you again, Alice."

"Alec," Alec replied. "I changed my name, Mrs. Graham."

"Hello, Aunt Dorothy," Delphine said, wondering why her friend chose now to speak in an alien, abrupt way. They went inside and as she inhaled the familiar scent of coffee and paint, Delphine hoped the developers would leave Dorothy alone. This house had been a source of magic for her and Brian when they were kids. The many odd ornaments and lack of arrangement spoke not so much of sloth as of a fond accumulation. There was the old Toby jug, the little brass owl she'd given Dorothy long ago, graduation pictures of Isabel and Alice, Alice holding baby Elvira on one arm and her diploma in the other hand. A photograph of herself with Jake at his christening stood on the mantel. Familiar objects, all anchored in their places, all offering the security of memory. Two of Dorothy's own paintings hung on the wall between the windows. She called them "non-representative still lifes." Tortured fruit and broken crockery were set on a bright green lawn in one, and in the other a moon shone evilly down, casting a beam of light over three battered oranges. She sat down beside Alec on the unevenly cushioned sofa.

Dorothy gave them each a glass of yellowish wine. She didn't bother to ask whether they would have preferred red. Sitting opposite on her rocking chair, she leaned towards them, speaking softly as if there might be someone else in the room – under the table or behind the bookcase.

"I met a man today. Such a coincidence! I was coming back from Oakville. A woman I used to work with is in a home there, Alice. Anyway, the man helped me off the GO Train. I kind of fell into his arms and he told me I reminded him of his grandmother. I was a little put out of course because no one wants to be taken for a granny, for God's sake, even at my age. But I had to thank him and we got talking and he told me about himself and so."

Dorothy seemed barely to have aged in the last couple of decades. Her hair, slightly tinted, was brownish grey and her complexion, hardly ever touched by creams and enhancing products, was youthful. She would have made a good model for a cosmetic ad. But her mind was apparently slowing down. There was clearly more to be said about the stranger but her brain, like an overloaded hard drive, had frozen for the moment.

Alec said, "This is unusual wine."

"Thank you."

Delphine looked around and as her eye lit on the picture of herself with the infant Jake, the room lost some of its comfort.

Yes," Dorothy went on, bringing herself back to the matter. "Pierre, Pierre Jones his name is. He told me about himself. Downhill. I mean he went downhill for a while after he sold the family business and invested in all that dot.com stuff in the 90s. Or was it 80s? Anyway. He's moved here from Quebec, or was it Wales, to take over a little publishing company. He seemed excited about it."

"What kind of books does he intend to publish?"

"He's taken over the list. Mainly memoirs. That kind of thing. He's looking for material and that's partly why you're here."

Delphine began to wish she'd stayed home. She felt increasing irritation with Dorothy and her schemes, her little plots and suggestions, her knack of making people do what she wanted even against their will. "It sounds interesting," she said.

"The thing is," the old woman went on, "after we've talked about the dinner, I want to try something out. You'll be my test audience. I'm going to serve small things to eat. And you can drink and nibble while I read you some of my letters. I want some feedback before I show them to Pierre. It'll give him a chance to put out a worthwhile book and make money for the company at the same time."

"You don't know anything about him," Alec said. "He might be after your money."

"Then he'll be disappointed, dear. I have none."

The doorbell rang.

"I'm sorry," Delphine whispered to Alec.

"It's okay."

Then Isabel and Elsie and Kate came in together, talking.

At once, Alec stood up. "I came to see how you were," she said to Dorothy. "I have to practice for the club tomorrow. Thanks for the wine."

Before Dorothy could grapple with her and tell her she had to stay and talk to her mother and sister, she was gone.

Kate held on to Elsie and Elsie looked out of the window and said, "You shouldn't try to fix things, Dorothy. Things you know nothing about."

"I didn't know she was going to come," Dorothy said.

"You invited her," Delphine stated, hearing the tears in Elsie's voice.

Quietly the new arrivals sat down and Kate began, "This is a meeting about the dinner, right?" She brought out a notebook. "I've been doing some research into the eating habits of Afghanis."

Dorothy started to recite, "'When you're wounded and left on Afghanistan's plains, And the women come out to cut up your remains.'"

"Stop!" Delphine burst into tears.

Isabel, looking around as if she were in a theatre, said, "Is this be cruel to your friends day, Aunt Dorothy?"

Kate took her daughter out to the kitchen and they could be heard murmuring.

"You sure know how to empty a room," Elsie said.

Oh Omar!

"I'm sorry. These days old bits of poetry come out at odd times. Prompted, you know, by something. Triggered. It's involuntary. I'll learn more cheerful poems. 'God's in his heaven.' 'My heart leaps up.' 'Glory be for dappled things.' That's not quite right, is it?"

"For heaven's sake, Dorothy," Elsie snapped. "Let's get on with this. We've committed ourselves and we have to do it right."

"I think I got committed whether I like it or not," Isabel said.

"And you should've told Alice it was a family gathering," Elsie continued. "Given her time to get used to the idea. Not to mention me and Isabel. You do not think."

Dorothy decided not to say sorry or to tell both of them that they should get over it and act like human beings. Instead, she returned to the matter at hand. "I was telling Delphine about this man called Pierre. I met him on the GO Train and we went for coffee. He's something of an entrepreneur. He might be able to help. I told him about the space on Queen."

"Hold on," Elsie said. "We are supposed to be doing this. If we let a man take over, it's not our event. You should've discussed this with us. You made a unilateral decision, Dorothy. I don't like it. He's probably a middle-aged guy who'll see us as three old trouts and run it to his own advantage."

"All right. All right. I'll tell him we don't need him then. I only thought we might be glad to have a little extra help. It seems to me that we've taken on rather a lot. And he's sixty-something if you must know."

Kate returned followed by Delphine. They sat down and Kate got out her notebook again.

"Let's make some lists," she said. "I've been looking at what is going on there and what people traditionally eat. I don't think we need to go too far in that direction. We have to remember that the guests will want to enjoy themselves and eat something they're used to."

"My freezer is full of goat," Elsie said.

"You've gone ahead and bought goat!"

"It was on sale."

Isabel said, "It seems to me that you're all acting unilaterally. If you can't have a consensus about the menu, what's going to happen about everything else?"

Kate passed around a piece of paper that read, "Menu: Mixed green salad, beef and pasta casserole, rolls, pie and ice cream."

"This is so old-fashioned, Mom," Delphine said.

"We can make goat stew with couscous and have fresh fruit for dessert," Elsie said. "Those goats are not going to be wasted."

"Couscous has to be served the minute it's done."

"Rice then."

"We'd better have a vote."

"I don't think I want the responsibility of being a voting member," Isabel said. "More wine anyone?"

Kate tore up her menu and let the bits of paper lie on the rug.

Delphine asked, "Have you set a date?"

Elsie answered, "The best time for me would be early June. Don't look at me like that, Dorothy. It's just that I usually do have more appointments than either of you so I looked at my diary before I came."

"I'm going to go to the Kuril Islands," Kate said.

Dorothy fetched her calendar from the kitchen.

"How about the tenth?"

"Where are they, Aunt Kate?" Isabel asked.

"She's fantasizing," Elsie said. "Let's pin this down."

"The tenth, everyone?"

"And the place?"

"Pierre thinks –"

"We are excluding this man," Kate said.

"Unless he knows of somewhere free – complete with chairs and tables and cutlery and plates. I absolutely refuse to have anything to do with paper plates and plastic cloths."

"What Pierre knows is publishing. He's looking for interesting manuscripts."

"Are we writing a book or organizing a dinner?"

"Could you give me a hand, Isabel, please?" Dorothy asked.

The two of them went out and in a moment the younger woman returned bearing a tray laden with crackers and cheese and pâté. Dorothy followed her carrying three shoeboxes.

"My writing," she said, hugging the boxes before she set them down on the table beside her. "Letters."

"Aunt Dorothy!" Delphine exclaimed. "You must have hundreds."

Dorothy said, "Examples of a lost art."

"Who are they from?" Isabel asked politely.

"From me, of course."

"Letters you haven't sent yet?"

"I don't know their addresses. The people I write to. And in any case, some of them are dead. You've all got wine? Help yourselves to the edibles. I just want your opinion. That's all."

Delphine took the second bottle of GoldCrest and filled the glasses to the top.

Dorothy brought several sheets of paper out of the top box and said, "This is a recent one. 'Dear Ms.X , I am not sure that you know what you are doing. You are young and rich and people buy magazines just in order to see what you are wearing, if anything, and whether you are getting married or divorced this week. You no doubt became famous before anyone had time to instill some sense of responsibility into your simple head. Just being you is not enough. Your beauty will fade and all the Botox in the world won't stop you from becoming passé. I suggest that now, before it's too late, you try to do some good in the world. Consider Princess Diana.'"

She read on. There were letters to the prime minister, to President Bush and to other politicians. "This one's to the pope. 'Your Holiness should perhaps adopt a dozen orphans (your house is surely large enough) before you make pronouncements about contraception. Protected as you are from real life, you can have little knowledge of sex. For your information making love is very enjoyable and good exercise too...'"

She finished her recital with part of a letter to the chairman of a large finance company: "'Dear Thief, While I realize that you have a different title on your office door, the truth is that because of your actions, or lack of action, thousands have lost their savings. Old people are desperate. I have walked by the mansion you call home and seen the Mercedes and BMW parked outside. I know the size of your obscene bonus.

As a shareholder, I would like to see your fat face looking out through the bars of a grille.' That's a copy of the one I actually mailed a year ago. His lawyer called. I pretended to be my daughter and told him my mother was in South America."

Rumour had it that, now in his seventies and clinging to his position as CEO, the man was about to be indicted for tax fraud.

Kate said, "Well." And the word hung in the air.

Isabel said, "I think they need answers. I mean responses."

Delphine roused herself from a comatose state and looked at her watch.

Dorothy said, "I can't send them and expect people to reply. I'll get coffee. Who wants decaf?"

She went to the kitchen and stood near the door to listen to their comments. She wished there was a way to turn up the sound. She heard Delphine say, "So she sits here writing these letters to people she doesn't know." And then Elsie murmured softly, " I sometimes wonder..." The rest of her comment was inaudible.

When Dorothy returned with the tray, Kate said, "You've been writing these letters for years?"

"I like them," Isabel said. "You could make them into an epistolary novel. Jean-Louis Barron's letters are being published next year. But he's very well-known. Was. I mean his writing."

"Thank you, dear."

After that, they talked about the chilly weather, the war in Iraq, the price of gas and then how late it was. Dorothy sighed. They were choosing to ignore what they probably didn't understand.

As they were leaving, she said, "With your advertising skills, Delphine, you might have a few ideas to help with promotion for the dinner. And there'll be invitations. We want them addressed by hand. It looks classier."

Elsie said, "We should look for a another venue."

"The Queen Street place has a kind of desperate look. Maybe it's exactly the right ambiance."

"That's a fancy name for a foul smell and inch-thick grime."

Kate kissed Dorothy's cheek and said, "Well," again in a tone of voice that implied that it wasn't.

Omar dear, I'm tired. I'd like to have some of the special tea they serve in Arab countries and lie back and relax in a hamam and run my fingers through a box of real Turkish Delight. They sell a rubbery imitation of it here, but I want the soft sugary kind that dissolves on the tongue and that you no doubt keep by your bedside in a gaudy box.

All in all, it had been a fairly successful evening, even though Alice had taken off like a frightened rabbit and the rest of them hadn't said anything about her writing. She'd expected a little enthusiastic feedback. Maybe when they'd had time to think about the letters, she would hear from them. Elsie and Isabel hadn't finished their wine. She poured their leavings into her own glass and sat down to arrange her collection. The clearing up could wait till tomorrow. She reached down into the first box and pulled out a yellowing paper.

Dear Winston,
One of the reasons my father came to Canada besides, as I

now know, wanting to be with my Aunt Kathleen, was that your spirit seemed to go out of England when peace arrived. It was as if all those giant barrage balloons that hovered in the sky during the war had deflated with one great sigh and covered the country with their grey material.

In 1945, people expected instantly to have bananas again, to have comfort and money and good weather too. And when this didn't happen they threw you out with the bathwater. "Cometh the hour. Cometh the man," they say. The war was your hour and you knew it. You weren't always right, but you had the gift of making people think you were.

And what would the old cigar-smoker have thought of the world now? He was a fighter, but would he have chosen to engage in the current conflicts?

$\sim$

Kate was driving her daughter home because Alec had taken Delphine's car. She couldn't prevent herself from asking how the two of them were getting on together.

Delphine said, "She sleeps in Jake's room and comes in late. She sleeps in and watches daytime TV." She'd lost her high school friend and gained a musician, a sax player who was in no hurry to move out and who returned noisily at two or three in the morning. Her son in his wilder days had been more considerate. As she lay awake in those early hours, Delphine made plans to speak sharply to Alec and tell her to move on. But on those days when she came home from work and found that Alec had made a salad and poured wine, she found herself grateful and could only say thank you. Then they talked about the "doll," about his latest email message and his future academic success.

Kate said, "It's a pity she can't move in with Elsie."

"Too much baggage. Aunt Dorothy's letters. Weird. Do you think she's okay?"

"At university she was a good writer. I guess she's been using her talent."

"And putting it in a shoebox?"

"Lots of writers do that."

"It seems like a waste that's all. Maybe she'll begin to write novels and surprise everyone. Become a bestseller at eighty-five."

Delphine had made up her mind to sit down with Alec and ask about her plans. She did see that some of her distress at Jake's departure had been swallowed up in the surprise of Alec's arrival and was grateful at least for that. But she wanted to live by herself, to learn to get used to it. Alec had brought her own burden of resentment and distress with her and now it lurked about the house like a strange unwelcome animal.

She said good night to her mother, watched her drive off and went inside. Alec was sitting at the kitchen table looking surly and eating toast and peanut butter.

"I'm sorry. Dorothy didn't tell me it was a family meeting."

"You must've known, Delph."

"Look. It's all right you staying with me but you're in the same city now. Your mother. Isabel. Elvira."

"I think they have to come to me."

"Even your daughter?"

"I'm getting around to the right approach. Elvira hates me. I know that. I'm looking for my child through a thick curtain of guilt."

Delphine tidied the dishes in the sink, made herself a cup of ginger tea and said, "I have to work tonight."

"Dorothy hasn't changed. I always think of her as a

maiden aunt. The kind you get in old-fashioned English novels. Virginal."

"She's been married three times!" It was easy to think of Aunt Dorothy thrashing about in bed and emitting ecstatic cries. "She's never seemed like a lonely woman."

"Then she's fortunate."

"Why don't you just call Elvira?"

"Why don't you shut up and have a glass of wine. That piss you're drinking isn't going to stir your creative juices."

∾

Kate's cellphone rang and woke her from sleep. The bedside clock told her it was only four-thirty. Jake? Delphine? In a moment she was on her way to Kabul to bring the wounded boy home. She said 'hello' and listened. And listened. She wasn't sure when she closed the phone whether to laugh or cry. She wanted to laugh because it wasn't about Jake; therefore Jake was all right. And then she did begin to laugh in a kind of vengeful way that she knew was wrong. It was sad, sad. No laughing matter. She got up and went to the kitchen and put the kettle on. There was no going back to sleep after news like this. She wanted to call Elsie, who might well be lying awake cursing the dog next door. Instead she made a cup of mint tea and put two shortbread cookies on a plate. It was not, absolutely not, she said firmly to herself, a celebratory feast. Who would she tell first? Delphine might already know and Brian, who had always taken his father's side, certainly would have been informed. The news had to be absorbed and the late judge's request considered without advice from anyone else. As she ate the cookies, she wished she had another friend, one less intimate, less knowing, to whom she could talk. A friend who wouldn't tell her what she should and shouldn't do. There was always Marian in the gift shop, who didn't really listen but often responded with an offbeat though helpful comment.

She looked up to see whether it was worth going back to bed. The clock was gone from the wall. The round clock with Mickey Mouse hands that they'd bought at Disneyland thirty years ago was not there. Who would come in and steal just that one thing? The rest of the apartment appeared to be in its usual state of ordered untidiness. She checked the locks and the windows. Then she saw the clock lying almost under the far counter as if it had been thrown from its place in anger. If it had fallen naturally, it would have hit the microwave oven and dropped broken onto the floor beside the mat. The poltergeist again. Another inexplicable event. The subway trains beneath the building six floors down didn't cause tremors, and earthquakes were rare. "Who are you?" she asked. "Why are you doing this to me?" There was no reply from the mischievous spirit.

Two strange events before daylight. She took the tea and cookies to the easy chair under the lamp and picked up yesterday's newspaper. She would read her way into the morning and ignore the imp of *schadenfreude* that was dancing in her mind.

In her despair, the maiden tied up her golden tresses and fastened them with a black ribbon, a sign of mourning for the knight who had gone on a fruitless journey. He, foolish fellow, thought it was all for glory and a better future and that he would come back with a name, fame and if he was very fortunate, a fortune. All those rewards had been promised him by the woman who lived near the well and people believed her simply because she was old.

That was the gist of the story Dorothy had just read to Elvira's class. *To be continued.* She closed the book and looked at the enquiring faces around her.

"What was the name of the horse, Miss?"

"We haven't got to that yet, Gavin."

"Horses don't have names, silly."

"They do so, don't they, Miss Edwards?"

"That's all for today, children," Elvira said.

The bell rang on cue. She helped the two smallest into their jackets, and others who were capable of dressing themselves drifted towards her trying to look even younger than they were.

"I can't do my zipper up."

"What's a fortune?"

Something that is told. Something that is received. A blessing. A wonder. Something that has to be good. Sometimes a lot of money.

"It's in the next chapter. You'll find out next week."

"Can I have a fortune?"

"Goodbye. Todd. Alison. Ezra. Lisa."

They drifted out through the doorway, a wave of red and blue and pink surging towards waiting adults. Elvira watched to make sure that not a single child was left standing alone looking about in despair, abandoned.

"I'm not sure about that story, Aunt Dorothy," she said. "I don't think it's on the approved list."

"The sooner they learn words like *mourning, fruitless, misfortune*, the better. The words will sink into their minds and, when they get a little older, they will understand the difference between the first part of the day and the sadness of bereavement and that it is not only a November apple tree that is without fruit. And what do you call it when you are waiting and wishing for something and the time passes and that thing hasn't happened or been delivered? What must you never lose, children? Hope. H.O.P.E."

Elvira straightened the little chairs and found a ribbon, a nickel and a toy car on the floor. Tomorrow there would be all the excitement of lost and found. The goldfish in the tank were mouthing their little nothings. She dropped food into the water and said, "Good night, Rudolph and Barbie," as if relapsing into childishness herself would make her life easier.

Dorothy noticed the black ribbon in the girl's hair, the dark skirt and blouse she was wearing. She looked bereaved, or perhaps *bereft* was a better word. She and Alice should be shut in a room to yell at each other until they found a way through the dark forest to love.

"Have you time to come to SITV with me, Elvira?" she asked. "Did you drive today?"

"I don't have a car. Are you going to be on television?"

"I want to ask about advertising. I'll drive you home after."

"I need to stop in the staff room first."

"I'll wait outside."

Dorothy wound the car window down and listened to the sound of the older kids coming out of the school, the ones who didn't need to be met and taken home by hand. Murmuring, laughing, running, leaping. Some of them already had the dangerous look of knowledge in their eyes. And all of them knew that it was only six weeks till the long summer break.

Elvira came out arguing with her friend Jenny.

"I don't want to," Elvira was saying.

"Come on," Jenny said. "You need to have some fun."

"I'm not going to that arcade again. The noise those machines make gives me a headache, and the kids there are frightening."

"They're just quick, that's all. Anyway, this will be different. We'll have coffee first."

"My aunt's waiting for me."

She got into the car and waved to Jenny through the window.

"The kids like fairy stories," Dorothy said as she drove off.

"Fairy stories are okay as long as they have the right message. Kids need to know about real life. Why Mummy is sometimes cross. Why Daddy comes home late from the office, smiling and staggering, with lipstick on his shirt."

"You want to tell them there's no safe place?"

Dorothy heard a sniffle and glanced sideways. Elvira was holding a Kleenex to her nose.

"I'm sorry," she said. "Sorry."

"Come on, Elvira. Why now? It's been years."

"It's the little ones," Elvira said. "I know I was ten years older than they are now when it happened, but I see them run to their mothers and they have no idea that their mothers might up and leave them one day without any warning. Just a few words and a note and go."

"Well," Dorothy said, "you're not going to be much of a teacher if you go on like this. Maybe you should go back to college and then teach in a high school."

"Then they'd all be teenagers whose parents have split up already."

"No hope then."

Dorothy noticed that Elvira moved her foot to an imaginary brake once or twice and paid no attention. She'd kidnapped the unhappy princess and was taking her to the castle dungeon. There was no place to park outside the building so she drove along the street and found a space beside a meter.

"I've asked you to come with me because people don't always see older women. They look right past us. We get ignored. You're my front. Watch and learn."

"I'm sorry I'm such a drag. It's because I know she's here in the city."

"And one of these days you have to talk to her, Elvira. She's probably afraid of your rejection. You have to make the first move."

At the reception desk, Dorothy said, "I'd like to talk to somebody about advertising an event."

"Marlyn down the hall on the right will take care of you."

Down the hall in a small space sat Marlyn at her desk. Marlyn was perched on a large blue exercise ball. Elvira and Dorothy were standing side by side in front of her.

Marlyn turned to Elvira and said, "Can I help you?"

Elvira smiled and replied, "Mrs. Graham here would like to ask about your advertising rates."

"Tell her that we don't charge for local events but we need the information a week in advance and we can't promise to broadcast it but will do our best."

Dorothy said thank you and emerged from the invisibility zone. She wondered whether Marlyn's father had been a fisherman but decided not to ask.

"We don't do bake sales," Marlyn continued, "only real events and it's free but the manager decides whether to do them or not."

And the next event, Marlyn, is when I puncture your ball and you end up on your ass. Dorothy was wondering whether to go into her you-too-will-be-old-one-day speech when Elvira turned to her and yelled, "You set this up!"

She was pointing at two monitors high on the wall. There was Alice in duplicate sitting on a couch being interviewed by another woman.

"You're all against me." The girl ran out into the corridor.

Marlyn looked at Dorothy as if it was something she might have known: Another old woman up to her evil tricks. And Dorothy, knowing she wouldn't be able to catch up with Elvira, sat down to watch Alice.

"Could you turn the sound up, please, Marlyn?"

"It would disturb everyone."

Somewhere there had to be a listening room, a green room. Dorothy wandered along the corridor till she found a door with a red light over it and went inside. She could see Alice/Alec, her saxophone in her hand, sitting across from the interviewer, smiling.

"You left the city eight years ago, Alec?" the interviewer said.

"It seems longer."

"You were married at the time."

"That's right. That was before I knew."

"You're not meant to be here," a man hissed at Dorothy.

"That's my niece. An honorary niece."

"Nice for you but you have to get out. Now. How did you get in here? I'll have security come and get you."

"I'm going."

Dorothy walked out of the building and the sounds of the saxophone followed her: A dark street on a wet night. A detective in a belted raincoat. Somewhere a blonde was waiting in a shady hotel room.

Hotel! She could check it out and still be home by five to report on it to Kate and Elsie. The traffic was building up to early rush hour, but she found a parking spot two streets away.

"I'm sorry." The manager said fifteen minutes later walking her to the door as if he feared she might steal his computer. "It's not our kind of event."

Pierre, wrong-again-Pierre, had assured her that any large hotel would be glad to lend space for a charity dinner. Not this charity dinner. Not this hotel. The charge for room and service was far too high, and then there was the matter of the food the hotel would insist on providing along with staff and wine. TEWP would have to charge a thousand dollars a head to make any profit at all.

She walked through the lobby towards the side exit and then stopped, was stopped, in her tracks. Her feet were glued to the red carpet. Her legs were pillars of stone. He was there. He was, in the solid flesh, there. The newspapers had said filming would begin in Toronto next week but that his scenes would be shot on location in Turkey. Yet he was here now. Here in her city. The grey hair, grey moustache, heavy eyebrows, the brown eyes, skin the colour of light toast: Him. He put his head down on his hand as if he too was tired. She was breathing the same air. Now she noticed the velvet ropes by the staircase and the minders and body-guards standing around like statues, little wires coming out of their ears. They were not looking her way. This was her opportunity. Heaven-sent. Should she or shouldn't she? What approach to take? She could go and stand before him with her toes turned in and offer up an embarrassing line about always having loved his work, or she could go up to him and demand to know why he hadn't replied to the letters she'd never mailed. She might lie and say, You don't remember me, but we met once in Cairo. She preferred that cool approach and had she been wearing her silky blue pantsuit would have moved in on him at once. It would then be up to him to be polite and either tell her he remembered or say he'd never seen her before in his life. Either would do because at last she would hear his voice clear without the filter of a movie soundtrack.

She turned away in order to gather herself together. She pushed her fingers through her hair. *Be still my heart!* After all, he was not a god. He was simply a lucky man who had been able to spend his life doing whatever he wanted. Women had fallen to him like apples from a tree. His last movie had not been a success. Trading on his looks and his accent, he likely got an inflated price for both. She began to feel angry. She would go up to him and ask what earthly use he was to anybody any more. How had he dared to become this aging version of the handsome young doctor who'd rattled along in the train across Russia? Was he now simply a total waste of space?

He would say, and she could hear him saying it, *My dear, I have given pleasure to millions all over this sorry world.* The truth of that statement reduced her heart to mush again. He wouldn't mind that she was wearing flat-heeled shoes and a raincoat that had lost its belt. She turned to go towards him and pay homage and say, *You have given me much joy in my life, Mr. Sharif, and I would like to send you some letters.* But the plush armchair was empty. He had vanished. She felt betrayed.

At the reception desk, she asked to be put through to Mr. Sharif's room.

"No one of that name here," the man answered with a patronizing smile. She was no doubt the fiftieth woman who had asked for the old actor that day.

She did consider lingering in the hotel lobby for the rest of the evening and watching for a TV camera, a herd of journalists, another chance. But her old friends would arrive and find the door locked and tell each other that she had started down the slippery slope of forgetfulness.

As she drove home, she pondered the hesitation that had caused her to lose the one moment she might have had to speak to her idol. Did life offer many second chances? The movie scenes were to be shot next week. She might spend a few days lurking in the street where the action was to take place. She hoped somebody was going to clean the city so that Omar might walk on tidy sidewalks. It had become a shabbier place lately. There were papers and cans in the gutters and dust and noise from construction all around. What impression would it give to a man of his cosmopolitan sensibility?

She shook his image from her mind. A squirrel ran down a tree that was in its early summer glory. And her two friends who, like her, were well into the autumn of life and verging on winter would be at her door in five minutes.

She picked up the mail from the mat. Nothing from Pierre. She decided to allow another week to go by, seven days exactly, before she called him about her correspondence. She'd sorted her letters in order of date before she handed them over. In the twenty-five-year stretch, they made a neat historical document. One of the first was to Ronald Reagan.

Dear Mr. President,

I'm glad to know that you are paying attention to the Cold War, to the leftover hysterics of that period. It's over, Mr. P. Get your country to move on. I suggest that you, while you're about it, encourage schools to teach more Russian and German literature and any other foreign works that will introduce students to the civilized side of other nations. I would not, however, recommend Dostoevsky as a starting point.

Did Ronald Reagan have any idea who Dostoevsky was? Did he see the point of reading at all? Too late to ask him now. The poor man's mind had drifted into that dread limbo and left him thought-less. She couldn't remember why she'd started that particular letter and then continued to write so many others. It spoke perhaps of loneliness, a need to talk to someone else even though there would be no reply: Conversations with an empty chair.

And now the question was, should she tell her friends about her nearly close encounter, or would they think she was crazy? They shared pretty well everything. The only secret she and Kate kept from Elsie was their old fantasy that Richard might be the third child. He wasn't exactly the right age, but while his nose and teeth were no part of the genetic pattern, his hair was pale brown and his jaw did jut out slightly. They had watched to see if their friend's husband grew as he aged into a replica of Dorothy's dad, Dennis, but he had become stocky and ruddy-faced, nothing like the tall Yorkshireman. DNA tests were expensive and truth would have spoilt their game.

She only had time to put out mugs and plates on the tray and there they were, coming up the path. Her best friends, her sisters in the combat of life. Enter two clowns, she thought as she gave each of them a hug.

Kate said, "You look flushed."

Dorothy said, "I've had an experience."

Elsie said, "That artist. You sleep with him."

"Don't be ridiculous."

They sat around the table and Dorothy got out the folder marked TEWP. If they were going to be stupid she wouldn't tell them about Sharif at all. Their loss! Elsie was wearing her working outfit today, jeans and an old green sweater. She'd printed out a sample invitation and Kate had picked out a logo in the shape of a hand reaching out in a helpful way.

"I think where we begin," Dorothy said, "is with the people who are always asking US for money."

"They ask us because they need it. We have to reach out beyond them."

"We also have to arrange the dinner," Kate said.

"To be successful, a fundraiser has to offer people something in return for their money."

"After the dinner we might hold a celebrity auction."

"And just which celebrity are we offering as the prize?"

"Be serious."

"I can get the maestro," Elsie said.

"And he would do what?"

"A symphony concert plus wine and nibblies. Three

hundred bucks a head. Donations. Split the profits with the orchestra."

"Too highbrow," Kate said.

"We won't make much impression with a bake sale."

"People want something for their money."

"They get to feel good."

"I think," Kate said, "that we should get people to sponsor something like a walk, a run."

Dorothy let the two of them argue and then suggested, "A trip to Afghanistan."

"Who'd want to go there?"

"You don't persuade people to give money to send you on a trip."

"Maybe, if we went, if the three of us went, we could come back and make a TV program about it and ask people to give."

"That's what gives charities a bad name," Kate said. "You spend more than you take in that way. We want to show that we can do it differently."

"All the same, that's an idea, Dot."

"Don't call me that, Elsie."

"Now the Conservatives are in again, we'll need all the charity we can get at home."

"It's still a minority government. Nothing will change."

"I miss Chretien. There was something sexy about him."

"Your choice in men, Dorothy, has always been unreliable."

"I don't think so," Dorothy replied, thinking of Sharif. "I haven't met the right ones. Perhaps I've expected the wrong things from them. And they from me. That's what it's all about. Like Christmas really. You hope for one gift and you get another. Often something you never wanted."

"My poltergeist has struck again. The kitchen clock."

"I never liked it," Dorothy said. "Do you think you need an exorcist?"

"And that's not the only thing. You'll never guess who called this morning."

"The dinner, girls," Elsie said. "Let's stick to our sheep, or rather our goat, before we get to the idle chat."

"I saw him," Dorothy said, letting it out before she could stop herself. "He's here making a movie."

"The space on Queen could be okay. What are you talking about?"

"Omar Sharif. He's here. He was sitting in the lobby of the Royal York. I could have touched him. But when I turned around, he was gone."

"That's nice," Kate said, tight-lipped for some reason. "Will they provide plates and cutlery and glassware?"

"There isn't exactly a 'they,'" Elsie answered. "It's empty. A large empty space."

"So we have to find chairs and tables and every last little thing! How are you going to cook the goat?"

"If you use plenty of herbs, I gather it tastes like lamb."

"He was there."

"Maybe we should have rice and couscous. A choice."

"Are you telling me how to cater, Kate? I do have some experience."

" He was sitting in a red chair."

"I saw the Dalai Lama when he came here. Our eyes met. It was a holy kind of experience," Elsie said. "As if he was looking right into me. I felt inspired for days afterwards."

"You said we should we get on!" Kate put in.

Dorothy was annoyed. Why couldn't they just allow her a moment and enter into her excitement? If she'd said she'd seen Brad Pitt or some other ephemeral godlet, they might have reacted with awe. She gave up.

They made more lists and assigned tasks. As she was seeing

Kate and Elsie out, she called after them, "I did see him!" When even your best friends don't understand what something means to you, what hope is there?

She put the dishes away and then sat down to consider the mad idea of going to Pakistan and then trying to cross the border via the Khyber Pass. Three elderly women. Three unwise women riding camels. If they were kidnapped and held hostage and killed, it would certainly raise WANT's profile and be a lasting benefit to the country. It might be the best possible thing they could do and surely wouldn't be difficult to arrange. What were their lives worth beyond this point after all?

To what do we look forward except decline and discomfort? And that includes you, Omar. Creaking joints, unreliable digestive systems, fading vision, disappearing voices, that's what. On the other hand, I do want to continue to aggravate the developers by staying on here. I'm depriving them of the opportunity to build a low-rise building with ten units each valued at $450,000. Do the math, Omar. And I want to see what happens next in the Alice/Delphine story. Will Alice now Alec meet Elvira who is after all her only child? Will Elsie and Richard take Alice now Alec back into the fold? It's all a soap opera. Just like your glamorous life if it were set down in simple sentences.

Coming back to charity. Maybe I can persuade Elsie and Kate that a trip to Afghanistan and a possible gruesome death at the hands of black-robed brigands will be a worthwhile fundraising effort.

Their slaughter would bring the state of that country to the attention of millions around the world. Their pictures would appear hourly on TV and journalists would haunt their grieving families and try to catch tears on tape. Money would pour in to WANT. In a year, the soldiers would be able to go home leaving a place fit for – what! Dream on, Dorothy!

Kate was still annoyed with herself next morning. She could have shouted Elsie and Dorothy down and forced them to hear what she wanted to say. Perhaps she was afraid of their response. And right now, she felt in a childish way that she wouldn't tell them at all. Screw them! Standing behind the counter in the hospital gift shop she wondered why she'd ever taken this job on. The air in the building was filled with vague murmurs of sorrow and pain interrupted now and then by the loudspeaker calling for this doctor or that. *Ready in* OR. An unconscious patient was about to be cut open and his entrails disturbed by a stranger's hands. The late judge might become just another man drifting along a corridor wearing a gown that didn't fit, pushing a drip on a stand, going out for a smoke. What were all those years of living together about if she couldn't feel compassion for him now? The iron in her soul was on the verge of melting, if iron could melt.

A security guard came in and asked her if she'd seen an old guy in yellow pyjamas. When she said no, he ran to the front entrance. Had the patient escaped and climbed onto the bus to town? A group of business people with briefcases walked by talking about the new Emergency Centre, a warehouse of a place set aside for centralized triage. The idea was to send serious cases to the appropriate hospitals. Broken legs, wasp stings and slight injuries would be treated on site. In the papers, there were already angry letters from doctors and nurses. The Health Authority responded that once they got used to it, the plan would ease their work considerably. To which the medical staffs replied that yes, it would, because numbers of patients would die before they ever got to be seen: It was ignorant bureaucracy once again imposing its will on something it knew nothing about.

Kate sold a pink baby jacket to a young man and a chocolate bar to the little boy holding his hand. Silently she wished the family a happy future. The chocolate bar would not prevent sibling rivalry in the years ahead but it would sweeten the moment. *What shall we call your baby sister, honey?* She had said those very words to Brian as together they looked down at tiny Delphine, and he'd replied, "nothing." Was it in that moment that her son had decided to be daddy's boy? When Brian called last Sunday she knew his father had already been in touch, seeking sympathy from his child the way unhappy old men do.

She looked at her watch; lunchtime had gone by. She was hungry and Marian hadn't arrived to release her.

"Hello, Aunt Kate. How much is this?" Isabel was standing at the counter holding a crocheted shawl.

"What does it say? Twenty-five dollars."

"It's for a friend. I'm really here with the group about the new ER plans. They're meeting with the management. I backed out of the room. It's so boring. I have ideas but they don't want to hear them. If it gets built in my lifetime we'll be lucky."

"That's a pretty colour."

"I'll take it."

Kate was putting the shawl into a plastic bag when Marian came hurrying in saying she was sorry to be late but parking was the pits and she was down the far side of the building. "I know I could come on the bus and save time, but every time I go on public transport, I catch a cold. People cough and wipe their hands on the seats and – hello?"

"This is my friend's daughter, Isabel," Kate said. "We're going for lunch. You can go back to the group later, Isabel."

They walked through the long corridor to the cafeteria and Isabel chose a table as far away as possible from doctors, from sickly patients who'd dragged their IV stands with them to have coffee or some forbidden treat.

"Tell me about Paris," Kate said when she brought over the coffee and two tuna sandwiches.

"Thanks. I had a muffin at the break."

Kate looked at the soggy sandwiches and lost interest in them too.

"What happened was, Aunt Kate, this man. You know I went especially to see Jean Louis Barron's house and the place where he wrote because I love his work."

"He certainly knew how to tell a story."

"He knew how to live a story. All this time, I thought he was a faithful man and that Marguerite was his only love and that he stayed with her and all that stuff in the books..."

Kate looked at Elsie's daughter and wondered how she had grown up to be naïve and to remain so at forty.

"Mother doesn't understand. If you're going to Paris, she said – well you know how she thinks. But there was this guy in the house, Barron's house, in the study. And he told me he was a grandson, though Marguerite didn't have any children."

Kate said, "It's possible that the man was lying." *An actor hired to hang about in the great man's shrine and destroy the illusions of true believers. But hired by whom?*

"I looked at his face. There was something. A kind of resemblance. And he told me that Barron had loved someone else. And there were twins who'd been put into a home when they were babies so he could keep the secret from Marguerite. How could he do that? It makes him a monster."

"You still like his work. That doesn't change."

"But when you've admired someone for so long, thought they were one thing and they turn out to be another."

Tell me about it.

"And then, the weird thing is, yesterday I met the guy, Pierre, outside my office building. He was passing by, he said. I did go for a drink with him in Paris. I guess I told him where I worked. He's moved here now from Quebec, he said. But he never mentioned that when we talked."

There were days when Kate wished the world were populated with older people, men and women full of experience for whom there were no surprises and who didn't believe in coincidence.

"Don't look at me like that, Aunt Kate. He's old. Sorry."

"Old doesn't mean there's no life in him, Isabel. It must be Dorothy's Pierre. The man she met on the train."

"Then that's really weird. A bit creepy in fact."

Kate bit into the damp sandwich – always too much mayonnaise – and looked at the younger woman. "If you want to know what's really weird, Isabel, I had a call from my ex-husband," she said, eager now to tell her story.

But Isabel had caught a glimpse of her colleagues going by outside. "I'd better join them," she said. "I think the new ER should be attractive. Nice drapes, paintings, themes, quilts. Homelike and not some sterile factory. But no one listens to me."

She hurried away and left Kate aware that she must tell Elsie and Dorothy about Robert before she blurted her news out to a passing stranger. She took her copy of Flann O'Brien's *The Third Policeman* from her bag and sat back to enjoy a few minutes of quiet absurdity.

Chapter 3

STILL IRRITATED BY HER FRIENDS' lack of interest, Dorothy sat down at the computer and began to write to the queen. *Your Majesty, I've been thinking about you lately.*

And that was true. For some reason, royal images had been flickering through her mind: Princess Elizabeth in her ATS uniform in 1943. The princess with her parents in bomb-shocked London. The young queen mourning her uncle-in-law who'd been killed in a different kind of warfare. To whom did she turn in times of stress?

Although I tend towards republicanism, I have great admiration for you.

Is it possible in your elevated position to have any real friends, people you can relax and joke with and in whose company you can, if need be, belch or fart without embarrassment? These friends, say you had two of them, might have prevented a couple of the unfortunate marriages in your family by speaking out. Of course my friends, Kate and Elsie, didn't stop me marrying Alfred Sparrow though they were right. I went ahead because I loved him.

I have to tell you that, wonderful as old friends are, they are not always perfect or even reliable. In fact, they don't always listen. I think if you caught sight of me in the crowd and we exchanged a glance, you might imagine me as a friend. Sitting with you in your smaller sitting room I could tell you about almost meeting Omar Sharif, the actor. Perhaps you know him. Perhaps you have been fortunate enough to experience him in the flesh. I don't mean 'carnal knowledge' of course. You are too much in the public eye for that.

Anyway, I hope there is someone close to you who tells you if something you wear doesn't suit you or that you looked silly in the hat you wore to Ascot. Friends can be a comfort in many ways.

More later.

She pressed the *Save* key and opened her email. Jake's last message had said in a joking way that he and Ali were learning to play the local football game and had "not been shot yet." What did that mean? Was he wounded though not by gunfire? Slashed with a sword perhaps? Was Ali a warlord who had him in captivity?

"When you're wounded and left on Afghanistan's plains."

She certainly wasn't going to send him the rest of that poem. Censorship. Reprisals. A long arm reaching even to this short street in Toronto, almost a desert in its own right. At least, deserted. "Jest lean on your rifle." He had a bleak view, Kipling. But then he'd been there. He knew. It was nothing like that old movie, *Carry on up the Khyber*, which had almost given her father a heart attack from laughing so much. She and Kate had had to support him as they left the cinema. Warfare was still "carrying on" up the Khyber Pass, and it was no joke.

There were no new messages.

Dorothy felt tired and put the kettle on. She would indulge in a little daytime television, something her protestant soul still found sinful. Days were for working, for getting on with things. But this was an occasion. She moved the small coffee table alongside the couch so that she could put her feet up and still reach her cup of valedictory tea. The remote control device in magic carpet mode whisked her instantly to Washington D.C.

What pomp! What ceremony! The cortège of black cars moved in slow time. A horse – the dead man had loved horses – walked in funeral time, its saddle empty, empty boots in the stirrups facing backwards. It made her cold to watch the family group in their dark clothes standing, waiting, shivering. Umbrellas appearing now. And the widow small, intense, was like a black spider at the centre of it all.

With all these primitive trappings they were seeing an old chief off to his last reward, whatever that meant. And death had to be considered. It was, after all, a fact of life. It was present in her only prayer: Let me die before I go bald, incontinent and mindless. And death had presided over her birth, taking her mother and leaving her to her sad father's care. *But that was long ago, Omar. I'm over it, okay.*

The deceased president had suffered from Alzheimer's for a long time. Better off where you are now, Mr. Reagan, that's for sure. All glory gone. The good is certainly living after you at the moment but historians and other pikers will get around to the debit side of the ledger soon enough. How do they train horses to walk at funeral pace?

She took a sip of the green tea Elvira had given her. For some reason the girl had taken to bringing her little gifts. Did she at this late date want some kind of an attachment? She already had a grandmother, two in fact, and surely didn't need another. But the Edwards family seemed to keep their feelings in some kind of refrigerated compartment. And now, possibly having a mid-life crisis at seventy, Elsie was obsessed with the idea of her other daughter having a child. All three of them were slightly off-centre these days. Alfred Sparrow's words, "It's all downhill from here," didn't only refer to the lie of the land.

It seemed economically right for my dad to share a house with his brother's widow, my aunt Kathleen, and her daughter Kate. So Delphine's mother, Kate that is, and I grew up

*together. Are you still with me? And I couldn't help being
jealous of any attention my dad paid to Kate. I was truly
sorry, though, after I let her hamster out into the snow. I'm
still puzzled as to why he left her the camera.*

The music was sombre. "I've been a widow too, Nancy.
My aunt was a widow almost all her life, but not necessarily
single." She and Kate had learned about not doing it with
your brother's widow at Sunday School. As they grew older
they'd wondered exactly why they'd been sent off there every
Sunday, rain, snow or shine, when it was obvious that their
parents, like a lot of wartime people, were non-believers.
And then there was Kathleen's swollen belly. A trip to hospital. Had they imagined it like two hysterical girls from *The
Crucible*? In bed at night, they'd built up their story about a
sibling who was a stepbrother to each of them, born of
Kate's mother and Dorothy's father: A child growing up elsewhere whom they would one day recognize and move
towards like scraps of metal to a magnet. On the other hand,
Dennis and Kathleen were decent people and would never
have abandoned a child. Unless it was from the fear of having a scarlet I engraved on their backs.

Like I said, Omar, I'm trying to raise money.

Why was she sharing her thoughts with a man whose
friends apparently called him "Cairo Fred," and who had
gambled away sums that would buy homes, health, food,
water, for whole cities of the deprived and oppressed?
Perhaps, and she had to give him the benefit of the doubt,
he donated even larger sums to charity than he lost in casinos. And, as she was learning, charitable ideas are not
always easy to put into effect.

The coffin was inside the church now. The pieties were
being intoned for the passing of the soul of a man who had
held the power of world destruction in his hand and had
died a virtual imbecile. She turned off the TV and put on her

raincoat. Harvey Lent had been behaving in a vague and offhand way. It was time for a visit.

The WorldAidNow director's office was not plush. Here was no expensive artwork, no antique desk. The poster of Kabul on the wall beside the map of Afghanistan was dull, sepia and beige. He was sitting at an old, scratched table. The two chairs were not meant for comfort. The young woman at reception had better furniture. Harvey obviously took the hair-shirt approach, and quite right too.

He didn't look pleased to see her but asked her to sit down.

"We, my friends and I, aren't trying to do this because we have nothing better to do, Mr. Lent."

"I know that, Mrs. Graham. I do appreciate that you've chosen WANT for your – your fundraising efforts."

"Please call me Dorothy. I've brought you an invitation for our dinner. Would you like one for your wife?"

"My wife is an invalid."

"I'm so sorry."

He gave her a weary look as if he was thinking that of all the charities in all the world, these old women had to pick on his. Slowly he said, "Delivering food and goods in that wild country is so difficult. Warlords rule those areas. Bandits with Kalashnikovs stop every truck. We spend five times what it's worth to deliver one sack of rice."

"What did you do before this?"

"I don't see – well if you must know, I worked in the tax office."

"And," Dorothy said in her best cheerleading tone, "you decided to do something more positive."

"There was a time when I wanted to be a priest," he said as if it explained everything.

She had no answer to that but looked at him with new respect. Just because a man had a weaselly appearance, and after all that was not something he could help, it didn't mean that he was a weasel. He was trying to make a difference in a world where every step forward appeared to lead to two steps back.

"I've been told," he said, "that only someone on the ground can possibly understand the difficulties." He riffled his hand through the pile of letters and papers on his desk. Some of them, including a few cheques, fell to the floor.

"Exactly," she said. "Would it be very difficult to send someone out there as an observer, under your aegis of course? Someone mature?" She meant someone who, if killed, would not be much missed, someone whose future was short.

"If we start using WorldAidNow funds for travel, there'll be questions. There are questions already."

"Well, let's see what we can do with the dinner next week. Perhaps we'll raise a ton of money and then."

He looked at her kindly and nodded. He would be there. She said, " I think you'll be surprised at what we come up with. Give us a little time. What's your target figure for this year? To the end of this calendar year, say?"

"A quarter of a million."

"And so far?"

"Eighty-two thousand, seven hundred and three dollars."

"A little way to go. But the year isn't half over yet."

"And I haven't added in these cheques."

As she went out, she stopped to look at the map. Uzbekistan, Tajikistan, Iran, Pakistan. The Afghans had perhaps too many neighbours for comfort.

In a box in the spare room there were children's books from the time when Brian and Delphine and Alice and Isabel had been left with her on summer days. She took out Kipling's *Kim*, made herself a cucumber and tomato sandwich and sat down to read. "They met a troop of long-haired, strong-scented Sansis with baskets of lizards and other unclean food on their backs, their lean dogs sniffing at their heels. These people kept their own side of the road..."

"This is all your fault," Elsie was saying. "If I'd been in my right mind..."

"I don't think you have any idea what a right mind is."

They were sitting by the side of a road that wasn't a road, merely a sandy track. Dorothy knew that in a moment Elsie would say it was all her fault. And it was true that if she hadn't spoken so sharply to the driver of the small bus, speaking in French because she didn't know any Arabic, he wouldn't have made them get out and sit here on the sand to await God knew what with the sun beating down on them, Elsie wearing the only hat they had between them. The vision must be a mirage stirred up by the breeze. Camels. Women on horseback? No. Men in long robes on horseback. Their saviours. Robbers, Elsie said, but nonetheless got up behind the man on the black horse while Dorothy, surprised at her own agility, leapt up onto the saddle behind the other.

"They are robbers," Elsie repeated.

"They are Omar Sharifs," Dorothy replied, surprised that there were two – twins.

It was a lovely undulating ride that went on for the best part of a day before they were lifted off their steeds and deposited on couches in a tent the size of a wedding marquee and given small cups of coffee and tiny sweet cakes before, Dorothy had no doubt, they would be offered a steamy scented bath and then towelled down by the three handsome men who were sitting in a row facing her. She murmured happily. Elsie had disappeared. Perhaps she was already in the bath. Perhaps...

She woke up startled as the phone rang and the book fell from her lap.

"Dorothy, it's Elsie. Have you arranged for the chairs and tables?"

"I told you. The guys will be there at four. And they supply cutlery and plates."

"What's that going to cost?"

"Kate has the figures."

"Okay. Bye."

"Hi Kate, it's Elsie. Have you bought flowers?"

"I thought we were doing this as cheaply as possible."

"Three long tables, six small vases with something cheap and cheerful."

"I don't have six small vases."

"For goodness sake. Juice glasses. Use your imagination."

"No need to snap. What about the floor?"

"I've called the cleaners. I can't meet them there tomorrow. Can you?"

"Look, Elsie, I seem to be doing all the work here. Just because I make lists doesn't mean I have to do every damn thing."

"I think you're forgetting about the goat. And I've got a line on linen cloths."

" Good quality paper will do. We're in this to make money."

"I'm aware of that. Have we got the young people on side besides Isabel?"

"Delphine will come. But listen, Elsie, I want to tell you something."

Elsie had hung up. Kate called her cousin.

"Hello Dorothy. You've got the key to the place and I'm to let the cleaners in. Can you drop it off at my place? I'll be here this afternoon."

"I'll come by about three. I'm off to talk to Matt about his mural, and I think I've got a musician. I'm enjoying this. Are you?"

"No. See you later."

Kate found it hard to imagine that this place, this empty dark shell, could ever be festive.

It was a cavern fit only for monsters. She moved around in it expecting every moment that a ghastly figure would emerge from the shadows and grab her by the throat.

A voice from the doorway startled her.

"Hello, Dorothy?"

The intruder was tall, sixtyish, full head of greying dark hair, smiling, familiar, almost distinguished.

"It's me, Pierre."

"I'm Kate, Kate Charbonneau."

She and Dorothy were not alike. Her hair was a different colour and their features reflected different sides of the same family, and besides, Dorothy was three or four inches taller.

"Of course," he said. "It's dark in here."

"I'm waiting for someone," she said.

"Not a romantic rendezvous obviously. Would you like a coffee while you wait?"

Before she could lie to him and say no when in fact it was what she wanted more than anything, he had gone.

Another voice echoed into the space. "What a god-rotten place. You've got to be kidding. Mrs. Edwards says you're having a dinner here. There's lots of church basements clean and nice you could've had." Harry from Celestial Cleaners was standing in the doorway. "I'm not sure I even want to bring my vacuum cleaner into this."

"Do what you can, please," Kate said handing him the key. "And could you return that to Mrs. Edwards when you're done?"

"It'll take till the middle of next week to sort this out. I'm going to have to send for my assistant. Talk about Hercules. What day are you planning to eat in here?"

"The day after tomorrow."

"Good luck!"

On her way out, Kate bumped into Pierre, who was holding two paper cups.

"Let's go back to the café and sit down," he suggested.
"Maybe we need muffins too. In Europe they have no idea
how to make muffins."

Kate knew she should go home, there were place cards
to write, the "cheap" flower arrangements to sort out. And
these days she often needed an afternoon nap.

When they were sitting at the table, he reached for her
hand and turned it over. "I don't see Europe written here."

"I'm thinking of further east," she replied, wondering
why she had told him that. But he seemed to be one of those
people who manage to elicit information without having to
ask questions.

"Going to seek your soul?"

"Flora and fauna," she said, laughing at her own pre-
sumption. "It's a wild dream. Looking for a butterfly. And
in the Kuril Islands. But I think it's a matter of simply looking for the exotic and unreachable."

"We all do that at times."

"And you? Are you looking for something exotic in
Toronto? Dorothy said you'd moved here from Quebec."

"What am I doing here? Looking for you perhaps. I was
getting off the streetcar and I saw you going into that awful
building. What I'm doing in your city is taking over a small,
near-bankrupt publishing house. Insanity."

"Another dream?"

"Nightmare more likely. But writing is my background.
I'm actually related to Jean-Louis Barron. My father was a
successful publisher in Wales. I took over from him and
then, when I sold up, I decided to have an adventure. "

This was the man Isabel had met in Paris. And perhaps
that wasn't coincidence either. But unless he tapped their
phone calls and hacked into their computers, how could he

know where they were? That Dorothy would be on that train and she would be here at this hour? He'd said little about himself so far but his narrative was already suspect.

"I want to ask you something, Mrs. Charbonneau."

Here it came. She waited warily.

"If you were writing a novel."

"I'm not a fiction writer but I have studied literature."

"I think I knew that."

"And I have to be on my way soon."

His fingers were long, his hands unmarked by manual labour. His face was an open face, clear eyes, generous mouth, a mask that perhaps concealed a cunning mind. She had seen many a student with that look and knew not to take it at face value.

"And in this novel, there is a story about an older man who late in life falls in love."

"It's been done many times with varying ages of the love object." He said nothing so she went on. "I'm an admirer of Barron's work," she said. "I could have written my dissertation on him but chose to write about the younger women in some of Balzac's novels, in particular *Eugenie Grandet* and *Le Pere Goriot*. A well-ploughed field but I spent a term at the Sorbonne and thought I had something new to say. The arrogance of youth. Besides, there were areas in Barron's work that to me lacked – what shall I say – not authenticity but the kind of reality that engenders belief, sympathy." God! Why was she giving a lecture to this man? She hesitated and went on, "In particular, in *La Lune de Miel.*"

"Not one of my favourites."

"The character of Gladys, the English girl, isn't convincing."

"I never liked her. Why are you smiling?"

"Tell me about your publishing venture, Pierre."

"Your cousin's letters. I'd like to publish them but they're not a financially sound proposition unless she gives me a few more. If she really wants to see them as a book, she might have to invest a little money. Perhaps you could persuade her."

"I'm not sure anyone has ever been able to persuade Dorothy of anything."

"There's a nice biographical quality to her writing and besides, it could be a kind of period piece. I'm hoping to get a grant too but that's a lottery."

He moved his hands in an open gesture, staring at her. He looked very like Dorothy's father Dennis in that moment. Kate's common sense was shouting, no, no, no. But she had, on the other hand, always known that there was a third child and that one day he or she would come into their lives, hers and Dorothy's. And maybe here he was, drawn to them by an undeniable genetic thread.

"You should ask her yourself about the money," she said. Then she stood up and gathered her coat and umbrella. "I'm going to be late, Pierre. I really have to go."

"You've time for another coffee," he said.

Ten minutes later, or was it days, she found herself talking to this stranger about Robert, and at the same time wishing she wasn't. Engineers can hold back the flow of water going over Niagara Falls, but her words were spilling out in spite of herself.

"My late husband wants me to go back to him. He was a man of no principles at all. He was a judge but what does that mean really? He was a judge, but was he just? I often asked myself that. He never talked about his cases, but I read about them in the papers and sometimes I took files from his briefcase and looked over them. There were complaints about his inconsistency. I saw him crying once, but when I went near he turned away. I guess he'd destroyed someone's life that day."

Pierre was stroking her hand and pushing her thin sleeve up towards her elbow.

At the subway stop he kissed her cheek and said, "Enjoy the Islands." She walked quickly away and laughed to herself. The journey to Vladivostock and beyond was as unlikely to happen as was an affair with a man who had popped into their lives from nowhere and might possibly be a step-sibling. But at least she had got rid of her last ticket for the dinner. He'd promised to pay her for it on the night.

Dorothy believed that knowing the reasons for things brought happiness when any sane person could have told her, and Elsie had, that it's often far better not to know. Why else do people say that ignorance is bliss? She even questioned gifts. Why have you bought this book for me? This scarf is too expensive. But, Elsie thought, we all have our faults. Some people's are more aggravating than others and I'm sure hers are more aggravating than mine.

June already and what kind of a summer was this going to be? Still cool and wet, warmer on the west coast than here in Ontario. Climate change. Expiring wildlife. Peculiar family life. Isabel was designing a small shopping mall and an emergency ward and, if not pregnant, was discontented. Her daughter, her daughters, were not – she couldn't find a word that described them both. She had to think of them separately. To say they were not normal was too easy. She checked back through Richard's family, the ones she'd known, as she had done many times, but could find no trace of either gender uncertainty or chimerical wanderings.

At least Isabel and Mike weren't married so there was nothing there to dissolve if it came to that. A decent man, Mike. Kind, quiet, cheerful most of the time though his work told on him and there was sometimes a sad, faraway look in his eyes. They called him a social worker, but he was often dealing with the un- and the anti- social. He knew the heart of sadness, did Mike. His family, on the other hand, were adventurers, always finding new places to travel, losing money and making it. Among four brothers, he was the odd man out and the one least likely to end up in jail.

Her own family had been boringly hard-working. The Hallows weren't smart enough to make a fortune or even to keep what they had. December for them was a time of excusable extravagance. Easter meant new clothes and chocolate and yet another family feast. Charity had begun and ended at home. And the overspending at Christmas often meant paying bills till March and putting off the purchase of new boots or a new coat till later. She recalled skates that were too tight, hand-me-downs from sister Jane that she hated. But the memory of the good times remained and her bent little toes were perhaps a small price to have paid, though her inner jury was still out on that particular matter. One of her teachers had taught them about the true spirit of the season, reading *A Christmas Carol* to them, getting them to put on a nativity pageant, leading them to the Gospel according to St. Luke. After that, in her teenage years, the season had been coloured with guilt, knowing that in her home there would be a fat turkey and gaudily wrapped gifts under a tree weighed down with shining baubles. When she later understood that their celebration was built on credit, she resolved that when she had a family they would pay as they went even if the Xmas tree was a stick and the gifts small.

It had taken a while to get used to wealth. Luxury had come slowly to her and Richard. Gradually, the list of things that could not be done without had grown as money flowed in from the business. Unless – and sometimes she found herself wishing for the challenge – there was a repeat of

October 1929, her bountiful life would continue. Which was why, as she'd told Isabel who obviously didn't see the connection, she was going to get Celina to cook the damn goat. *Because I can afford it.*

She turned her mind back to the movie and watched as the sea roiled and the rain came down and the hero kept swimming and swimming beyond the limit of any ordinary human being's endurance. At last he found land, what looked like volcanic rock, an island. What a relief! He lay there exhausted and then got up to explore.

When the phone rang she said, "Hello?" It was Dorothy with one more question.

"It's about the seating. Am I interrupting you?" Dorothy asked. "You sound distant."

"I'm watching Tom Hanks try to open a coconut with a rock."

"I can call back later."

"My disbelief isn't suspended. He's a rich actor and before he gets to the last coconut on the island, I'm sure he'll be rescued only to find that his beloved has married again and has six kids."

"I don't think that's how it ends."

"It's my ending. Anyway. The seating. Kate has a list."

"Kate has lists like dogs have fleas."

"It's her way of coping."

"I only wanted to ask if you knew of anyone who's coming who shouldn't sit next to someone else. I mean people who hate each other."

"He's falling back in despair. Poor Tom. No. Well, yes. Ms. Gerdon shouldn't sit next to the two guys from the council. Keep her away from Lent. I'll go around with Kate. Don't worry about it. It's too late. There, you see. He's getting quite proficient with his bits of rock. Stone Age Tom! Night Dorothy."

The things they made actors do. *Dear Tom Hanks, Is this*

movie worthy of your acting talents? Ask yourself. Why not
wait for a script with some depth? Besides.

No! One-way correspondence was Dorothy's addiction.
Elsie could easily see how she too could fall into the habit.
But there was a slight madness in it also and one of the three
of them had to stay sane. So far, she only talked to others in
her head, usually arguments with delinquent workmen but
sometimes also with Alice.

Tom was drinking milk from the coconut and that would
sustain him till nature put the next gift in his way.

After she'd hung up, Dorothy poured herself another glass
of wine. Alcohol wasn't conducive to sleep, so they said, but
at least it was relaxing. In these evening hours she'd come
to know more about loneliness than ever before. She understood those works of art in which human figures hung
suspended in space, or were isolated in a crowd. The one
grey person in a mass of people in bright clothes. She'd seen
a picture of a Roman tomb with images of the faceless
dead... Come on, Dorothy, stop maundering and make yourself a cheese sandwich! What was it about that sharp-tasting
fatty food that was so cheering? She smeared the outside of
a slice of bread with margarine, laid it down in the frying
pan, covered it with pieces of cheese and put the other slice
on top. As she turned the sandwich over, the cheese, an aged
cheddar, began to melt and drip over the crusts of the bread.

She woke up next morning with a pain in her chest and
lay still for a while diagnosing it as a heart attack, cancer,
and then hunger. With her digestive problems, emptiness
was a bad thing. Acid juices would gnaw holes in various
tracts and food would spill out into unlikely spaces if she
didn't have breakfast very soon.

While she was eating her yogurt, Dorothy turned on the
computer. There was one new email message: *Hi Kate, I have*
a feeling that our dear friend is behind Elvira's hysterics.

She has a way of saying things that makes the kids think she knows something when you and I know she's just an interfering old idiot. Likes to get her fingers into things. If she'd had children of her own she might be more careful. As if the girl didn't have enough problems. And then there's poor Jake. Besides that, I think she's going a bit loopy. Look, this is too long. I'm coming over for coffee. There's a problem. Elsie.

Elsie had obviously sent this message to her by mistake. It was meant for Kate's eyes only. Or was it a cunning way of letting her know what they thought of her? "Loopy" indeed. What a silly word. She would show them *loopy*. As for "hysterics" the child had merely made her feelings known, and if a few more of the Edwards clan did that, they might be a happier family.

She began to write back angrily to say that the "children" were grown up and had minds of their own but decided instead to take a deep breath, get dressed, and turn up "accidentally" at Kate's.

She found Elsie in the lobby of Kate's building, trying the intercom. There was no reply.

"Perhaps you've forgotten the numbers," Dorothy said. "It happens at your age."

And there was Kate coming down the path between the carefully trimmed shrubs.

"Why are you here so early?" she asked and then, afraid, "Has something happened to Jake? Don't tell me here. Come in." She rushed ahead before they could speak and opened the elevator door.

"It's nothing to do with Jake," Elsie said.

"It's about me," Dorothy said.

"Why is it always you, Dorothy. It's about the damn dinner is what it is."

"Why did you send that email meant for her to me?"

"Oh God!"

"And who says Elvira had hysterics. She only ran out of the TV station because she saw her mother on the monitors."

"She ran, as you would have known if you watched the local news at night, straight into the lens of one of those camera crews that rove around the streets looking for stories from the emotionally disturbed."

"I don't see that was my fault, Elsie. And besides, what does it matter?"

"I'll tell you what matters."

"Will you both shut up," Kate shouted. "Sit down, there and there. What matters is that Jake's all right. I'll put the kettle on and then I have something to tell you."

"She's backing out of the dinner."

"She wouldn't dare."

"Let me speak. You both talk as if I'm a child. Using the third person when I'm right here. I've half a mind not to tell you now."

"She's," Dorothy began and then said, "I'm sorry, Kate."

Kate said, "He's having serious prostate trouble. My ex-husband."

"He wants to come back?"

"Of all the nerve."

"I'd tell him what to do with his prostate."

"Allow me to go on. He doesn't want to come back here. He wants me to move out West and live with him and help him through this difficult time. He called me and then sent a letter full of apologies and regret about his terrible mistake."

They all laughed then. Kate made coffee while they discussed various responses.

"His 'terrible mistake' has left him high and dry, I suppose," Elsie said.

"Dry," Dorothy said.

"He says the climate's great."

Kate said, "I suppose he is human."

"Don't start thinking that way, Kate."

"I'm not crazy. I told him I was sorry and left it at that. I'm not about to go and tell him I'll look after him."

"I should think not," Elsie said. "Be very, very careful. We're here for you. You know that. Don't answer if he calls. Don't do anything without talking to me – and Dorothy.

"Now I have to tell you something. Celina's quit. She looked at the goat as if it was human remains and refused to cut it up."

When Dorothy got home, she found another email from Elsie, this time for her:

We have to keep an eye on Kate. I couldn't believe it when she said he was human. We mustn't let her fall into that trap. I'm going to cook the goat myself.

So Judge Charbonneau was looking in the mirror and perhaps seeing death standing behind him. Had Graham perhaps, unknown to her, to anyone, been ill, informed perhaps of a fatal disease, and decided not to wait. No doctor had come forward at the time to suggest this.

In spring, or at any rate towards the end of winter, giant blocks of ice moved along the river to the top of the Falls, hovering there till they broke up or crashed and fell into the whirlpool below. It had been Dorothy's favourite time. Fewer visitors came in winter, and the spray from the great cataract covered the walls and street lights with magical coats of shiny glass. Graham had chosen a busier time to leave. That summer evening, startling three tourists from Ohio, he had climbed over the rail and slithered into the awful rushing water. Three days later, his body had washed up in the whirlpool downstream. The typewriter had never been seen again.

I went back to England in guilty mourning, Omar. It was 1961 and at first I thought that there was no "back" there.

She found the street in Halifax easily. The house where she had been born was part of an imposing terrace, a stone attachment of ten dwellings with slate roofs that sloped down a hill. Kate's house, the one where they had watched and waited for the men to come back, and where Kate's mother, Kathleen, had kept a canister of loose tea laced with cyanide on a high shelf, had been torn down to make way for a road. Kathleen, a kindly, gentle woman, had been prepared for the invasion that never came. *Would you like a warm drink, Herr Leutnant?* Dorothy hoped that Kathleen had burned the tea or buried the tin where it would never be found.

The war that had ended less than sixteen years before was already history and memories had dimmed. In a pub, she talked to a man who thought he remembered the brothers and a woman left on her own with two little girls. But he wasn't sure. There were so many young people in uniform and so many sad tales in those days. So Dorothy had trekked to Haworth to see where that tragic family had lived a century before and to consider the sheep on the moors. These woolly animals had to be the great, great, great, great grandchildren of the lambs she'd watched as a child. She wandered down a muddy lane between allotments and saw a man sitting on a stool patting the head of a goat that was making a sad sound. She asked what was wrong with it and the man, barely looking up, replied, "I've sold her kid, haven't I?"

After that she went down into the caves at Ingleton to admire the stalactites and stalagmites, and on another day climbed up Pen-y-ghent. But it was all landscape, just that:

She was a tourist in the place that had been her home for a short and violent time.

The church she'd come to see was an ancient building that stood on the site of an even older structure. Before she went inside she looked for her mother's grave. Distant memory drew her to the site. She pushed weeds and grass aside to read the words on the small stone: Margery Bowles, beloved wife and mother. And she cried, mourning not for the woman who'd died so young but for her own motherless childhood.

Softly she went through the porch into the church treading on slabs of paving, reading memorial tablets on the wall and the stained glass window donated by the Andersons in memory of their only son killed in 1918. Hearing music, she wandered through a door marked Vestry. A youngish man wearing a clergyman's collar and black shirt was ironing what looked like sheets and listening to a radio that was perched on a shelf nearby.

"Choir surplices," he said when he saw her. "We do the laundry ourselves to save money." He introduced himself as the vicar and was happy to turn the iron off and show her the parish register.

He took a volume from the shelf and turned the pages back slowly as if he enjoyed looking at the names of people who'd moved around in this place before he was born. The unknowns of the past. There they were: Dennis and Margery both of this parish, and John and Kathleen likewise. All of them had stood on this spot to sign the register. A double wedding. Three sets of parents, grandparents to her and to Kate.

"It's sort of circular, life, isn't it?" she said to the kindly man who was putting the book away.

"Indeed." he replied. "It goes on, repeats itself. Very little changes."

"That's depressing."

"But there are glints of gold, glints of gold."

He smiled at her in a way that had made her want to say things to him like, Can we go out sometime? Will you marry me? In seconds she had built a life in this quiet, lovely place. She was the vicar's wife dispensing tea and buns to parishioners. She would learn the local history, imbibe religion, teach Sunday School and become known as a saintly woman, her face remaining smooth over time, her hair white and abundant.

"It's peaceful here."

"We accept donations," he replied, and walked away.

"I've just lost my husband, " she'd said then, to hold him back for a moment.

He turned and told her how sorry he was and asked if she'd like to pray.

It seemed only polite to do so, and she had knelt beside him and repeated the Lord's Prayer and listened as he murmured comforting words. He offered her tea but all she wanted was for him to kiss her and hold her close and make love to her on the cold floor. As if he'd sensed her sinful thoughts, he quietly left her and went back to his ironing.

Fatefully, a few days later, she decided to go down to the south of the country before she returned home to Canada. She signed on for a bus trip around *Wessex*. The tour guide driver, a kindly, heavy-set young man from Plymouth who called all the women "my love," told his passengers that the church at the next stop was the one in which Hardy set his weddings and funerals. So there she was in *Tess of the D'Urbervilles* country, far from home and from everyone she knew. A young widow travelling on her own. Dorothy the Obscure. Then Alfred Sparrow, who had looked at her through the mirror as he drove his bus down a winding road with the sea many metres below at one side, turned and said to her, "Come on. Cheer up. It's all downhill from here."

Maybe it was those simple words that had led her to leave her job, rent out the house and move to England to live with him and help him run his company. Her father gave her a cheque, said he hoped she'd be happy and promised to come and visit. Kate and Elsie took her out to lunch and told her she was mad: You hardly know him. He might be a murderer, a drunk, insane. But she had spent a week on the bus with him and knew him to be kind and funny. And although it was the far end of the island from where she had begun her life, she'd felt as if she were returning to her roots. Dear Alfred. He had done his best and sometimes she'd regretted her hasty retreat. He introduced her to his family. They were married in a little chapel in Cornwall with two strangers as witnesses. His mother was displeased. His sister welcomed her with, "You won't like it here."

Just when Dorothy was getting used to the food, enjoying the evenings spent in pubs and acting as occasional tour guide while Alfred drove, his wife turned up and appeared not to be quite as ex as he had said. In their list of his possible defects, her two friends back in Canada had missed bigamist.

The phone rang interrupting her memories. She picked it up and listened. Listened and understood what Melissa was telling her. She made sympathetic sounds that were hardly words. Yes, she would go and visit. But first she had to cry.

∽

Delphine read Jake's letter again. There was much omitted. Perhaps that was the way with correspondence from loved ones. And then too, people nowadays were used to sending terse, ill-spelt messages to each other via email. A real letter,

one with descriptions and feelings and conclusions, was a
rare and lovely thing. She just wished he'd chosen to do his
charitable work in a safe place like Iceland.

Later she would write back and tell him that she was taking a little time off work and had set up as a consultant. Her
nights out with Alec had slowed her down. She'd been arriving late and tired at the office. The boss had suggested she
take time out, but there was no need for the boy to know
that. She now had to get on with it and find some amazing
and original revenue-producing ideas while Alec was away
in Boston.

She sat down and tried to figure out whether she missed
Alec or whether it was a convenient separation. Would she
mind if Alec never returned or wrote to say she had found
someone else? She also wanted time to explain to herself
what had happened. First there had been an affectionate
lying down together. And then a few moments of passionate
love followed by, on her part, moments of recoil. A sense of
what am I doing making love to my old friend Alice! Alec
was not a man. But she had produced in Delphine the same
rising of hormones, of excitement, as Bert and a few random
lovers had done. And she had felt, oddly in that moment, a
voice in her head whispering, I am not lonely now. After the
first strangeness, she had given herself over to pleasing and
reciprocal sex.

And she wanted Alec now. She wanted to call her and tell
her to return at once. She would not look at her askance in
the morning. There would be respect and care and perhaps
love. *Come back to me, sweetheart.* And there she was tapping at the window, Alec rendered back into Alice, wearing
a green dress and shiny gold earrings.

"Come in," she mouthed at the window. "You have a key."

But it was only Isabel. Delphine went to the door and let
her in.

"I want to talk to her."

"She's in Boston."

"My mother and the man she calls her husband..."

"Your father."

"He's gone crazy."

"What has he done?"

"Says he's about to make a new will leaving everything in trust to Mother if she survives him, and then to the opera company."

"Alec and you?"

"Alice was cut off some time ago. Me? He figures I'll get by, I suppose."

"Nothing?"

"*Nada.* I'm sorry, Delphie, I shouldn't burden you with this. I came to see my sister really. It's been good of you to give her a home these last weeks."

The pleasure was mine. "We're old friends after all. Is your dad ill?"

"A heart problem, like most men his age. The doctor says he'll live for years."

"He must be feeling mortal though."

"You mean is he losing it? He's gone crazy about opera. Mom says he studies each one for days before he goes to see it. Reads about composers. And he talks about nothing else."

It seemed a harmless occupation for a man in his seventies. But is any obsession truly harmless? It occurred to Delphine that her only obsession was her son, and he had left. Delphine made tea and they sat at the kitchen table as if they were friends. But they were only two women who'd always known each other sitting there exchanging questions and giving slight answers.

And then Isabel said, "It's not about the money, Delph. It's about feeling abandoned. As if I'm being punished for something I haven't done. I want to talk to Alice. When will she be back?"

"Isabel! If you ever talked to each other, you'd know."

"She's the one who won't talk," Isabel replied sulkily.

"In this day and age, it can't be because she's gay."

"It was the way she left. The going. Things that were said. And there's Elvira."

"Look! All Alec wants is to be accepted by you all. She thinks you all hate her, and that's not fair. You've had loads of time to forgive whatever you think she's done, and I really think you're all behaving like idiots."

Isabel glanced around at the walls, the shelves. And then she pushed her mug to one side and said, "What's going on with you and her?"

Delphine replied, "What do you mean?" aware that she sounded childish.

"I don't care, Delphine."

"It's our affair."

"Your affair." Isabel sounded as if she'd gone off into a dream. "Affair. Yes."

"You okay?"

Speaking quickly, Isabel said, "I'm fine. I'm just fine. If one more person suggests that I'm pregnant, I'll scream. I know you didn't. It's absolutely not what I have in mind. Mike and I don't want children. We're happy the way we are."

"I'm sorry about Paris?"

"I don't know why Mike had to bring that up at Easter. So I went for a drink with this old guy because I was upset. Mike was sleeping off his jet lag anyway. It's not as if. Anyway, Aunt Kate gave me her lecture about separating the artist's work from his life, but it's hard to do. Thanks for the tea."

When she watched her go off down the road, Delphine figured that there was more on Isabel's mind than the miserliness of an old man and the betrayal of a dead writer. She was hiding a secret. Delphine smiled. She'd had Jake at the beginning of her child-bearing years, and Isabel had conceived near the end of the cycle.

Isabel left Delphine's comfortable, untidy house and walked down the street looking around carefully. It wasn't a great neighbourhood. People could get mugged here or pounced on by aggressive dogs bred for the purpose. But the trees planted when the houses were built sixty years ago had flourished and they gave the place a park-like look.

Very likely in the next decade, this would be the coming area. The homes would be bought up and treated to expensive makeovers.

She wasn't sure whether she was glad or sorry not to have seen her sister. Alec, when Alice, had been a fount of common sense. She solved problems. Made things clear. And there was no reason why, now that she was "different," the quality of her mind should have altered. But the gap of years, the chasm they'd allowed to grow between them, was great. Alice might simply tell her to get lost.

She did, she had to admit to herself, hate the idea of Delphine and Alice sleeping together. If they were. The only hint of it was a vague scent of sex. It wasn't because they were two women. She knew she wasn't homophobic. It was more the strangeness of it. The oddity. An image she couldn't push from her mind. She absolutely did not want to think of her sister, the girl she had grown up with, as Delphine's lover. How to accept, that was the word, *accept*, it? It made her feel slightly sick.

And now this matter of Dad and his will. Why should she be treated like King Lear's misunderstood daughter? Did things happen the same way over and over? No way was Richard Edwards cast out onto the blasted heath of ingratitude. He had a comfortable home. Her mother was attentive to his needs. Isabel hadn't always liked him, especially when she was younger and he seemed to represent environmental destruction. But she had always loved him. The little Fathers' Day gifts his daughters had given him were still displayed on a shelf in his study as if they were costly treasures. He'd taught them to swim when they were at the cottage, played endless board games with them. So why was he casting her off, his forty-year-old best child? *I will confront him. I will ask for reasons.*

Yesterday, the props that held her life together had been her job, Mike and the prospect that her father's money would provide a cushion in her later years. Today one of those props was gone. Mike was reserved and distant. Her boss patronized her. Should she kick away the rest of the scaffolding and behave in what might be seen by all her family and friends as a totally irrational way? I'm tired of rational, she said half aloud. *And too young to start talking to myself on the street.*

She stopped in at the coffee shop, put her shopping bag on a comfortable chair to reserve it and went to the counter to order a latte. Self-indulgence. *Self-indulgence.* She deconstructed the words. I am indulging myself. I am giving myself a treat. Self. Selfishness. I will spend all my money and then be dependent on others. Mike was my love. Mike is remote. Has he a new love? Is he ill? What if he has a major, major problem? If I don't ask, I won't know. If I do ask, and I discover he is ill or about to be laid off, I will have to stay with him. Perhaps, quite simply, his work among the desperate is weighing him down.

"Your latté, miss."

Isabel drew back. The smell of the coffee was unpleasant and she'd forgotten for a moment where she was.

"I didn't order that," she said to the bewildered young man, and picked up her bag and walked out. The money they made, the prices they charged, the company could afford to pour one latte down the drain.

~

Hospital doors were like prison gates; you never knew if you were going to get out into sunshine again. Dorothy walked firmly to the reception desk and faced down the enquiring woman.

"I'm his cousin from Orillia. I'm expected."

"Fifth floor. Room 21C."

"Thank you." She hurried away before more questions were asked.

Leon Ericsson lay staring at the ceiling, bereft of speech and mobility. Dorothy sat down in the chair beside the bed. She put her hand on his hand. The boss, the chief, the one who had held careers in his hand, feared by some, revered by those who saw him as a maker of fortunes, lay powerless, struck down.

It was said that people in this condition could hear and that you should speak to them. What could he possibly care about? Did the tragedies of the world matter to him now? The stock market? The latest movie? Best perhaps to stick to the trivia of daily life.

"It's me, Dorothy, Leon. I am sorry to see you like this." She paused. Not the right approach. Okay. Here comes trivia. She had to suppress the tears in her voice before she could speak. "I've got myself involved in a fundraising scheme. With my two old friends. You might remember me mentioning them." Had sneaky Kate guessed about those late afternoon trysts and told Elsie? Nothing had ever been said. "I'm going to have to move out of my little house, Leon. I'll be sorry." Why tell him that when he was moving out of life? "You came there once when you drove me home. The doorbell rang when we were on the living room rug. We laughed. And laughed till we realized that we could have been found out." How remote that sounded, how distant, how silly. But she kept on.

"I was thinking, my dear, the other day about our times in the 'afternoon hotel.' That first time you took me there it was out of altruism. I needed a diversion, you said. I didn't believe you for a minute. You wanted me. I wanted you. We leapt on each other. Oh, it was good."

The spikes on the monitor in the corner appeared to move faster and become sharper. So maybe he could hear. She put her hand under the sheet and drew it back when she touched a plastic tube.

"Leon, I did love you for a while. At any rate on those afternoons. Do you think the others in the office ever knew? You always brought wine." How many times was always? "I knew it would have to stop. You had your family. I understood but it wasn't easy. I walked by our 'afternoon hotel' on the way here and looked in for old time's sake. It's grown shabby and will be knocked down soon, like us, to make way for something modern."

He seemed to look at her. She smiled at him. Certain romantic tunes still brought those stolen hours back with all their guilt and pleasure. Had it been passion? If so, it was more sly than grand. They used to leave the hotel separately, and next morning at the office, demure as hell, they would be Mr. Ericsson and Mrs. Graham again.

"Leon, darling Leon. Unfaithful you were. I hope your wife never found out."

The nurse came in looking first amused and then annoyed.

"Visiting hours don't start till three. You're not a member of the family."

"I'm an old colleague. We worked together for nearly

thirty years. I have an appointment for a scan downstairs. I thought I'd just pop in as I'm here anyway."

As she walked away, Dorothy took note of all the electronic devices around the nurses' station. Was there a microphone that checked Leon's breathing, his possible attempts at speech? She hurried to the elevator, not wanting anyone to see her cry, and wished the poor relic of her old lover an easeful death.

Lying on the table drinking a thick, white, floury concoction, she watched the two men on the other side of the window point out to each other the beauties or defects of her esophagus. The older man must be the doctor, the other, no more than a boy with brushed up hair, a student. They wouldn't divulge their findings on this day. The mysteries would be revealed at a meeting with Dr. Bartel next week. She gulped down the last of the fluid and imagined being told that she could have no more asparagus, no more cheese, no more wine. Ever. *This vile liquid contains every nutrient your body needs, Ms Graham. Not my body, doctor! My body likes cakes and ale.*

"That's it," the technician said. "You can go now."

The men behind the window gave no acknowledgement of her existence, no wave goodbye. To them she was only an interesting piece of tubing. And in moments another patient would lie there on the table, drinking, waiting to be told that eating was damaging to her health.

On the way home, she stopped at the Italian *Caffe* and ordered a cappuccino and a mozarella and prosciutto sandwich on focaccia bread. The three healthy, dark-haired young folk behind the bar smiled and laughed and shouted to make themselves heard above the sounds of anguish on the sound system. She'd never liked opera and certainly didn't want to take it in with what might be one of her last meals. *She died*

doing what she liked best. She and Kate and Elsie had made
a game out of that phrase picked out of obituaries of crocodile hunters and golfers and racing car drivers. At one time
they might all have chosen to die having sex. But now?
Eating? Drinking good wine?

"Turn the music down, please," she shouted.

No one paid any attention. In half an hour she'd moved
from being a body on a table to being a crazy person who
yelled in public places, a woman who ate large sandwiches
at ten thirty in the morning. She wished she'd brought a
jacket. The sun kept going behind threatening clouds.

She also wished she hadn't left the car at home. Every
now and then she made a virtue of choosing to travel by
public transport. On a day like today, feeling bloated and
invaded and sad, she decided to go home the easy way and
treated herself to a taxi. After all, how long was she going
to live?

A thick brown envelope delivered by hand had been
pushed through the letter box and was lying on top of the
mail on the mat inside the front door. She pushed at it with
her foot. It wasn't a neatly wrapped bomb from the developers, but all the same she was afraid of it. Maybe it was
her letters, rejected, unread, returned to sender. She held it
at arm's length as she carried it to the kitchen. With the
carving knife, she ripped open the envelope. What were her
letters anyway? The ramblings of a silly old woman? A
message to the world? An entertainment? It was indeed her
manuscript. She flicked through it. Someone had made notes
in the margins. There was a letter, an unbelievable letter.
Pierre was possibly going to publish her words. *We need, to
make a viable manuscript, a few more of these. Have you
anything else hidden away in your shoeboxes?*

The title he'd chosen, *That Said,* was better than the one
suggested by Kate, who had come up with Exhortations. It

would be set in cursive type so that it looked as though the letters had simply been written out by hand and copied. And it might do well, Pierre wrote. People are snoopy; they like to read other people's mail. It's as simple as that. Literary voyeurism. And your thousand dollars will be returned to you with interest.

Dear Omar,

Because I haven't finished writing to you, I didn't include your letters in the collection. Besides, they are really private and I'm not sure whether I should hand them over to Pierre. I will, in any case, send you a copy of the book, autographed.

And what would the old actor make of that? What would readers, her friends especially, make of *That said*? Like the doctors behind the window at the hospital they would perhaps see more of her than she'd intended to reveal.

She riffled through the real mail, the haul of letters responding to TEWP, and picked out the one that bore a foreign stamp with Arabic writing on it. Omar had responded to a letter she hadn't even sent! Computers transferred words around the world in seconds and hackers could move messages about without the writer even being aware. Her words had been plucked off the hard drive and hurled out of cyberspace into the earth's atmosphere like a falling star.

Dear Dorothy,

I do get a lot of letters but none quite like yours. I thank you for sharing part of your life with me and I enclose the picture you asked for. Your picture is now in my album. Yours in admiration, Omar Sharif. He would have written that sitting at the white desk in his Paris hotel room and then walked down to the lobby and given it to the concierge to mail along with a large tip.

The letter was, in fact, from Jake.

Dear Aunt Dorothy,

I'm sending this letter from a little area near the border with Pakistan. At first we were in a place where the people were well fed. But the families in this so-called "town" are so poor that it would make you weep. We have distributed the food sent on by WANT, *and the clothes. But there is never enough. By the time the load arrives here, some has been stolen, some given out to places on the way. I am learning patience. Don't tell my mother, but I have been shot at twice already, and one of the workers has been killed. My nickname here is Lucky because they miss me. That is, the snipers miss me.*

The countryside. Stark, high, cold, desert and mountains together. Words like bleak and harsh don't cover it. It is an exciting and terrifying place. It has occurred to me that people kill each other here with such abandon because the landscape makes man seem like an ant; a little thing of no account.

There is a woman here who says she knows you. Or knows of you. She's about your age and similar to look at. You'd never imagine meeting someone even connected to your life in this remote place.

Dinnertime. Everything with sand as usual. Love, Jake.

What woman? *More people know Tom Tit than Tom Tit knows.* Of course he hadn't thought to ask her name! Was the ghost of old Gertrude Bell still wandering around taking notes, or had an old school friend, lost, turned right instead of left? Was she the third child? She and Kate had only ever imagined him to be a boy.

Keep safe, Lucky, she prayed to the old Sunday School God. *Make the right choices.*

The letters for TEWP could easily be divided into two piles. There were those congratulating the three of them on their effort but sorry the writer couldn't attend the dinner.

Waste of time. The other, much smaller, pile actually contained cheques. Today's haul amounted to three hundred dollars. There were three letters for the to-be-passed-on-to-Lent pile: One was abusive. The second one was from an Afghan living in Ottawa who offered to come and help. The last was from a government agency saying that they might require a closer look at the organization.

She tuned out, poured herself a very small glass of wine and drank a few toasts: To *That Said*. To the journey. To Jake. To young Elvira. Again, to the journey. The wine had soured slightly, open too long. Indeed – to the journey. Harvey Lent had become more assertive and she had hesitated to tell him about the plan at first. When she finally did, he had, to her surprise, said, "Go. Yes. All of you if you like."

I'll stop in Paris en route. There was enough in the bank for one very long distance return trip and if she consented to sell the house – if she sold the house... She looked again at the map on the wall and traced her finger along the route a plane might take to Kabul. Mysterious place names. A country walked over by invaders, the uninvited. A place where even the stones were never allowed rest. She sighed.

So her publisher wanted more letters. The one to the queen could be included and there was a lot more to say to the pope. She hadn't given Pierre the ones she considered scurrilous or too confessional. Some, she had never printed out. She brought up the file and skimmed down the list.

Dear Kofi Annan,
Of course, when you retire, they will say you have not been a good Secretary-General but that's because you have had opposition from the ignorant and the backward. And we both know who I mean by that. The parlous state of the world is not your fault. Violence and aggression seem to be an accepted way of life in many places. And the wealthy

arms manufacturers are pleased. Their business provides employment for thousands, so they feel good about what they do. It's time, I think, for someone to shoot the horse from under that particular "horseman."

Dear Oprah,
According to a woman writing in the paper today, you affect all our lives. Well you don't affect mine because I don't watch your program and I have to say...
It might be a good idea to finish that letter in a pleasant and encouraging way. After all, to have your book discussed on that program meant instant fame and high sales figures.

Dear Mr.Chamberlain,
I don't recall hearing your voice telling Britain that it was "now at war" in September 1939 but Aunt Kathleen often mentioned the sadness of it, the hollowness. You were brow-beaten later and called an appeaser and my father couldn't mention your name without sounding bitter. So I grew up knowing who you were and what you had done. I think you were a man who hoped. You were blinded by hope and couldn't see evil when it was staring you in the face. If you were alive now, you might have found your niche.

Chapter 4

DELPHINE HADN'T WALKED in this part of town so late for decades. There were glittering lights now. In a restaurant window across the street, she could see a man and a woman lost in romance, lingering perhaps over brandy while the waiter wished they would go home and let him close for the night. But for all the bright store windows, she was wary. The city that for decades had been smugly pleased with its reputation for safety was so no longer. People had guns. People got killed. She stayed close to the buildings, though that could be a mistake if there were someone waiting to leap out of one of the alleys she had to pass. At least she wasn't carrying a purse. Her money and keys were in her zipped inside pocket. If she'd been sure of a space, she could have parked the car closer. She walked the last part of the way quickly.

The club door was open and the music drew her inside; come listen, come drink with us, come along do. She sat up at the bar and ordered a beer and tried to understand what she was hearing. She'd never much liked jazz, never known what it was about or how to listen to it, but the seemingly random, improvised notes gave pleasure to so many people that it had to make sense. And she hoped that it might inspire her, give her an idea for an advertising campaign that would make the stone-faced man in charge of BabyDew break into a jig.

In the half-light, she could make out Alec on the small stage in front of the drummer and beside the bass player. A man blowing a trumpet was beside the microphone, apparently half asleep or lost in ecstasy. She turned when someone sat down beside her; it was Elvira. The city had become a village where you were never alone. They didn't speak to each other for a moment but let the sound, lively now, stand in for conversation.

In a quiet moment, Elvira said, "Have you heard from Jake?"

"He's fine," Delphine replied.

"How do you know that? This minute. This hour. You don't know what he's doing right now."

This sprite had come to stir up her fears in a moment that had been calm; her mind far from war and destruction. She moved to an empty table further from the stage and beckoned the girl to follow. In the dim light of a candle, she could see Elvira clearly: She would walk through life searching for secure love. The abandoned child in the forest. The deserted princess. Her long hair was suited to the role as was the flowing top she was wearing with her frayed jeans.

"I suppose I tend to translate hope into reality."

"That's not very sensible, Aunt Delph."

"What are you doing out so late?"

"I'm twenty-one."

Indeed she was. Alice had married in her second year of university and soon afterwards had her own doll to bring in out of the rain.

"Do you enjoy teaching?"

"It's my first year."

The music took over again. Delphine thought she should be saying Delphic words to the girl, or at least something useful.

Elvira began to talk against the music, "I'm glad you're here. I just want to tell you that I've got over it. I was at a party in a café a couple of blocks from here and I told my friends I was meeting someone. And here you are. I want some champagne. I want my mother to see me drinking it. I want to say, Hello, Mom, and shout, Where've you been all my life, all this time, in my teenage years and when I graduated. But it's all right. Or it's all left. I was left but I'm all right. Get me some wine, Aunt Delph."

Elvira was drunk. Her friends shouldn't have abandoned her in the city so late at night. Delphine signalled to the waiter and said, "A bottle of Perrier, please."

"My mother said, 'There's something I've wanted to tell you, honey.' And she left. I was home by myself. And then my Dad came in and he cried and I cried and then six months later, he said, 'There's someone I'd like you to meet, honey.'

"If I hadn't come home early, she wouldn't have been there. Only the note on the kitchen table. A few months later, Dad took me to Grady's for dinner and I got dressed up thinking it was special and he told me he wanted me to meet her – my 'new mother.' I know I could have kind of behaved better but nobody told me how. I've never eaten lobster bisque since. I guess they're both entitled to – to – do whatever it was they wanted. But it hasn't made them happy. When people ask, what was the worst day of your life, I never know which one to pick. Do you like lobster bisque? Anything made with shellfish can be very poisonous. And I'm not shellfish. I'll answer if she talks to me."

Delphine reached for Elvira's hand and said, "Your mom and dad both need you. And so does your grandmother."

They listened together to a version of "You are the lovely breath of springtime"; it was obviously a night for ancient romantics.

"The truth is, Aunt Delph, the guy I really liked just went home with my friend Jen. What kind of friend is she? And she weighs a ton and has no taste in clothes. You must be worried about Jake. Poor Jake. All those bad people. And I guess this music doesn't help."

No it doesn't, Delphine thought. Jake was out there and every day there were stories in the news of attacks, accidents, kidnappings. Meanwhile here in this shadowy box the musicians were playing another nostalgic piece. She closed her eyes and began to follow the riffs and let the notes run up and down her nerves. All she wanted, all she'd wanted since her beloved son had left, was time on her own to fret. And the whole world was conspiring to prevent her from having a single moment to herself. When she opened her eyes again, Elvira had grown much older.

"She left," Alec said, "when I came over."

∽

Dorothy was watching the soccer game between France and Croatia. As Elsie and Kate came in, she motioned them to sit down.

"Look at that," she said, as the great Zidane ran down the field, evading opponents and kicking the ball just wide of the net. She muted the sound, turned to her friends and said, "Do we really want to go through with this?"

"What are you referring to?" Elsie asked. "Not the dinner, I hope?"

"It's a bit too late to back out now," Kate replied.

"So we stick a notice on the door. 'Help yourself to the goat stew. Gone fishing!'" Elsie said. "Out of your mind, Dot. I was at the hairdresser's this morning and Charlene asked that same question, whether to go through with it. She's getting married on Saturday and now she's not even sure she really likes the guy. I told her that only a fool never changes her mind."

"My point, Elsie! But for heaven's sake, you shouldn't meddle in the lives of strangers."

"People who wash and cut your hair aren't strangers."

RACHEL WYATT

Kate looked at them both and said, "So. It's tomorrow."

Dorothy sighed, "All the letters. What does it add up to? And what difference will one lousy dinner make?"

"Jeez!" Elsie said. "Don't make us all depressed. You started this, Dorothy. This is our planning brunch, if you recall. Our last-minute meeting."

"Some days," Dorothy said, "I wonder which one of us will be the first to go."

"You, if you don't shut up and get the bagels you promised us."

"I'm the oldest," Kate said. "I've got seniority."

Dorothy went into the kitchen and called, "Who wants hers toasted?"

Elsie was shaking her head. She whispered to Kate, "What's gotten into her?" Kate patted her friend's hand and said, "Fear of failure. She'll be fine. Check over these lists while we wait."

Dorothy put the bagels and smoked salmon and cream cheese on a tray. She arranged thin slices of lemon around the salmon and sprinkled a few capers on top. The capers were a little past their expiry date, but then so was she. It was early for champagne and she'd meant to save it for a celebration after the dinner, if the dinner was a success, but poured half a bottle into the jug of orange juice anyway.

"Natural events do take over sometimes," Elsie was saying as a crawler crept across the bottom of the TV screen telling of a hurricane in Florida.

Kate murmured, "What do people do when their homes are destroyed and all their belongings gone?"

"They sit down and howl," Dorothy replied as she came in with the tray. "Help yourselves."

"What they do," Elsie said, "is move on. What they do is go to another place. What they do is find out where to go for help. And other people find out where to go to help

those people and that's what it's about, isn't it? If we had
any sense of obligation, we would go to Florida and build
shelters."

Kate said, "Nice orange juice."

Dorothy said, "If France scores, it's going to be a problem for England."

"Look at those guys. How fast they can run," Elsie said.

"What about dessert?" Kate asked. "How come we
didn't think of it?"

"Don't look at me," Dorothy said. "I've had a lot on my
mind. We'll buy baklava and serve that. It's simple. Maybe
with ice cream."

"No ice cream. It's messy. Just go buy all the baklava
you can find in the morning, Kate. Enough for fifty. Go
to Davenport."

"How much will that cost?"

"Keep the bill," Elsie said. "Keep all the bills. And by the
way, I can't carry the pots by myself."

"Get Isabel to help you."

"She shouldn't be lifting heavy things in her condition."

"She is denying her 'condition,' and I have a bad knee,"
Dorothy said.

"We do not have time for pain, Dorothy. Uncle Dennis
used to say that, remember. When we were setting off for a
walk and you wanted to stay home and read and said you
had a headache."

"He said no such thing, Kate."

"Yes he did. It would be cold and you'd complain about
it and he'd sing some old soldiers' song about no time
for pain."

"He was my father," Dorothy said, instantly ashamed
that a fragment of childhood jealousy was there still and yet
unable to stop herself. "I think I know what he talked about
and the songs he sang."

Kate turned away and flicked through the pages of her notebook.

After the other two had left, Dorothy drank the rest of the juice from the jug, put her feet up on the sofa and watched the beginning of the next match. Through the roar of the crowd, she heard loud repeated knocks on her front door.

Elvira was there holding a very large jar of speckled liquid. It looked volatile.

"I was going to leave this on the step."

"Have you come to blow the place up, dear?"

"I can't come to the dinner. I told Gran I'd make the vinaigrette. I think there's enough here for fifty people."

"Come in."

"I have to go. I have to – I want to leave town."

Dorothy waited.

"They stopped me on the street. TV people with a micro- phone. They asked me what I did, and I told them. So they wanted to know. Well, I only meant to say parents should read to children but it came out all wrong."

"It'll be forgotten in three days."

"I meant what I said. I just didn't mean to say it there in front of everybody."

"You need a change, Elvira. Go to Europe, or travel around India. Be nice to your dad. Make him give you the money."

"I've thought about it. But I don't like sucking up to him."

"Asking parents for money isn't 'sucking up' and that's a vile phrase anyway. It's a perfectly natural thing to do."

Late that night, unable to sleep, Dorothy went to the living room and turned on the TV. There was Elvira once again tearfully urging parents everywhere to stay together no matter what, at least until their offspring were twenty. How many times were they going to repeat that clip for God's sake?

And what about a letter to Him? It would be like writing to Santa. Address: Highest Throne, Heaven. *Dear God, do you exist? And how will you let me know if you do? Although not a believer except in a superstitious sense, I admire those who go to church on Sundays and try to live in a decent Christian way. But my goodness how your words and images have been used to bad purposes. But if you know anything, you certainly know that. Speaking of my humble self, I have not been entirely good through my life but I am now, before the end comes, trying to be useful.*

Those deathbed scenes where the sinner sends for a priest never ring true to me. A bit late, I would say to the last-minute repenter, if I were you. But you are supposed to have mercy.

She went back to bed. Morning would be soon enough to get in touch with the Almighty.

Richard helped Elsie set down the third container of stew and gasped, "Are you sure about this?"

"I would have carried that, Mother," Isabel said, following her parents.

"It's too heavy."

"I'm not pregnant!"

"It's a drab place," Richard said as he was leaving.

"The hotels wouldn't let us provide the food," Dorothy told him. "And anyway, we're making a point. Besides trying to make money."

She watched as Elsie, in her irritating way, ran her fingers over the counter and glanced up at the exposed pipes in the ceiling. The paint on the walls had been scrubbed clean, but it was streaked with indelible stains and there was a strong smell of stale life, dinginess, mould. Elsie's mouth expressed dismay, then she straightened her shoulders and said, "You can get the box with the salt and peppers, Isabel."

Elsie had set her hand to the plough and would do what she had to do. It was her way. She was dressed in an outfit dragged from the back of the closet by the look of it. Long brown skirt, uneven hem, strands of beads, loose shirt in shades of gold and green. Perhaps she imagined herself an Afghan woman cooking for the whole village. Dorothy looked at her friend's feet to make sure she wasn't wearing sandals. She herself had thought the evening demanded a little formality and had put on her grey pantsuit, a blue shirt bought at the ReNew store and the silver bracelet that was Alfred Sparrow's only lasting gift.

She left Elsie talking to herself about which container to put on which of the burners on the stove and went to check the tables. Places for fifty-three. Paper cloths, paper napkins. It reminded Dorothy of those church suppers in Niagara Falls when Kate's mother had made dessert for the whole congregation. Peach pie and ice cream. The peaches were from the trees in their backyard. August always came complete with wasps and homemade grape juice and afternoons helping to put sliced and sticky peaches into freezer bags. She watched Kate setting out the knives and forks. They hadn't gone with plastic in case the meat was tough. There were small glasses for wine. The folding chairs looked uncomfortable. At least the guests wouldn't stay long. With luck it could all be cleared away by eleven and she'd be in bed by midnight.

Matt was unrolling his mural and tacking it to the back wall where people would see it as soon as they entered the hall. Hall, though, was too grand a name for this space. It had been useful once and even, occasionally, splendid, but was now a neglected, sad room. They were here to add cheer to it. There would be noise and laughter and chatter. A brief breath of life before the old place took on a different incarnation. Matt turned to her, silently pleading for praise.

Dorothy stood back, and then further back. Perhaps she should have asked for a preview or at least specified optimism. On half the paper, he had sketched in a bleak backdrop of mountainous terrain and framed it with mosque impressions at crazy angles. In the foreground, men on horseback were playing a polo-like game with what looked like a human head. On the other half, a pleasing field of poppies flourished. Or seemed to flourish. A closer look revealed a collage of ugly red mouths with black teeth. There were scary faces and some of the stems were strangling smaller flowers that grimaced in agony: An opium nightmare illuminated by a large bright sun.

"Oh," she said.

"What do you think?" he asked.

What she was thinking was that, knowing his work, she'd been out of her mind to ask him of all people to make a backdrop for this event. At the same time, she was wondering how to spell "aghast."

"If you ask me," Isabel said, coming by with the condiments, "it will put people off their food."

"You've got the shock effect right, Matt," Dorothy said. After all, what was it all about if not to startle people into recognizing a need?

"What I'm aiming at is a sense of energy and destruction and then maybe revival."

"I see that," Dorothy said. "Yes. There's something of Goya and maybe Delacroix and then a hint of Rousseau."

He laughed. "You don't know what you're talking about." He was leaning forward tacking a corner of the paper to the wall. In spite of the fact that he was into his seventh decade he had a lean and lithe body. He was wearing jeans that were free from paint spots and a white shirt that spoke of hope. Perhaps among the guests there might be one who would give him a commission. She hugged him and before she could stop herself, asked when he was going to come and repaint her bedroom furniture. Her tongue seemed to have become sharper over the last year or two and slightly disconnected from her brain. This wasn't the moment to remind him about the bank's rejection of his proposal for the lobby of their new building and of his need for money.

"I'll do it," he said. "Okay!"

Elsie came in and said, "I'm putting the rice on."

"It's too soon."

"No, it's not. In half an hour fifty people will arrive wanting a dinner for which they have paid one hundred bucks. They will not want to linger in this place. We should have the food ready."

"There's wine," Kate said.

"If you can call it wine," Elsie replied. She turned to stare at the mural, shook her head and returned to the kitchen.

Matt followed her. "So what do you think of it, Mrs. Edwards?"

Kate watched the artist go after Elsie. Money attracts, she thought. Elsie, the magnet. But Elsie was resistant in the way that people who get rich later in life often are. She could see them coming, the flatterers and sycophants, the hard-luck storytellers, and knew how to hold them at bay. Elsie and Richard donated rather than gave, and the sums were likely to be in five figures. Hands-on charity like this event was a rare thing in her life and Kate admired her friend for doing it. It could easily turn out to be a disaster; food poisoning, sickness from inhaling mould spores, people demanding their money back. Three elderly women held responsible for a fatal outbreak of E. coli.

"Where's the dessert?"

Dorothy's voice startled her.

"I'm not sure there's space yet. I left it in the car."

"There's room. Why don't you bring it in? We don't

want to seem as if we've gone down the road to buy it at the last minute."

Kate looked outside. The warm rain had slowed to a drizzle. She put her coat over her shoulders and ran out to the parking lot. On the way back she slipped and the top tray fell onto the wet sidewalk.

"Fuck!" she said, and leant down to pick up the pieces of baklava while trying to hold the other trays level. She'd warned the others about planning anything on a Friday.

"Dogs've probably peed there," a voice said.

She straightened and looked at the man. He was holding a ragged umbrella and wearing a suit too large for him and a woollen toque. His beard was ratty and his eyes were red from outdoor living or drink or perhaps tears. He held the umbrella over her while she gathered up the fragile pastry and set the trays down on a bench. She felt in her pocket and found a two-dollar coin.

"This won't get me dinner," he said.

"Maybe there'll be leftovers."

He took a piece of the undamaged dessert and escorted her to the door.

Isabel came to take the trays from her with that look of withheld impatience as if once more she'd fallen into the trap of helping her mother and her crazy friends with a mad plan.

Kate hung up her jacket and noticed another problem. "Not much room here for coats and umbrellas."

Dorothy said, "We expected it to be fine." There weren't half enough hooks, and wire hangers would bend under the weight of damp raincoats. She imagined some of the guests trying to pull sodden garments from a pile on the floor as they left. But it would be okay. It had to be okay. They had collected the money. People had said yes, they would come. There was food and there was wine.

Kate, moving around putting the handwritten place cards on the tables, said, "If enemies are sitting side by side, they'll have to get over it for charity's sake."

"Harvey will have to be at the centre."

"I don't see why, Dorothy."

"We're doing this for him."

"I'm not sure he's thrilled about it."

"If he can think of a better way to make five thousand dollars, let him."

Matt was helping Elsie fill a vat with water for the rice. "Does anybody use this place now?"

"Occasionally," Elsie said. "It used to be a funky restaurant. All these exposed pipes. Brick wall. Then it was a soup kitchen and that was moved over to Bathurst or somewhere. It's been empty awhile. A haven for rats and cockroaches, I should think."

"Nice!"

"They have to eat somewhere." She shook a handful of salt into the water and put the lid on the pot.

"You guys," Matt said. "You're amazing. I mean the three of you. You could be just sitting around watching soaps. And you do things."

"The alternative," Elsie said, "is not doing things." She had no time for the man but tried to like him for Dorothy's sake. He had a shiftless look, a pudgy face, wide eyes; the sort of man who appealed to certain women. Other women.

"You make me think it's never too late. I'm considering portrait painting. Yours is just the kind of face."

"If we cook the rice for exactly the right length of time," Elsie said, "there'll be no need to drain it. Each grain has to be separate and soft but not too soft, and then we stir in the butter."

"There's nothing for the vegetarians," Isabel said from the doorway.

"Let them eat rice," her mother answered.

"If I'd paid a hundred dollars..."

"It's for charity!"

Isabel backed away but Elsie went on, "Those people are starving and dying and they have no clean water and no nice things at all and we go out and drink martinis and we eat steak and sea bass and I hope you remembered the coffee urn."

Dorothy said to Kate, "Why isn't Delphine here to help? I thought she was going to do the flowers."

"She had a rush job. Something to do with boots or pandas. She said she'd come later. Besides, you can't blame her for not wanting to think about that place."

"Jake is an aid worker. He'll be fine."

"We have to hope so."

Dorothy felt the sting of that remark. Both mother and grandmother still held her responsible for the boy's adventure. But he was twenty-three for heaven's sake and did have a mind of his own. He could have said no. She patted her cousin on the shoulder. Kate was still in mourning for her own life. Her husband, the judge, was out there in the warmer place, alas not hell, ill now and deserted by his nubile love. It was time that her sadness turned to a sense of energetic outrage that would bring her back to reality.

"These daisies are pathetic."

"They were all I could get yesterday."

"Come, Kate," Dorothy said. They walked to the far end of the room and looked at the three tables arranged in a U-shape. The place was festive now. From a distance the paper cloths did have a slight appearance of linen. The chairs waiting for bodies were welcoming. It was going to be a party.

Isabel called out, "Have you been in the washroom?"

They followed her to the back of the hall and down a short corridor. She opened the door wide. There was graffiti on the walls; water, if it was water, pooled on the floor around the toilet. A chipped wash basin and an absence of toilet paper completed the picture. Sanitary arrangements hadn't figured in their careful plans.

Dorothy stood back and recalled a phrase of her aunt's when confronted with any sordid situation. "It's far from the home life of our dear queen."

"We've got ten minutes before they get here!"

Kate shrieked, "We can't clean it in that time."

"Exactly," Dorothy said. She ripped a piece off the end of the nearest paper tablecloth and wrote Out of Order on it.

"Stick it on the door, Isabel."

"What with, Aunt Dorothy?"

"Be creative."

Dorothy had envied Kate and Elsie their daughters especially when, as young mothers, they'd brought their little ones to visit. They were borrowed children she could buy gifts for and take out for treats. She would always love them but did wish that Isabel had been endowed with more common sense. Even as, years ago, she had briefly wished that Kate's daughter had been a good girl. But then Jake had arrived and brought joy with him.

"We've got five minutes before the early ones arrive."

Matt had found a corner behind the huge fridge and dragged Isabel into it.

"Get off me. I want a couple of pins, tacks, please."

"A kiss for the artist."

When Dorothy came in, they were embracing.

"Where's Mike?" she asked. "Wasn't he supposed to help?"

"He had to work."

No doubt lying on the couch watching the baseball game. And had very likely said something along the lines of, *Let those three witches do it. It was their idea.*

"Let's hope it's that old stove giving off that smell," she murmured and left them to it.

A man holding a balalaika put his head around the door and said, "Where do you want me?"

Isabel didn't look at Dorothy as she walked past her.

Kate called, "Harvey Lent is here," and went to greet him. Her job was to introduce him to the two city councillors and to the owner of the building. Gratitude was required.

Lent walked around the room looking at the paper napkins and the cheap cutlery.

"The thing is," he said, "to encourage people to give again. Charity can't be a one-time payment, unless you're talking millions. It's a matter of repeated giving. They have to give and give and then, when they die, give more. So that's why I'm going to make a short speech and collect money at the end."

He obviously disapproved of their plan to make the dinner stark and simple. Harsh reality was not his way. Give them fine wine, good food, entertainment and they will pay and pay again. Make them uncomfortable and they'll never write another cheque. "I call the givers my rabbits," he said. "You have to stroke and flatter them. Entice them. Make them feel loved."

Kate, looking at the room, sympathized with the man. He was imagining a great affair with the minister arriving in a limo and pictures of himself with various VIPs in the weekend papers. To divert him she said that she was planning a trip to the Kuril Islands.

"What do they need?" he asked.

"Nothing, as far as I know. I simply want to go there."

"Far away," he said as if he understood that sometimes there was nothing for it but to go beyond the horizon.

Louisa Gerdon came in and Lent went towards her. He took her wet raincoat and hung it on a hanger.

"Good of you to come, Councillor," he said.

She looked slowly around, like a camera panning the scene. "Brilliant," she said. "You've made it look truly authentic, Harvey."

"We tried," he answered. "This is Dr. Kate Charbonneau, one of my helpers."

A dozen people were in the room now, looking for their names on the cards. Another swarm arrived as if they'd planned to make a multiple entrance. Jackets and umbrellas filled the entry. Dorothy felt overwhelmed. They were actually here. They had come. She'd imagined finding a host of excuses in her email next day. *I felt sick. I had to wash my hair. My cat died.* But here they were, jovially greeting one another as if, instead of being in this bleak room, they were at one of the grand hotels, standing on soft carpet being handed champagne in flutes, a string trio playing in the background. She was so grateful that she wanted to go around and thank each one personally.

The crook Gervais who was certainly not on *her* guest list got hold of her arm and said, "Let's talk about your little house."

Elsie had tears in her eyes. Matt had captured the desolation of that land and the desperation of the lives lived there. She turned away from the others and stood with her back to the wall, surveying the arrangement of tables and the people hovering around them. There were the red cloths they had chosen and cheap glass vases holding a few daisies. Economy had ruled. The place looked like a cafeteria for the homeless. She was about to have a crying fit such as she hadn't had since the night before her wedding.

Two voices were arguing in her head just as they had done then. But her mother was not standing over her with the coronet of camellias saying, *We have gone to all this expense. He loves you. You love him. The guests are waiting.*

How could her mother have helped now: Your friends love you? You are helping a good cause? The guests are arriving? Forget that it looks tawdry and that people will say why is Elsie Edwards involved in this mad scheme? Just remember that you're doing it for a desperate people. But I am desperate too, Mother.

She felt a hand on her shoulder and nearly jumped out of her skin. But it was not her mother with the coronet and veil, it was Dorothy asking if she was all right.

"Nerves," she replied.

"It'll be fine," Dorothy said. "'All manner of things will be fine.'"

"Do you have to keep quoting stuff? None of it ever makes any sense. I left something in the car. I'll be back in a minute."

Later she would blame the car. She sat down in the driver's seat. The key appeared in the ignition as if by magic, the engine fired, the wheels moved. Fifteen minutes later she was home.

Richard was sitting by the fire, bent over his newspaper like a lonely old man. Elsie wondered why, in all their time together, she'd never called him Rick or Rickie. Mainly she supposed because he wouldn't have liked it. He looked up and saw her and smiled. He had a certain smugness about him always. But then, as far as she knew, and it was pretty far, he had behaved well through his life. He was honest and faithful and forbearing – except in that one very large thing. And perhaps she hadn't behaved well in that case either. Had a kind of jealousy prevented her from sticking up for their daughter and explaining her choice to him, being a fair go-between?

She smiled back at him and admired the room. In the past weeks she'd barely been aware of the furniture, the cream and gold wallpaper, the silky drapes. The dahlias in the

Chinese bowl on the lacquer table were fresh. Deep red and yellow, their crowded petals curved over each other sensuously. On the credenza in the far corner, the wedding photograph had pride of place among pictures of the children when young, Isabel at her graduation, herself and Richard with the Governor General, with financial bigwigs. She lingered over the word *dignitaries*, liking it.

Richard was still looking at her. She reached for his hand.

"You're back," he said.

"I think so."

"Where would you like to go for dinner?"

"Anywhere they don't serve goat," she said. "Give me ten minutes to change."

Matt was putting congealed rice onto plates. Kate was ladling stew on top. There were already ten full plates cooling on the counter. Isabel was running in and out delivering food to the guests. Dorothy slowly carried three plates at a time, one in each hand and one balanced precariously on her forearm.

"Could I have a glass of water, please?" a man asked, setting off a chorus of me-toos.

They hadn't thought of water glasses. It was going to be a question of choice.

"Pour the wine, please," she said to Lent.

He found the bottles and went up and down the table pouring white and red alternately. There was a busy exchange of glasses. Finally he took all the bottles from the kitchen and set them up and down the tables.

"Water?"

"In a moment," Dorothy replied, wondering why in hell the man couldn't forget. "We want you to have the food while it's hot."

She wasn't surprised to see Pierre there, sitting next to

the crook Gervais and clearly having an amicable chat with him. Were they in cahoots? When she had time, she would consider her suspicions of both men.

The musician began to play slow rhythmic Eastern music. Everyone was served and it became quiet. Dorothy looked at the people around her. We've done it, she thought. It wasn't so difficult after all. We could put on one of these every month and make sixty thousand a year minus expenses. One or two guests began to cough and gasp and demand water. She tasted the stew. It was fine. She took a forkful of rice and nearly spat it out. Too much salt. Far too much salt.

"In Afghanistan," she said to her neighbour, "they cook in sea water."

"It would have to come quite a way," he said. "I wonder which would be the shortest route. Through China or Pakistan. Or Iran."

"It was a figure of speech," Dorothy replied.

"Don't worry," the man said. "No one has great expectations of these affairs. The meat is okay."

"It's goat," she said.

"Delicious," he replied, poking about in the stew as if expecting an eye or worse.

There was a murmur in the room and Dorothy sensed a balloon of thought hanging over the collective heads: *This is revolting. Why am I here? I could have been watching* TV, *at the game, anywhere else at all.*

Isabel whispered, "Should I bring out the baklava?"

It would make them even thirstier but at least it was sweet. Dorothy went to the kitchen to find a water jug. Kate had begun to clear the plates. Matt was sidling up to Louisa Gerdon, no doubt to suggest a mural for city hall. The musician was playing an even sadder tune. The guests were drinking wine as if, indeed, they were in a desert. A cheerier atmosphere began to take over.

Someone shouted, "Play a Cossack song."

The musician obliged with a rousing tune and people began to clap their hands to the rhythm. It was all right again. And then Lent had to ruin it by telling the musician to stop and banging his fork on the table. For a while no one took any notice of him.

"This is an Afghan meal," he shouted.

The musician struck a chord on his instrument.

"In that part of Asia, goat is a staple food."

The musician struck a minor chord in contradiction.

"We're here to do what we can to help those brothers and sisters who share our planet but who have none of our advantages, none of our wealth." He looked at the musician, daring him to touch a string.

A man called out, "I've been there. It's not like this."

Harvey said, "We didn't want to go too far towards reality."

He's quick on his feet, thought Kate.

"And just whose fault is that?" Louisa Gerdon shouted. Her views on colonial intervention were well-known and far from pacific.

"If we weren't there, it would be worse," a woman said.

"They don't want us there."

"The Brits, the Russians. What good did they ever do?"

"Why don't you read history?"

"Why don't you shut up?"

Harvey yelled, "Please everybody, we're here to enjoy an evening of..."

He was drowned out. Fearing that food would be thrown, Dorothy and Kate removed the remaining plates.

"The Afghans can look after themselves."

"Sure, with all that opium!"

Isabel was handing around pieces of baklava when three

men came in from the street shaking rainwater off their tattered coats.

Kate went towards them.

"She said there'd be leftovers," the man in the toque said. He saw the baklava and turned to the guests and shouted, "Dogs've peed on that."

Dorothy was beside them now. "Come right in," she said. If anything could save the situation, it might be these three ragged intruders. She turned to the guests. "These are some of the people we are trying to help."

She cleared a space for them, making people move to give them chairs. Kate brought them stew without rice.

At that moment, a man with a camera on his shoulder came in and stared around, pointing his lens at the musician. Beside him, a woman with a microphone searched for a celebrity. Harvey Lent went towards them smiling, ready for his close-up. He said a few words to the woman in charge but she paid no attention. The camera was turned on the homeless men as the older one said, "Who eats this shit?"

"Act like we're not here, everybody," the woman said.

People began to talk again. Politely they watched and didn't stare as the unexpected guests stood up, each taking a bottle from the table, and went out into the street again. There was applause as if it truly had been a staged scene.

Harvey Lent whispered, "Nice touch," to Dorothy.

The producer introduced herself and Dorothy recognised Marlyn from SITV. "I do this evenings," she said. "And this is in aid of?"

"Sending food and clothes to a poor village in Afghanistan. WorldAidNow&Tomorrow is a well- respected organization..."

Harvey Lent moved into view and shouldered Dorothy aside. "We are grateful for all donations of money. The situation there is..."

The cameraman moved to take in the mural and Matt appeared and began to talk into the microphone about his use of colour and his preference for bleak subjects.

Isabel was asking if anyone wanted coffee until Kate shook her head. There was no coffee, only an urn.

"Suppose my mother's had an accident," Isabel murmured.

"She cut up the goat," Kate replied as if that explained Elsie's absence. "She's probably sitting by the fire at home."

People were beginning to rummage around for their coats and umbrellas, preparing to leave. Dorothy stood by the door.

"Thank you for coming."

"Interesting."

"Thank you so much."

"Something to think about."

"Will you be doing this again?"

"Certainly."

It was only quarter past nine. The crook Gervais had stayed behind and was piling the plastic glasses into a heap on the table, rolling the paper tablecloth to make a package of them and throw them out.

"That was a grotesque affair, Mrs. Graham," he said.

"Thank you," Dorothy said. "That was our aim. To make people aware. Please don't put those glasses in the garbage. We'll need them for our next event."

Kate's feet were hurting. She'd made excuses for her daughter but Delphine really might have come to help. The whole evening had been a fiasco, and there was Dorothy putting a spin on it while she had this mountain of clearing up to do. I've been a sheep again, she thought. When had she abdicated her role as leader? Being the older one, she'd taken charge when she and Dorothy were growing up, half-orphans they'd called themselves. (At college, Elsie had envied them their single parents because she had too many: This is my mother and Frank. This is my father and Sylvie.) That was then when the hot war was too close and the Cold War about to begin and there was no peace. Like now. She looked around the awful kitchen, then picked up a plate and began to scrape the wasted food into a large green bag. It was perhaps time for her to take the other two in hand.

Matt was taking down his mural. "Not great exposure," he said. "I did manage to leave a few of my cards around. And yes, I will come and paint your goddam furniture, Dorothy. You pick up the paint. I suppose you want a shitty beige colour."

And Dorothy was aware again that she'd offended him.

The musician was waiting to be paid. She gave him a twenty-dollar bill. He looked at it with disdain. She gave him a fifty and he twanged his instrument, kissed her on the cheek, and said, "That was fun."

Isabel followed him out.

"Where are you going?" Dorothy asked.

"Home to pee," she answered.

Dorothy went into the kitchen. They hadn't made a clearing plan. Kate was scraping, scraping, scraping. Dorothy opened the door of the fridge and looked into a huge mound of lettuce.

"Do you know how to make lettuce soup?"

They leaned against the counter and laughed. They became hysterical, near to tears. All they needed was a magician to make all the dishes disappear.

"It'll still be here tomorrow."

"But will we?"

"Mom!"

And there was Delphine, smiling. "They're sending him home. Jake is coming home. I just got an email."

Dorothy and Kate shared a moment of stark fear. Wounded? Maimed?

"The bosses said he shouldn't have gone there with so little training. He's to go on courses."

The kitchen became a clean place full of light. And Delphine said, "Pack the dirty dishes into the big cooking pots. We'll do them in our dishwashers. How many garbage bags have you got? Come on Alec."

And Alec, who had been lurking behind the door, came in to help.

Dorothy didn't realize how tired she was until she got home. *I am old, Omar.* The fourth toe on her right foot had independently decided to be arthritic and was hurting like mad. She took off her shoes and sat back on the couch, not sure that she'd have the strength to make it to bed. Her legs ached and her head felt as though someone had inflated a balloon inside it. She and Kate and Delphine and Alec in a spirit of celebration mixed with despair at the job ahead of them had drunk wine out of the bottles on the table as they cleared and sang and found ways to dispose of the garbage. They'd discussed the idea of dumping all the cutlery and all the plates on Elsie's doorstep in revenge for her defection, but Kate voted against it. And it was midnight when they quietly deposited the lettuce and all the empty bottles outside the Salvation Army hostel. After all, each bottle was worth a dime and the lettuce would be useful for sandwiches. Thus they had reasoned as Delphine and Alec, standing on the sidewalk, sang a hymn, softly so as not to wake the sleepers inside, and Kate murmured, "My late husband always spoke well of the Army."

I'm too exhausted to sleep, Omar. Do you remember that song, "Too much in love to say goodnight" it went? Or was it "too much in love to go to bed"? You must have had nights like that. Not wanting the moment, the hour, ever to end. A time when simply being with the beloved was enough. You wanted to stay awake so as not to miss one second of this strange delight. A delight tinged with mourning because you knew that once you slept and daylight came again, it would never be the same. Lying side by side, or dancing, touching, holding, stroking the beloved's hair and not quite believing in the magic: That's how it was. I had my glorious times too.

But enough! My legs are tired. (I should have my veins seen to but am afraid of the pain.) My hands ache. The dinner was in some ways a success and we shall go on. We shall go on. Now, if we could hold an event with you as guest of honour...

Goodnight, dear friend.

∽

"I'm glad you're here early. It's going to be hot." Kate was at her kitchen counter putting muffins on a plate.

"We have added this up over and over and the figure remains the same," Elsie said. She was speaking pleasantly because she had deserted her friends at the dinner and could imagine what they'd been saying about her. All the same, too much had been spent and they had to face up to it.

"I'm happy to pay the musician out of my own pocket," Dorothy said.

"No. That's not the point. We have to work it out exactly. What we spent. What we have left to hand over to WANT."

"I gave Lent a cheque," Kate said as she brought in the

tray and set it down on the coffee table.

"For how much?"

"The whole amount."

"For heaven's sake, Kate. Why did you do that? We have to deduct our expenses. If he's already deposited it, we'll have to ask him to give us the rest back. It'll be embarrassing," Dorothy said, aware too late that she should have acted as sole treasurer.

"He asked for it after the dinner and I just didn't think."

They were at Kate's because Matt was painting at Dorothy's. The apartment was tidier than usual. The piles of books that were usually leaning towers had been straightened and put in some kind of order. Magazines were arranged neatly, the top of each one showing above the next as if they were in a medical waiting room. Dorothy felt afraid for her friend.

"That is so – so unprofessional, Kate," Elsie said. "I mean you know better than that. You wait to see how much you've spent and then you hand over the cheque with a bit of ceremony, not as if you're slipping the guy a bribe on the sly."

"It's done now," Dorothy said. "We have to work around it."

"Well you're the ones who have to go and get the difference back from him. He won't be pleased."

"Okay. Okay," Kate said. "I'm sorry. I'd drunk a fair bit of wine because of the rice. If you hadn't put so much salt in it, Elsie."

Elsie turned her back and looked out the window. Dorothy poured coffee for her and put milk in it.

"Does anyone want butter – well, marg? These are banana and nut. I haven't made muffins for years."

"They're good," Dorothy said. She pressed the keys on the calculator again. "It really should be more."

"Fifty people paid one hundred dollars," Kate said. "Therefore we began with five thousand."

"Not exactly."

"What do you mean, Elsie?"

"The thing with a charity event is that you have to have important people there. Make it look good. You start with a couple of well-known people and then others come."

"You gave tickets away!"

"To Louisa Gerdon and maybe a couple of others."

"So right off we're a few hundred down."

Dorothy picked a piece of walnut out of her muffin and said, "I gave two tickets away."

"The real amount we'll be giving him is?" Kate asked.

"Nine hundred dollars," Dorothy replied. She shook the calculator as if she could make it alter the figures, but the rent of the space and the chairs and tables, the cost of the goat, the wine, the dessert, all added up to more than they'd first reckoned. She'd gone over the numbers in her head and knew that the little machine was right.

"It's not nothing," she said.

"I would have paid nine hundred bucks not to go through that awful evening."

"You skipped out."

"Who did the cooking?"

"We could've raised that amount at a bake sale."

"We forgot the bill from Celestial Cleaners," Kate said. "Two hundred dollars."

"Okay!" Dorothy said. "Chalk it up to experience. We will move on."

"You will move on. I have to get to my tai chi class. I just hope this doesn't cause trouble for anyone, that's all."

Elsie picked up her purse and walked out.

"Elsie!" Dorothy called out but the door closed. She didn't understand what right their friend had to be so snippy or why she was talking about trouble as if trouble would surely come.

Kate was saying, "In an odd sort of way, I liked it. It was so awful it made me feel better than I've felt in a while. I know that wasn't the object but I realized I've been behaving stupidly. I didn't even like him at the end, you know, the late judge. I hadn't liked him for a long time. But it was pride. I was rejected. And what did his leaving say about all our years together? Were they a wasteland, a total waste of time? But it came to me in that horrible place when I was eating the goat that if you're rejected by someone despicable, then it doesn't matter." She burst into tears but was smiling.

Dorothy put her arm around her and said, "You're fine, Kate. And you will be fine."

"Elsie's mad. I could cash in a GIC and pay for all this and then Lent could keep the cheque I gave him."

"He shouldn't have asked for it. We'll sort it out."

"Well, I'll make it up to a round thousand."

On her way home Dorothy stopped at the pharmacy to pick up her prescribed pills. Dr. Bartel had told her that it would be a while, a long while, before she needed surgery, but for now she should be careful. The warm muffin and strong coffee were making their presence felt. She sighed. *Have you seen Niagara Falls in winter, Omar, when great blocks of ice gather in the river before crashing down into the pool below?*

She stopped the car halfway down the street. What was going on? They were dismantling her house without warning, without letting her know. Had she signed something at the dinner, given permission to the crook Gervais in a drunken moment?

Two ladders and a plank were set up along the front wall. She drove the last few yards quickly, parked the car and hopped out and yelled, "Hey there!" But it was Matt who was standing on the plank stroking the wall with a large brush to a background of screeching sound that blared out from a radio on the ground.

"You're supposed to be painting my furniture," she shouted up to him.

"This is my gift to you," he yelled back. "You're going to love it."

She went inside, closing the door carefully so as not to shake the crazy man off his perch.

Before she did anything else, she had to sit down and write a letter to the person who had been on her mind since the night of the dinner.

What good, dear Ms. Afghan mother of three, have we done for you? I imagine you to be called Alami and am not even sure it's a Christian name in your country. And what kind of assumption is that? Of course you don't have Christian names. I want to know if your children are able to go to school. Do they have three meals a day, assuming that the structure of your day is built around food as mine tends to be? Do you and your husband, assuming he's not in the army and assuming too that he looks a little like Omar Sharif, have sex on a regular basis? Well, as you have three children, probably. Do you enjoy it? None of my business, right?

My apologies for assuming so much. For all I know, you might be proudly looking out over acres of poppies and anticipating a bumper harvest. Or have three grown sons who fight alongside the Taliban.

Either way, I hope things turn out for the best.

Yours in sad ignorance of what that best might be, Dorothy Graham

The panda was peering through a forest of bamboo canes. *Come to the Art Show A must-see event.* The little face reminded Delphine of Elvira, a child teaching other children. Isabel and Elsie should have done more for the girl, but they were caught up in their feelings about Alec, and Elvira had resisted them both with all her might. Like all unhappy families, they would have to find their own way out of the bamboo thicket – or not. She outlined the animal, added colour and printed the page. It might not be original but it was pleasing and fun. She went back to the computer and decided to multiply the pandas until there were hundreds of them, more than existed in the world, wild and caged. She added in a few humans and then more humans than pandas. Her screen was full of faces. She put a smile on the face of the original panda and went back to the first image. She printed all the versions and laid them in a row on the desk.

If Jake were here, he would look at the pictures and tell her what he thought. He'd always had a good eye. She decided to submit two designs to the committee and let them choose. Meanwhile, the Ontario government wanted a bright and forward-looking suggestion for its new schools program. Make it appear, the very civil, civil servant had said, that soon every child will do math with ease, read and write fluently and be able to pinpoint Ingushetia on the map. A magic wand might be the appropriate symbol. The Future of Education? Do your children know where you are?

At least, she thought, I know where my mother is. She is walking up the path.

She opened the door and Kate came in quickly.

"I should have gone to Ottawa with them."

"I don't think so, Mom."

"Dorothy's impulsive. And if Elsie gets on her high horse too they'll do more harm than good."

"Come and look at these designs and tell me which you like best."

"You're diverting me."

"I'm diverting us both."

"I've had a sense lately that Dorothy is keeping a secret and I can't help wondering if she is seriously ill and might take stupid risks because she doesn't care any longer."

"She wouldn't get Elsie into trouble. She does have some sense."

"And Elsie was in a strange mood. She's waited all this time to have a mid-life crisis."

Delphine said nothing. All three friends appeared to be going through some kind of mental upheaval. Fear of death, perhaps.

"I like the panda by itself," her mother said, looking at the pictures. "What about the education project?"

"What's new to say?"

"Say what people have always said. Just say it differently."

"Opening doors. Not closing them. That kind of thing."

"Knowledge is freedom."

"A window on the world..."

"I'm working on a strange manuscript for Meeks. I wanted to do something absorbing to take my mind off those two wandering into a bureaucratic wilderness, but it's not helping."

"I imagine them being invited to speak to Parliament."

"Parliament is on vacation."

"They'll be back on Friday, Mom. Stop worrying. They're grown up. And stop walking up and down for goodness sake. Come into the kitchen. I'll make coffee."

Delphine ground the beans wondering if lifelong friendship had prevented the three older women from actually maturing. There was an element of being twenty years old in their lives that now and then seemed to engulf them. She saw her mother glancing at the note beside the phone.

"Dad called me," she said.

"I'm not going out there, Delphine. I won't be cruel about it. I could say he can rot for all I care, but I won't. I could say he's made his bed et cetera but I'm not saying that either. He'll have to look after himself. Many people do. A lot of people are old and lonely and they get by. Your brother is nearer though I can't see his dear Megan offering to help. Look how useless she was when Brian broke his leg. *Help! Help. What am I going to do?* "

"Dad only called to see how long the waiting lists for surgery are here."

"Oh no!"

"I told him up to a year."

After her mother left, Delphine knew she could have spent the day, the week, the month pondering the complications of family life. What were her own responsibilities? He was her father. Without him she wouldn't exist. He had given her money to help her when Jake was born. He had encouraged Jake and given him books and toys. She could put bunk beds in Jake's room or build an addition on the house. She tried to push aside the picture of herself tenderly nursing her father through cancer and dementia for two decades until she herself was frail and crippled, but the pandas on the screen became a multiple image of a sick and lonely elderly man. *Okay, Dad! After Jake gets back, I'll come out to see you and we'll make a plan.* She keyed in the "late judge's" email address.

～

Dorothy was staring at the war memorial and picturing the widows and veterans who had come to lay wreaths in honour of all the heroes. The Canadian doctor who'd seen the poppies blow "In Flanders Fields," had written his famous poem in despair at Ypres nearly ninety years ago. Now a young woman very like Delphine was looking at the flowers and crying. And Jake was seeing poppies blow in another war zone five thousand miles away. It continued. It went on. She felt shaken and wanted to hold on to something for support.

Elsie took her arm and said, "Come on. We haven't come to Ottawa to stare about."

"And how many pictures of the tulips have you taken, Ms.Tourist?"

The brave tulips, splendid in their many colours, a gift from the grateful Dutch, were a different kind of memorial.

"The secretary said three o'clock. That's what you're wearing?"

"Obviously. These are my best white jeans."

Elsie, assured in her beige and brown pantsuit and straw hat, said, "We have to figure out what we're going to say."

"Going to say?"

Wearing a long white skirt and turquoise top, Dorothy was with Dmitri Ostrevsky leaning over the rail of the ship while he pointed out the stars and told her he liked sad women. The man's attentiveness, not to mention his accent, had brought Dorothy back from never-again into the land of possibility. And there had been moments of delight.

"Dorothy!" Elsie said. "What exactly are we going to say?"

"He's only a man. We're both of sound mind. I think we can talk sensibly."

"The points we have to get across are..."

Dorothy tuned the words out as she walked with her friend towards the square building a few blocks away. Dmitri had licked her tears like a cat. But his tongue was smooth. Kate and Elsie had told her at the time that it was much too soon to get involved with another man. She had to let go of Sparrow the bigamist, they said, before she stepped into the arena again. She'd returned to Canada by ship instead of flying as a way of putting distance between herself and Alfred, the man she thought she could have loved, if not forever, then for a very long time, and had fallen into the arms of a charming exile.

"It's too hot," she said.

"We should have brought water."

"It's like a desert."

"Stop complaining.

"I was only saying."

There was no need for Elsie to be quite so sharp. There was no need for her to repeat that she was out of her mind to come on this trip with someone who had no plans. You look ahead. You figure it out. You don't go blindly on and then blunder into trouble. Dmitri hadn't been trouble at first. Love and money. Those were his immediately apparent attributes. Where was he now? *Step into the day, Dorothy. The past is yesterday's problem.*

Elsie had possibly imagined herself arriving in Ottawa as a kind of Lady Bountiful, hatted and gloved, shaking hands with a few natives, holding the least unhealthy-looking baby in the group and making nice speeches on behalf of WANT. Dorothy expected, and in fact rather hoped for, confrontation and argument. There would be difficulties. They had been warned...

Towards the west in the far distance loomed a range of unfriendly mountains. Closer, the colours were brown and beige and occasionally black. They reminded her of the many jungle print shirts and jackets and purses and pants hanging up in womenswear stores. A fashion that had lasted much too long. But the colours here were muted and had a fascinating ripple effect to them. When she got home, she would paint this landscape on a large canvas and call it Lost, or perhaps Nowhere. She and Elsie were walking barefoot across acres of hot beige sand...

...The sun had become an enemy and there was no sign of an oasis. Elsie was right to be afraid. They were still a long way from Kandahar. The village they'd left was north of here. They had to keep going or die of heat and thirst. If they couldn't reach the city before sunset, there was no hope. Elsie disappeared and she was alone in this wide new world. Alone. At peace. Feeling wonderful. In a cloud of dust he rode towards her on his camel. Leaning down from the saddle, he asked if he could take her to his tent and give her small cups of rich coffee and soft, sticky dates. "Yes," she said. "Yes."

A man on a black horse stopped beside them.

Dorothy took the proffered bottle gratefully, wondering why it wasn't a goatskin and not caring how many mouths had sucked from it before.

"Are you all right now, Dot?"

Elsie's face loomed large against the light.

"Are we there yet?"

"We're in the lobby. Sit still for a minute. You'll be all right."

"I'm fine."

Another man offered her coffee.

"Thank you, Omar," she said.

"Omar!" he replied.

"Dorothy?"

They knew her here. It was going to be all right.

Voices around her were talking about an ambulance, a hospital. She looked around for the patient. The brilliant images evaporated. Outlines sharpened.

"There you are, Elsie," she said, sitting up. "I'm all right now. Sorry. It was the sun."

~

Kate was watching Isabel and Isabel was watching her father. Richard had fallen and hurt his back and was not feeling well. He wanted to know exactly where Elsie was. What was she doing in Ottawa? It was his place. For years, he had stood before committees and made presentations. See, over on the wall his signed photograph with Chretien. And there he was again, part of a family group with Trudeau. For a newcomer, the place was uncharted territory, inhospitable. Isabel reached for one of her father's mottled and veined hands.

"I was planning to take her on a cruise," he said.

"You'll be able to do that when she returns."

"Kidnap victims are never the same after. They fall in love with their captors. And besides..."

Kate didn't want to let him wander into *besides*. There was nothing in that place but dread.

She said, "People don't get kidnapped there. I heard from Elsie this morning. They'll be fine. Back tomorrow." She'd told Elsie about Richard's trip to the hospital, the wait in emergency, the pronouncement: No bones broken. But she hadn't mentioned the man's confusion.

Richard Edwards, self-assured businessman, successful in all his endeavours to date, asked in a shaky voice, "Are you sure they're not in Kandahar?"

He was the one remaining husband of the four they'd had between them, five if you counted Alfred Sparrow. Kate wondered what held this particular union together, why no surprise or shock or sudden affair had broken the tie. She'd thought her own marriage secure until the day she came home early from a meeting and found her mate packing a suitcase.

Kate told Isabel to call her if she needed her. But Mike was coming to spend the night and between them they would manage.

As she made her way home, she passed the travel agent's office. Sheena waved her in but she kept going. She had seen love that morning, seen it in Richard's face, in his fear and his inability to think now of anything at all except his wife. And Isabel, the good daughter, was sitting with him tenderly. It was no time for exotic butterflies and near-mythical islands.

She pushed the code into the panel beside the door of her building and went into the lobby. Pierre Jones was sitting on a bench inside. He stood up as she came in and smiled.

"How did you get in? "she asked and knew she sounded irritated.

"Every burglar knows that it pays to be well-dressed and have a foreign accent, Dr. Charbonneau. Especially when he bears gifts." He handed her a bunch of anemones.

She hesitated, not wanting to invite him up to her place, but he was already holding the elevator open door for her. She appeared to have no choice. But she did have a choice. She could close the elevator door on his arm or be pleasant to the handsome stranger.

He stood beside her in the kitchen as she made tea and sliced lemon and cut in half the brownie she'd bought as a treat for herself. She told him about the butterfly again and about Henry Vorster who had not replied to her letter.

"You wouldn't like it if you went. And what do you need of exotic locations when I am here?"

She laughed. He told her that her smile lit up the space. To hold him at bay she began to talk about Dorothy's letters.

"I bet you could write a book," he said. "An autobiography for instance."

"I have written books. Academic books. And my life has been ordinary."

"No life —" he began.

She offered him more tea to stop him from uttering the usual trite comment.

After he'd gone, she googled him and found out very little. There was no mention of any new publishing venture or any literary relationship. A few weeks before, she'd conjured Jean-Louis Barron onto her screen and found nothing except the well-known biographical material, the lists of his books and a lot of critical comment. There was no suggestion that his great novel, *The Woman who Drowned in Lake Geneva*, contained any reference to his life whatsoever. And yet Pierre had told Isabel that much of it was true, driving Isabel into uncertainty about her dead hero and all his works.

Was Pierre simply a wandering liar? A modern troubadour who wove himself in and out of people's lives at whim? "You don't understand, do you?" he'd said as he left.

Chapter 5

"TENTH FLOOR," ELSIE SAID. "You sure you're up to this, Dot."

"I'm fine and if you keep calling me Dot, I'll call you 'Little Else.'"

"Come on. We have to be serious."

The door to the office was closed. Elsie turned the handle and went inside. A man and a woman drew quickly back from an embrace.

"I'm Elsie Edwards and this is Dorothy Graham. We're to see Mr. DeLisle who I believe is the head of this organization."

"He is. But he's not here."

"We told him we were coming. We have an appointment."

Dorothy took in the scene. An untidy office. A young woman wearing a neat pantsuit, her lipstick smeared. The man, older, expensive jacket, amused at having been caught, smiled and said, "He must have forgotten. They're out back. A reception. I'm sure you'll find him there. Go back to the ground floor, out the main door, turn left and it will bring you to the parking lot and turn right and you'll be in the gardens."

"Thank you," Elsie said. She closed the door and they heard laughter.

Men! Dorothy thought. And women! And there were a lot of them in the green treed space at the back of the building. The crowd was daunting. A tent the size of a baseball pitch filled half the lawn.

Here was strangeness. Four men in battle fatigues were standing around. A low table in the centre was spread with food. This was something to write to Omar about. Here perhaps were the dates, the little cups of coffee, the cakes of her imagination. She had dreamed it into reality. That was power! Soft music was drifting into the air. Bees began to hum in Dorothy's head. The men changed shape. Their outlines waved and flickered. *The liquid in the bottle given to me by the horseman was not water, she said to herself. We have been drugged. We shall never get home again. These villainous looking men have captured us and will use us for their pleasure.* She heard the gabble of foreign languages.

Someone offered her a cup but she pushed it aside. Then her hearing became clear and she understood what the men were saying. The one who appeared to be seven feet tall demanded to know what they were doing there.

"We've come to meet Mr. DeLisle. We have an appointment," Elsie said.

"Can I see your invitations, please?"

"This is Mrs. Edwards. I'm Dorothy Graham, and we're here on behalf of WANT. We've come because we need to find out why it takes so long for the money and supplies to get to the right places in that poor benighted country. And we want to take a trip there ourselves."

Elsie said, looking the man up and down, "We've come to Ottawa specially to speak to Mr. DeLisle and also, if possible, to the Minister of Foreign Affairs or his aide."

"You haven't got an official invitation. You have to leave."

He walked away and Elsie said, "We're not going to get much help here."

"If we sneak around they won't notice. We can eat lots and then we won't need dinner."

They moved as if they were going back the way they'd come and smiled at the giant who was watching them. He nodded his approval. And then they saw *him*. The obviously important person, the guest of honour. He was wearing a green gown over his suit and a forage cap on his head. Either side of him, close to his right and his left were bodyguards with wires sticking out of their ears. Elsie whispered, "It's him. It's Karzai."

Dorothy quickly pushed her way through the crowd and said to him, "What are you doing to protect charity workers in your country and to prevent money and goods from being stolen and...?"

She was grabbed by two men who took her to one side. She saw cameras and shouted, "Charity! We work for WANT."

"Irresponsible. Totally counterproductive."

Elsie moved. She went to the table and picked up a cup and threw the contents at the guard who had Dorothy's left arm in a lock. The cup was snatched from her hand.

"Manners," one of the men said.

They were taken forcefully back to the lobby of the building where two other men came to speak to them.

"Who are you?" Dorothy asked.

"We are WANT. I'm Jim Johnson from Montreal. And this is the president, Jean-Marie DeLisle. And the last thing we need is to deal with idiots like you. There's something very important happening here today."

"These are the two who've been bothering poor Harvey Lent," DeLisle said. "We did have an appointment. Sorry I missed you. If you come back at five..."

Elsie said, "We're here now. We've come all the way from Toronto. We want to go to Afghanistan ourselves to find out where the money goes and why the food distribution is so poor."

"And," Dorothy said, "if you don't give me something to eat and drink very soon I'll tell them you're living like sheikhs with dancing girls and opium..."

"You shouldn't even be here, woman!"

"My name is Dorothy, and as my friend just told you we're here to talk about visas for Afghanistan."

"Kabul isn't Kansas, Dorothy."

"Dorothy!"

Here I am, dear Mr. Sharif. The smell was not incense, not camel dung, not canvas. It was strangely and pungently sweet. The voices around her were pleasant and she was lying in a hammock while soft breezes played over her face.

"Heatstroke," someone said.

"Stroke," she heard.

Kate knew that she was mentally, if that were possible, holding her breath. No word from Delphine. Jake could have been home by now even if he'd flown the long way around the world. To divert herself, she went to the computer and brought up the pictures of the Kuril Islands on the screen and stared at the volcanoes. Now that she had work, did she need the unattainable? She imagined a plane in the air over Japan, Jake reading a magazine, now and then looking out the window at the Islands and the sea far below. She sat still for a moment and enjoyed the view.

The little light was flashing to tell her she had a message.

From: Elsed@global.com
To: Xkate@redwood.ca
Hi Kate. I know she's coming to see you this morning. Tell me what you think. She had a strange kind of attack in Ottawa, quite out of it. I don't think it was a stroke. Mother had strokes and this was different. Maybe it was, as they said, the heat. She didn't seem able to focus. The whole trip was a disaster and as for going to Afghanistan, well the moon is just as likely. And now Richard isn't himself. Thank

you for coming around, by the way. Isabel said you were a great help. He's much better and the doctor has given him new medication. I'm staying close to home till this stupid hearing. Don't think it was your fault by the way. We should have made plans about the money and there's a lot more to it than our little cheque.

Back to Dot. I wish she would get out of the house today and stay in a hotel or with me. Maybe she needs to be in a place with 24-hour care. I hope it hasn't come to that but I guess we have to consider it. If she seems at all vague, let me know and we'll make her go to the doctor.

Come around later if you have time. Love, Elsie

Kate put her head down on the desk for a moment. Hermits had no friends. People who built grass huts in the wilderness left their laptops at home. Cellphones could be thrown into Lake Ontario. Distance lent enchantment. But her friends were home again.

She pictured a three-legged race for a trio but then realized that the one in the centre with both legs tied would be carried along by the other two, a dead weight. For the past few years, she had been that middle one. *I am about to change.* The intercom made its squeaking intrusive sound. Kate hobbled over to the speaker. "Come on up, Dorothy." It was time to get back to friendship and chaos.

Dorothy was having misgivings. "I know I sometimes go too far. Maybe I've always had too much energy. Was I like that when we were growing up? I didn't mean to get the organization into trouble. Nor Harvey. Kate, come out from under all that paper and give me some advice."

"Me give you advice?"

"And come out from that cloud of pathos."

There was a pause as if Kate were trying to switch modes like a computer changing from Works to Word. Dorothy waited. She half expected a deluge of tears and comments about lack of understanding. Or perhaps Kate would get up and walk out.

To pre-empt either she said, "You were always the cleverest of us. I need you."

"I haven't been doing nothing," Kate said. "And I'm not pathetic."

"I know."

"For once, Dorothy, you actually don't."

All right, I'm a know-it-all. But speak!

"First of all, about the case. It won't come to anything. Once they see that the accounting mistakes were 'honest' ones, and that no criminal acts were involved, they'll throw it out. The good publicity from your mad attempt to get at Karzai will balance out the bad. People are sending money. When you're there only speak if you're asked to, and say as little as possible. We are after all on the side of the angels. No harm will come to Harvey Lent."

"Are you sure? Because I'm afraid the top people will use him as a scapegoat. I've come to like him."

"And aside from that, I'm working again. Don't look like that. I may be over seventy but I still have a brain. Harris and Meeks have taken me on as their academic editor. I've had to do a lot of reading to catch up with what's going on out there and I'm enjoying it. I'm pleased that I can still do it."

"Congratulations," Dorothy said, tamping down a small green imp of envy. "How did it happen?"

"Young Meeks was in my class years ago. We met by chance. I went to a lecture on Foucault at Hart House. He asked what I was doing with my life and I told him I was spending time regretting my marriage and talking to a china dog. He laughed. And three days later he called. Then he sent me a trial manuscript and so."

"I think we should have a drink on this."

"I think I should try to find these receipts and maybe then have a drink. And it will have to be tea because I haven't bought any wine this week."

"All right, Kate," Dorothy replied.

"I've got the clippings of your trip here too."

"I wish I'd been wearing my other shirt."

"I wish you'd been wearing a hat."

"I'm all right. They made a fuss. Never drink wine while sitting in the sun. My dad told me that."

"Don't tell Elsie, but before I got this offer, I was weighing the idea of going to Victoria. Just for a week or two."

"For heaven's sake! You've been saved."

Dorothy looked at her friend. She was engaged in life again, the kind of life that suited her best.

"Did something happen to Elsie while you were at that reception?"

"You mean this plan of hers to give dinners at home? It's a feeling we all have. That we're ineffectual. She wants to have an effect. Soon. While she can. That's how we got into arranging the dinner. Pressure of time."

"You mean the energy of impending doom. She's like a mad thing. Rushing here and there. No time to talk. I worry about her."

Dorothy had begun to worry about herself. She worried about falling down in the street, being run over or collapsing in the supermarket and now kept a card in her purse that stated her address, her blood type and the names and phone numbers of her two "contacts." As long as they didn't all crash in the same accident, recognition would be available. She really didn't want to end up on a slab with a label around her toe that read Jane Doe. After cremation, she wanted a party. She'd chosen the music and put a cassette in the envelope with her prepaid funeral contract. "See what the boys in the backroom will have," would send her on her way.

"And tell them I cried, and tell them I died of the same."

When she got home, she dug out the letter she'd written to Marlene in the singer's last reclusive years.

Dear Ms. Dietrich,

What was it about you? You were no angel, but you offered heaven to your audience. During the war, when you visited the troops and sang hymns to the transient love of perilous times, you gave those men a pass to take love where they found it. Generals loved you. Corporals loved you. And all ranks in between. You offered hope and the gift of sexual possibility to the soldiers when death might be waiting for them the next week, the next day. And you were rightly honoured for your war efforts. There are statues in public squares to leaders who did much less.

My dad kept an old 78 rpm record of yours in his closet. I found it and your picture when I was clearing out his room in the Home. He didn't take much with him when he moved from the house, only what was most important.

In that husky voice, whether you were wearing mannish clothes or a clinging silvery gown, you made love to us all when you sang.

Chapter 6

"IF ONLY EITHER BUSH or Blair ever said anything about the Iraqis being killed every day," Elsie said to Kate, "I would support them. They are unconscionable hypocrites."

"You don't have a vote in the US, or in the UK either."

Elsie was beating goat cutlets with a hammer. "I have simply realized," she said "that very little matters except the truth. You have to keep hitting at it. I'm going to bake it with garlic and herbs."

"I'm reading an interesting book about Kashmir."

"Come along, hand me that plate."

Kate went into the living room to say hello to Richard. He was sitting by the window looking out.

"Cardinals," he said. "I've always liked them. Pretty little things. Blue jays squawk too much." He lowered his voice. "I wish she hadn't gone there. She's not the same. She looks after me quite fiercely. Tells me when to take my pills and when to go to bed. I told her not to go there. It's a wild place, uncivilized, rooted in ancient tribalism. Shoot you as soon as look at you." He had become an uncertain man. A wavering, whispering man.

"They only went to Ottawa."

"That's what she says, Kate. And now you see, she's cooking as if we're running a restaurant. To understand a people, she says, you have to know what they eat. You have to understand what they kill for nourishment. Obviously they first eat what's plentiful. As people did here with buffalo. As the Inuit do with caribou and seals. Then you discover what is a luxury to them, as caviar and truffles are to us. What they will go a long way to find, or pay a great deal for. I worry about her sanity."

Kate left him and went back to the kitchen. The world was a shaky place indeed. People changed from day to day. Elsie was muttering to herself and pulling the leaves off stalks of rosemary.

"I want you to know, Kate, that I'm not out of my mind. The way Richard keeps looking at me I feel he's going to have me put away or at least have me psychoanalyzed. I can almost hear him telling his golfing buddies, my wife hasn't been the same since she got back. With some pride, of course, because how many of their wives have had their pictures in the paper and been written about. What's so annoying about men is the way they make fun of you at the same time. But that's not what I'm talking about. You've only to watch the news to see people living in ways that are not human, to see savagery, bloodlust. And I am angry. More, I should say, simmering. Look into the soup there and see if it's still cooking. I think mainly what I'm angry about is my own ignorance. We used to go to Sunday School and some things stick in your mind. There's a line about 'He that hath ears to hear...' We had ears but we weren't hearing. We weren't even listening. I'll tell you something. I'm going to make people listen."

She was bringing the hammer down heavily onto the board and Kate wished she would stop. Selfishly, she wanted Elsie back in her former shape, dressed elegantly even when she was chopping up tomatoes for spaghetti sauce, talking about her crowded social calendar, worrying that her outfit wouldn't be ready in time for the Opera Ball.

"Our little charitable efforts. The parties. Auctioning off a Mercedes. Do you realize how obscene that is? How totally contradictory?"

"It makes money," Kate ventured to say.

"Sand," Elsie replied. It was as near as she would come to shit. "From now on, I won't be here very much. This dinner is the first of a series I'm planning across the country. Afghan Awareness. And then I'll begin in the States."

"I wouldn't go there with an idea like this."

"If only five of those who come tonight invite ten others, think how this could spread. Think of the effect. Ripples."

But Kate was imagining her friend wearing an orange overall, shackled, encaged, her fingers entwined in a wire fence.

Richard came into the kitchen and looked at the pile of meat on the counter. "Do you have to do this, sweetheart? You're tiring yourself," he said. "Why don't you just put all this in the freezer and then we'll have dinner at the club."

"You don't know what's going on there," his wife replied. "If you did, you wouldn't say that. You don't have to be here. It's between you and your conscience."

"Then I think my conscience and I will dine out."

"Suit yourselves!"

In that moment, Kate determined to go back to Travel World and make arrangements to go to Asia.

Harvey Lent standing at the table with his lawyer appeared taller. The role of suspected thief suited him better than that of beggar. Dorothy bent her head to prevent herself from smiling at him in encouragement as if she were his accomplice and they had plans to run off to Fiji or Zanzibar together with the loot. Elsie, beside her wearing a red linen suit, was dressed to impress. Kate had stayed behind. She had an appointment, she said, and they could get on without her.

"Am I to understand that forty thousand dollars of the money collected on behalf of WANT was somehow misplaced by Mr. Lent?" The inquisitor was a man of hard edges. Beady eyes, thin fingers, sharp nose.

The lawyer bowed his head in assent.

"And there was no record of this?"

Again the little bow and a scarcely audible, "Yes, sir."

"It seems as though Mr. Lent was wanting something for himself."

The few people in the room tittered.

"In these times, that is not a great deal of money."

"If it were only two dollars, it was mismanagement or theft, taking money from a charity meant to help the poor and deprived in a foreign country."

"Money was not taken in the sense of stolen, sir," Lent's lawyer said. "It was merely misplaced. If you look at page 113 of the accounts for last year and the corresponding page for this year, column three, you will see that the figures have been moved and are on the next page and then..."

Dorothy wasn't sure how long she could stand to listen to it all. How did these people ever get anything done when all they did was talk? It was theatre of the absurd, absurdly formal when the whole matter could have been sorted out in half an hour over coffee and donuts.

Then she heard the man say, "It was the interference of the three women that caused this misguided enquiry. My client is a hard-working man who has done nothing wrong."

It was enough. Dorothy stood up and moved to the desk. "We three took this on, sir, in order to make a contribution. And we did make money, entrusting it to Mr. Lent who by the way has not, in my opinion, been wilfully misusing funds. Money gets sucked into a huge hole in that country. The little that gets through does make a difference. And that's why we have to keep on. WANT has supplied food and other goods to several very poor villages. There is a kind of poverty there that we, sitting in our warm homes, cannot comprehend."

"And I'm to understand that you wanted to go to Afghanistan yourselves?"

"Two of us, yes. Using our own finances. We wanted to know whether the deliveries were being made and to whom and why there are so many stumbling blocks. All we want to do is send what people need and before it even gets on a plane there are a dozen people in Ottawa holding it up, wanting permits, official invitations to this and that, eating dates and drinking sweet, dark coffee."

And besides, Omar, by whom and when was it decreed that we in the West have to wear skirts and suits and ties and such restrictive clothing? Robes are much more comfortable and democratic when you come to think about it. Except that it must be hard to keep them white. White dazzles the eyes.

"Mrs. Graham?"

She was helped back to her seat as if she were an invalid. Elsie touched her hand. Hardly listening to the voices, she recalled pictures in her old Sunday School prayer book. The artist couldn't have known whether Jesus wore flowing robes or a loincloth but she'd gone with the robes. Then she heard Elsie say it was over, and that there'd been no need for the hearing in the first place. The discrepancy had been explained. Harvey Lent was cleared of any wrongdoing and in fact commended for his efforts.

As they left the building he came over and thanked them and said he hoped to see them again soon. Sincere or not, it was friendly.

Outside, the sun was shining. Sparrows were chirping and squirrels were darting around. Dorothy wished her mind would settle down. She felt as if someone had shaken her head and created a storm of swirling sand in her brain.

"Let's have coffee," she said to Elsie. But Elsie replied that she had too much to do before tomorrow evening and she had to get home.

When Dorothy woke up, she realized that she'd fallen asleep on the couch, had been asleep for hours. It was already beginning to get dark. Her mind was crowded with images of her life: Morning after morning to her desk in the office, picking up a coffee at Tim Horton's on the way; days of paperwork; a few early evenings in the hotel with the boss; the house on Carlson Street in Niagara Falls; and Plymouth Hoe where Alfred had pointed out to her the spot where Drake played his famous game of bowls. She let her mind linger on the grassy Hoe. She hadn't kept any of the letters he'd sent in the first year of her return. She would have opened them now and read his desperate words: *Dear Dorothy, All is sorted out. Please come back to me. Dear Dorothy, what does it matter if we're married or not? I love you more than anything in the whole world.* But for all she knew the unopened letters were full of recrimination, anger at her quick departure.

The doorbell rang. Who was calling so late? She picked up the brass owl and went to open the door a tiny crack.

Alec was standing there. "Are you ready?" she asked. "You promised to come and hear me play, remember."

Dorothy didn't remember; her mind was still in the past. "I'll go change, " she said and set off up the stairs.

"You're fine the way you are," Alec called out. "We have to go now or I'll be late."

I'm fine the way I am. Dorothy picked up her purse and followed Alec down the garden path. When they got to the club, Alec went backstage and Dorothy found herself sitting at a little table in a twilit room, not quite sure whether she was still dreaming or not. A young person emerged from the smoky haze and asked her what she'd like to drink. What did people drink here? She looked around at the tables and saw cone-shaped glasses lit by candlelight; cocktails. The waiter was waiting.

"White wine," she said, forgetting to be specific and knowing that he would bring her something cheap and sweet and awful. After a few moments, there was applause as the musicians appeared. No announcements were made. A secret sign between the quartet on stage was all it took to start them off. Jazz had never been a language she understood. But she listened now, closed her eyes and let herself feel the rhythm that throbbed in the room like a shifting heartbeat. And then she allowed herself to scan the players.

The drummer shook his head up and down as he beat his drums; the sticks like hammers moved across and up and down, sideways, fast. The bass player was black and very tall. Even from her corner she could see that he was intense, that he held the instrument like a lover. But the saxophone player. The saxophone leant and swayed into the music, its plaintive sounds leaching out into the space, drawing souls towards it like a pied piper. *I am your god, follow me, follow where I lead.* The notes reached with long fingers into Dorothy's heart. I should have known of this before, she told herself. Should have been invited to this party years ago. Jazz is a magic place. It is roundabout and swings. It is every man and every woman and every life.

The waiter poured more wine into her glass. If he had asked her permission, she hadn't noticed. She also hadn't noticed that a man was now sitting at her table. She came out of her trance and looked at him.

"You're on your own," he said.

He had a round face, a familiar look and, as far as she could see in the dim light, was wearing a blue jacket with a rose in the lapel and a white shirt.

"I'm all right," she said.

"I was watching you. It's your first time, isn't it?"

He'd broken into her shell and now no doubt wanted to disrupt her evening. The red rose was perhaps a signal to someone he'd chatted with on the Internet and was expecting to meet. She had no password to offer him, no night of love.

"I'm waiting for somebody," she said sharply.

"For me, perhaps."

Then she recognized the voice. It was only Pierre after all. How did he know where she was? What did he want from them all? It was not as if they were rich or had anything in the way of influence to offer. Did he keep watch? Did he tap phones? Was he here to talk about the letters?

"How are you, Pierre?"

The waiter came over and said, "This guy bothering you?"

"Not yet," she replied, and Pierre laughed.

"There are a few of us sitting together," he said and pointed to a group a few tables away which, as far as Dorothy could see in the dim light, included a half-naked woman and two other men "Would you like to join us?"

It was a long time since she'd been out so late, so long past bedtime. She'd entered the night world of shadows and familiar strangers and melancholy music. A colony of a different species lived in the dark underworld of her city.

"I really am waiting for someone," she said and wondered, when Pierre had moved away, who that someone might be and whether he or she would turn up.

Chapter 7

KATE KNEW SHE WAS LATE but the road sloped downward and as she ran from the parking lot her foot slipped and all the baklava fell onto the wet sidewalk. A dozen crows rushed to the feast, pecking and cawing. She batted them away and picked up the sticky cakes, spat on her finger and wiped them and tried to arrange them in neat rows. A chorus of old men shouted, "Dogs've peed on those." She wasn't sure whether to offer them the baklava but decided it would be wrong to give damaged goods to poor men and walked away.

She woke up confused. She'd fallen asleep after lunch in her armchair, the sun beating in through the dusty apartment window. Elsie and Dorothy had been vague about the meeting. Why wasn't Jake home? Was Robert down in the lobby with all his possessions? She recognized the crows in her dream as a flock of worries. She looked at the clock propped up on the sideboard and saw that it was past time for her appointment. There had been no call from the receptionist demanding to know why she was late. Did they not care?

Standing up, she looked at the clock again. The sun, striking the glass, had distorted the figures. It was only one thirty. She had half an hour to get herself to the spa for an afternoon of being cosseted. That was Elsie's word. *Cosseted.*

Rushing from the parking lot, she hurried inside *Just For You* and was enveloped in the scent of exotic spices. In fact, she thought, it probably smelled like a brothel. She was led by a delicate flower of a maiden to a bank of lockers and shown the shower and the personal robe and slippers and instructed to go through a green door when she was ready. Soft music surrounded her and led her on.

It was the middle of the afternoon and she was lying in a scented bath and allowing her thoughts to wander where they would. She had passed over Robert and was considering the offer to republish *Signs and Symbols* that had come in the mail that morning from the university press. Her book had been out of print for years, but now apparently there was renewed interest in historical context and early Canadian fiction. Then she let her mind travel to her fantasy islands, the panpipes' call of a distant and little-visited destination.

The healing salts in the water were soothing her back muscles. She moved to one side to let the jet play on her hip and her thoughts shifted to family matters.

Dorothy had sounded strange when she called that morning. What was she doing going out to a nightclub? And why was Pierre there? He was weaving a thread around them like a spider, perhaps keeping them all in his web for later use. She wasn't sure what to think about his having also collected Elvira, who was young and not too bright. She had misgivings. There was something too persistent about the man. Was he really a 'family stalker'? Was he family?

His age was about right. He would be six years younger than Dorothy and seven years younger than her. His height and colouring fitted the family pattern. He made himself out to be the descendant of a famous man, which is what dispossessed children sometimes do. What an odd selection of men she, and sometimes Dorothy too, had over time and without their knowing, auditioned for the role of third child. Was this Welsh-French hybrid the one? "Taffy was a Welshman. Taffy was a thief." But what did Taffy want to steal?

And Jake was safe. The monster had not swallowed him. The jets had stopped and the water began slowly to drain away. There was no sign of the attendant. The warmed robe was lying on a chair a few feet from the bath. Kate put her arms on the sides of the tub and pushed to raise her body so that she could step out on to the floor and go to the massage room as she had been told to do. Her slippery skin slid around the slippery surface of the bath and her arms seemed to have no more strength than two pieces of string. Only one thing to do. She turned her body so that she could kneel up but the sides of this wet shell were too smooth and she slid back. She had no purchase. She tried to reach the towels on the floor but they were too far away. Come on, she said to herself. She thought of all those missed opportunities to go to the gym. She tried again but her arms were simply not strong enough to raise her hundred and forty-three pounds of solid weight.

Last resort. She called out, "Help!"

Vanna came in smiling. "How did you enjoy your thalassatherapy, Kate?"

"I can't get out," Kate said.

"Don't you worry."

She put her arms around Kate's upper body and heaved. But the slipperiness worked against her and at every slight gain, Kate slid further back.

Vanna called out, "Marie. We've got a heavy one here."

She sat on the edge of the bath and said, "You need to do weights."

Kate wished she had a weight in her hand to throw at this slim girl in her blue outfit. She felt helpless, captive, humiliated.

Marie came in, annoyed. "I'm in the middle of a massage," she said. But she laughed when she looked at Kate. "I guess we need grab bars for you old ones."

"Come on," Vanna said. "One two three, heave."

With their arms under her shoulders they pulled Kate up and finally she was able to step out of her slithery prison and onto a mat.

"There you are, sweetie. You just put on that robe and come to the aromatherapy room. Then you'll have the pedicure. You'll feel so good."

The two sylphs left.

"Sweetie" put the robe on and sat down. Whatever kind of delight might be waiting, Kate knew she couldn't face it. All the attendants were no doubt giggling, making remarks about a beached whale: an old woman with drooping boobs and fat thighs. But in the pocket of her robe was the key to freedom. She slipped out of the room, past the sauna and found the lockers. Not caring that she was still damp, she dressed quickly, picked up her purse and made for the exit. She was not fast enough.

"Hey," Vanna called. "Come here. You haven't..."

But Kate was on the street walking as quickly as she could. For all she knew, they had sprinters trained to bring down escapees and take them back for further torture. When she reached Better Beans, she asked for a pot of Earl Grey tea and sat down to get her breath. A failed sybarite, she wasn't made for luxury. It served her right for allowing herself to relax before Jake's feet were safely planted on Canadian soil again.

Delphine had slept in. Her mouth felt dry. This was why she didn't stay up late. Her life would soon fall into total disarray. Suppose she'd been due to make a presentation at the ministry. She got out of bed and went to the kitchen. The night before, she and Alec had opened a bottle of duty-free gin and talked as they drank. Alec, recovering from the shock of being pulled over by the airport security guards and searched, was still in bed. Delphine put on her robe and went to the kitchen. She made toast and coffee and then took a tray upstairs to Jake's room. Only once or twice when he was ill had she brought him meals in bed. She opened the dark blue drapes and let the sun in. There were clothes on the floor, sheets of music on the dresser and beside them a picture of Elvira as a little girl. Alec shook her head from side to side and opened her eyes. What kind of day was it? What time?

Alec sat up and there were traces of tears on her face. The airport security guard who had searched her had taunted her for being a coward; Canadians were afraid to go into Iraq. The body search was deliberate humiliation and there was no redress. Delphine had suggested lodging a complaint but Alec said that would only bring on more persecution.

Delphine put her arm around her friend and said, "You'll be okay, honey."

"Perhaps they treated me like that because they knew that I abandoned my most precious gift."

Delphine couldn't think of an answer, a reassuring answer. Finally she said, "You can't alter the years, can't wind time back. You just have to go on."

"My daughter won't talk to me."

"She liked your music."

"What the fuck does that mean?"

"It means, I think, that now she's seen you, she'll keep thinking about you. Put herself in your way again. It was a big step for her. And there's family."

"Family is like a great sucking cloud that sinks down over everything. People despair if they have a family and can't live up to its expectations. And people despair if they have no family. They look around for comfort. Things happen."

"She needs you."

"She has her father."

"And her stepmother?"

Alec picked up a piece of toast and nibbled around the edges.

"I'm going out to find real work."

"It's Saturday."

"I have to play tonight. You've been great, Delph. I shouldn't've moved in on you but I didn't know what else to do. I'm sorry about your job."

"I'm beginning to get more work. If I get the May-Star account, I'll be in clover.

"Move over. I'm in clover. Not catchy is it? If I try too hard, nothing happens. The really good ideas come when you're doing something else, thinking of something entirely different or up to your elbows in laundry. It's a question of how long you can afford to wait for the magic moment."

"How long have you got?"

"Till Tuesday."

"And it's insurance. Are your loved ones taken care of? That kind of thing."

"My loved ones are in clover when my life's over."

"Are you stuck on clover?"

"Their logo is a four-leaf."

"Then get right away from it. Think dark. Think post-mortem poverty."

"What a gruesome phrase."

The doorbell rang and Delphine knew at once that on the front step stood a soldier and a clergyman, both of them, heads down, here to tell her in practised unison that her son had been killed in the line of charity. They would hand her his belongings in a plastic bag and offer to send a counsellor to help with her grief. He wasn't a soldier so there would be no ceremonial return in a flag-covered coffin along the Highway of Heroes. She could pick his remains up at the airport. Tears came into her eyes. She walked slowly down the stairs and hardly had the strength to open the door.

And there before her was Jake himself. Perfectly whole. Sunburnt, smiling.

He kissed her and said, "I'm starving, Mom. What's for lunch? I'll just put my stuff in my room."

∽

Jake was home safe and sound. For the time being. Dorothy wanted to open a bottle of champagne and spray it all over Matt as she had seen racing car drivers and football players do when they won their contests. "He is home," she said. "He is whole. I'll have a party to celebrate."

But Matt, standing out on the street beside her, was staring at his work. He'd been depressed since the dinner and more so after the council's ruling that the house could now be demolished. "Waste of my talents," he said. "Like in the Bible, I've buried them."

"I think that referred to money, not to artistic gifts."

"All the same," Matt said. "All the same."

He'd used sexual imagery to illustrate the frenzied strivings of city men and women in their race to be first, to have the most money and the biggest office in the tallest building. "I'm calling it 'Before the Fall,'" he said.

"If you were to paint a few more walls around the city, you might do a guided tour."

He was about to call her stupid again. She could feel it and drew away from him. Then he put his arm around her. He looked like an old child and she wanted to stroke his hair.

"You have had a brilliant idea," he said. "And I want to make love to you."

"Ah," Dorothy said. She wanted to say, it's been a while, I'm not sure, I don't think so, I've forgotten how. But in a moment she remembered, and she wanted him, and her body wanted his. She turned to him and smiled. She did for a moment imagine being in bed with him, lying under the sheets naked, whispering Omar to him. But she said, "I'm going to the movies."

So, Omar, I went to Kate's and we watched you being old and dignified and eventually dying on the small screen. I liked that you were teaching the boy about the Koran. Kate hated it. She said it was a sentimental tear-jerker made to exploit the current situation. Perhaps she needs to go out more and try to meet men, men her own age, and have sex. There was no point in beating about the bush. Forming a relationship – what did that mean but meeting someone, talking for a little while and then getting into bed?

Dorothy hadn't expected Omar to turn up at her home. Unsent letters only go so far. But there he was, looking through the screen. For a moment she held an image of his face imprisoned behind wire. He smiled. She went towards the door. And opened it.

"Good evening," he said.

"Please come in."

"You invite strangers into your home?"

"We have a long relationship."

"Ah."

"Please sit down."

He was wearing a dark suit with a faint grey stripe, and a shirt open at the neck. His face was smooth.

"The picture on the wall?"

"You're an art inspector?"

"My name is Mahmoud Al-Haroun," he said. "I'm here about the funding for WorldAidNow&Tomorrow. My office is concerned."

"Why have you come to me?" Dorothy asked, accepting him for a non-Sharif.

"You made it your business to go to Ottawa."

"We wanted to do our bit. To raise money. Make people aware."

"Sometimes people become aware of more than is good for them."

"Before we go on with this," Dorothy said, "I'd like to see your credentials."

The man produced an Ontario driver's licence. It looked valid. The picture resembled him. He then showed her a business card bearing his name, an office address and, centred neatly in capitals, the grim words, SPECIAL SERVICES. There were places downtown where she could, if she wanted, get just such a card printed with her own name on it. It would only lack the government crest.

Dorothy said she would make coffee. He said that would be kind and followed her into the kitchen. She decided to attack before he did. "The amount that gets to that poor country is sixty per cent of the total raised. And when it gets there, another thirty per cent is lost in bribes, in theft. We wanted to know how to improve the situation."

On that April day it had seemed such a simple matter: There was a need. She and Elsie and Kate had made a plan. Through their efforts, children would have food and water. Schools would open. But now she imagined those dollars being taken away in sacks by men on horseback. Men reclining on fat cushions in their houses in Kabul were sitting on cash others had worked hard to harvest.

She said, "And what exactly are your special services? It sounds like one of those escort arrangements, and I have to tell you I'm too old for that kind of thing unless you're just suggesting we go to a concert or a play together."

"Don't come the stupid old lady with me, Mrs. Graham. You know very well what it means. And you also know that in these times anyone who crashes a party where important people are present and approaches a leading foreign figure is bound to come under suspicion."

"We only wanted to help. And it's easy to explain. The whole thing cost so much more than we thought and Kate handed over the cheque to Harvey Lent before the dinner. We wouldn't do that again. I mean we'd wait till we collected the money. We didn't think. Do you take milk?"

"No thank you."

The man sighed over his coffee cup. They sat and looked at each other. He bore no resemblance to Omar Sharif except for the colour of his skin and his eyes. On some days that might have been enough, but this man brought accusation with him and she feared where it might lead. She sank into the pit of despair: The three of them, three old women, had only caused trouble with their charitable effort. They could have done more by doing less.

"You're going off track again. Just why did you try to get so close to him, to the man you thought was Karzai?"

"It's such nice material. His gown. I wanted to touch it. I'm moving to a new place soon so I'm thinking about drapes."

"Mrs.Graham!"

"And maybe cushions to match."

The poor man lived in a totally serious and possibly dark world. She said as gently as she could, "You're wasting time here. You know very well that it was a momentary impulse. We had no designs on him or anyone else. Do you really have nothing better to do than bother me about this?"

"Lent didn't send you to Ottawa?" He looked about him as if she might have hidden the man in a closet.

"Harvey Lent is a difficult man trying to do a good job." Too late she realized she'd reversed the adjectives. It was happening more and more lately with numbers as well as words, and she knew that the less said to a man who was basically a spy the better, so she closed her lips.

"He hasn't been in his office this week."

She turned away.

"Look. You went to Ottawa. You saw the people at the top; you crashed the reception for the Mayor of Kandahar. My department also becomes involved when we sense opulence, overspending at home. People with tickets to exotic destinations."

"We don't..."

"Your friend, Dr. Charbonneau, has plans to go to the Far East."

"My cousin Kate is an armchair traveller. It's a hobby. And your card doesn't look authentic to me. Get out or I'll call a real policeman."

"And then there's the man who calls himself Pierre Jones."

Dorothy sighed. Her power to frighten had obviously waned with the years.

"He's my publisher," she said, enjoying the words. "I've written a book."

Did a flicker of new respect appear in the man's eyes? She wasn't sure. She wanted to ask him about Pierre but held back afraid of digging herself into a pit.

After the spy had gone, leaving behind a sense that all hers and her friends' communications had been read and even their unspoken words overheard and written down, Dorothy sat on the couch to think. Had their effort been simply a selfish desire to seem important? Had they gone blindly into a world of which they knew nothing? Had they forgotten that "Do unto others as you would have them do unto you," really means, "Do unto others as they would like to be done unto," and that older women should stick to bake sales, to door-to-door canvassing? The doorbell rang again. Had he come back to search her house for clues to a desperate other life?

But it was little Elvira standing there holding a package.

"Come in, dear. Come in. You've got over that frightful TV thing?"

"I'm talking to my friend again. She set me up, you know."

"It doesn't do to lose friends. Sit down. And to tell you the truth, I was feeling depressed. You might be able to help."

"This was outside, by the door."

An unidentified parcel. Had the three of them brought terrorism to the city? But there was no need to send for the bomb squad: It was clearly addressed to her and marked with Matt's own logo, a leaping hare. She set it aside. There was no telling what it might contain, and she wasn't about to open it in front of the child.

"How are you, Elvira?"

"Fine, thank you."

"Sit there. Look around. I'll be back in a minute. You like red wine?"

Elvira wasn't sure what she was supposed to look around at. She'd seen the room before several times. Nothing ever seemed to change. It was a fixed set. But, obediently, she glanced at the stack of books on the coffee table and at once saw what she was meant to discover: The mock-up of a title page attached to a handwritten preface. *That Said: Letters from Me by Dorothy Graham. Dear Reader, If I haven't written a letter to you personally, it is because you are not famous or infamous, not a celebrity, just someone like myself going about your life unnoticed and crawling along below the radar. The letters collected here have never been put into envelopes and mailed. They express thoughts directed at people I only know from a distance. I hope it will give you as much pleasure to read them as it has given me to write them.*

"Oh," Dorothy said, as if surprised. "My little book. It's

nothing. I hate that last sentence by the way. Pierre wanted it there as a polite gesture."

"It's impressive."

"If it sells a hundred copies, I'll be surprised. He's a desktop publisher, I gather, which means it costs practically nothing to produce. Only the cover and binding and so on. And I still have to write a couple more letters. I'm annoyed that he rejected my letter to the pope."

"You wrote to the pope?"

"I was only pointing out a few of the fallacies he imposes on his flock. He lives entirely among men and yet pronounces on same-sex relationships. As for abortion. Well, I'll get angry so I'll stop." *And another thing, Your Holiness, if you and a few others would stop saying that yours is the only god, the world might be a lot less bloody.*

"It's exciting to have a book you've written. And the dinner idea was great. Sorry I couldn't be there. Did it raise a lot of money?"

"It raised awareness."

"I came by here while you were in Ottawa and I met Matt Windridge. He was painting your house. I really like him."

"I'll tell him."

"I told him. He invited me to visit his cottage and said he'd give me art lessons if I wanted."

"I'd watch out if I were you, dear. Artists aren't like other people. They can be unreliable. But anyway. What I want to ask you. It's just a favour and you can say no. You see we've had a little problem with major fundraising. Trying to do things in large efforts. We're going back to small. I haven't discussed this with the other two yet but I'm sure they'll agree."

"You could arrange more dinners."

"To tell you the actual truth, dear, it cost us quite a bit. Who'd've thought goat could be so expensive? They look quite large but by the time you've cut off the legs and the head, there's not a lot left. And then the guests drank an awful lot of wine.

"The thing is that if every schoolchild in the city brought a quarter to school, it would add up to thousands of dollars. Now I can't spearhead this but you, as a teacher, you could start and publicize it. We could get Delphine to do an advertising campaign. Say the money's to help build a school in a village in the hills there."

"The principal doesn't like us asking the kids for money. Some will bring more and make the others feel bad. And some parents won't allow it."

"Tell your principal it's about education for the uneducated."

"I really came to ask if you'd come to the last-day-of-school party. The kids asked for you. Then you could talk to the principal yourself."

When Elvira had gone, Dorothy took the string from the package. String instead of tape. That was Matt. She took the brown paper apart, and there was a small print of a couple in bed. Not a young, lithe couple, but two people with veined legs and, in the woman's case, knotted finger joints. She stared at it. The colours were unnatural. Her body was bright pink. His was light blue. Their faces were turned towards the viewer. Both were smiling in a kind of demonic delight. She began to feel outraged. She truly wanted to feel outraged. She wanted to phone him or to drive straight to the cottage and throw a brick through his studio window, but outrage was slow to come.

She couldn't help herself. She started to laugh and the more she looked at the grotesque figures, the more she laughed. She laughed even though she knew it was a long overdue farewell gift and he was saying, It's over, baby.

She took her wine over to the desk and began to write:
Dear Unknown Artist,

I want you to know that I bear you no ill feelings. (Scarcely true but then what is?) You taught me a good deal about perspective and colour and how to look. Seeing is not only believing, though some would argue that it is. Seeing is also understanding, if you have eyes to see. If this is beginning to sound like the New Testament, bear with me.

You have felt for a long time that your art is unappreciated. You've been the Suffering Genius, unrecognized and with no descendants to reap the great sums your work will surely bring in after your death. Let me tell you something. Your work has gone unrecognized because it lacked the spark of humanity that is in every great work.

Now you are pleased to have walls to paint. Commissions. How are you going to discern between decoration and true art? Fact is, you can't. Not only that but the people who are giving you these sizable sums are going to want some say in what you do. They will burden you with those killers of the artistic endeavour: restrictions. No sex. No violence. Nothing controversial, please, Mr. U.A. You'll be fighting your way through a thicket of "taste."

But listen; it's okay. We had a few good little times. The picture you sent me is unkind but alas true, so maybe you have something after all. And I do wish you well.

Your unknown pupil

∽

Meeks and Co. were paying well for her work, but Kate had only gone through a third of the first manuscript. She worked hard because her goal was shimmering ahead of her. In the mornings, she awoke to the green of the Kuril Islands, to the blue Sea of Okhotsk and to the knowledge that the money she was earning would help her to underwrite the journey. In thought she transferred herself over the sea to Europe, thence to Moscow and beyond. She struck out a gerund and then the hundredth unnecessary adverb.

Jake looked up from his language textbook and said, "I've decided to go back there after the course. In the fall sometime."

Kate looked at him; he had taken on the features of his grandfather, the absconder, and since his return from Afghanistan he laughed less easily. The experience was there now, imprinted in his mind. She wished that a close-up of the world's suffering had been kept from him a little while longer.

"Would you like a cup of hot chocolate?"

"No thanks, Gran."

After the shock of finding his bed occupied had come the surprise that the interloper was Elvira's mother. Not that he minded, he'd made clear, but the room had been his space always. He'd assumed lifelong ownership. And he was upset.

"Coffee?"

"No thanks. I want to get back to the same village if I can. There's this problem with WANT's funding. There are other NGOs that do a lot of good. I'm thinking of going to the UN maybe and applying there. Or Gran, don't tell Mom but I'm thinking I could do more good if I joined the army."

"I think you should go back to university."

"I've seen truly desperate people. I've seen aid workers trying to hand out food and medicine but it's like pushing a stone uphill. You sort one place out and then a few guys with guns..."

Even grandsons couldn't be kept back from their desires, their vocations. Couldn't and shouldn't. She refrained from saying "a man's gotta do what a man's gotta do." But there crept into her mind a scene from *War and Peace*; Prince Andrei lying on a stretcher gravely wounded and Natasha...

She blocked out the image and said, "I wish you could find a safer place to work, dear." The sentence had slipped out instead of the praise and encouragement she had meant to offer him. "Would you like to come with me to the Kuril Islands?"

"Not this afternoon, Gran. I'm going to see Elvira. Aunt Dorothy says I should talk to her and persuade her to talk to her mother."

"Is that a good idea?"

"Somebody's gotta do it."

He kissed her and left. And left her thinking that if she hadn't given Pierre two thousand dollars towards the publication of Dorothy's book, she could set out on her trip sooner. Perhaps, since he had apparently found an investor, she could ask him for it back.

~

Dear Omar,

I am not calm at the moment. I'm sure you have some high-priced lawyer to give you advice when you're in trouble. Am I being selfish wanting to stick to my home? Graham and I bought it the year after we were married. My dad lent us a few thousand dollars. When Graham walked out– which you must have figured by now is a euphemism for killing himself, though why he had to take the typewriter with him as a weight I've never understood– he left quite a few debts behind. I didn't drive him to it though there were people who thought I had literally driven him to Niagara that night and shoved him into the river there above the Falls. How could I have persuaded him to hug the type-writer as he went over? So when I went to England to get hooked up with a bigamist (I don't suppose the word bigamy exists in your language), I rented the house out and

*kept on renting it for a couple of years till I could afford to
live here again.*

She sat back to examine her feelings. They appeared like
strands in her mind. Blue for a lingering sense of futility. Red
for anger. Orange for desire. Yellow for weariness. She fished
around for the shade of hope but nothing came forth. If she
could only follow the orange thread to Matt's cottage and
lie in bed beside him quietly, then content the colour of milk
might flow over the whole landscape and she would be fine,
and would drive back home singing songs of satisfaction. But
the red thread was dominant.

The dreaded letter from the council had arrived. There
was no more time. The crook Gervais and his partner
Robinson had won their case. It was no longer economically
sound for one person to occupy space that could be covered
in low-cost housing for the disadvantaged. A woman of her
sensitivity, a woman who had gone to Ottawa to make a
plea for the people of Afghanistan, must understand this.

Sneaky bastards. Playing every string on the violin. She
wanted to write back and tell the council that G and R devel-
opment had no thought of building low-cost housing. As
soon as they got the go-ahead, they would erect fancy condos
with hot tubs and Italian marble floors for the well-to-do.

It was a muddled, crazy world. She needed advice. To
give in or not to give in.

*So, the house, Omar. It's small, you might say shabby,
two storey, detached. Three bedrooms. The smallest one is
crammed with family history. Photos and letters and gifts
and things my dad and I brought to Canada with us. I could
begin to sort it out, or I could let the wreckers' ball shatter
the contents to smithereens along with the walls, pound it
all into the ground. Just as homes I see on the news every
night are being pounded into the ground. My home, really,
is of no significance. Except to me.*

She didn't erase the letter. She read it over and grimaced at the self-pitying tone of it. At least he'd never see it and she felt better for writing it. She was about to add some justifying lines when she saw that it was time to get ready for school.

There were four people standing outside her house staring at Matt's mural, talking to each other seriously as if they were in an art gallery. One of them was taking photographs. She ignored them and got into her car. She hoped the developers would be forced to incorporate the wall into their new, awful building.

The classroom was decorated with streamers in blue and red and green. The kids had learned how to fold and paste strips of paper around other strips. They looked at their work and pronounced it beautiful. No interior decorator could have been more satisfied. It was Ezra's fifth birthday, his turn to choose. He stood up and said, "I want the beetle story." Some of the other children groaned. They'd been together now for almost ten months and had learned how to express dissent. Ezra always wanted this particular tale. Perhaps he would grow up to be an entomologist.

Dorothy took the book down from its shelf and began to read: *Mrs. Beetle was having a bad day.* It was a simple story. While she read, her own life continued to occupy another part of her brain. *Mrs. Beetle's son Billy had fallen into the puddle again.* The children laughed. Dorothy considered the threat to her home and wanted to cry. Why had it taken her so long to take in the realization that her house was condemned and that she herself might not be around much longer? *His mother dried Billy's back and polished it and made it shine.* She was about to accompany him to school to speak to the boys who had been unkind to him. Like everyone, Mrs. B. possessed the power to do good or to do harm. It was a matter of choice. Every day for everyone it was a matter of choice.

She closed the book sharply. There was a cry from Ezra. "That's not the end." He was near to tears.

"I'm sorry," she said. "I'll go on."

Mrs. Beetle told the class that being kind was easy but when they come to knock down your home, you have no recourse but to stay there and let them knock you down with it, bulldoze you into the damn ground.

Elvira took the book from her gently and continued the story but the class had lost interest. They were looking out the window at the face of a man who was smiling and waving. Child-snatchers didn't make themselves so obvious. She shook her head at him. He grinned and signified that he would wait.

"Is he your boyfriend, Miss?"

"A kind of cousin," Elvira replied.

It was lovely outside in the sun. Dorothy walked over to a bench and sat down in the shade of a maple tree to watch the children drift away. After a while, Elvira and Jake came out of the school together; tomorrow's people, their lives stretching ahead of them like rainbow-coloured ribbons. Talking to each other, they glanced at her and waved. She waved back and went to her car. The vinyl seat was scorching hot. She lowered the window. It was time to get the air conditioning fixed. Through the rear-view mirror she could see the kids arguing. Elvira stamped her foot and turned away. Jake began to jog towards the road.

The girl stayed where she was and then, when the boy was several yards away, Dorothy heard her call out to him.

⁓

Elsie was still thinking over Kate's stupidity. What possessed her to give a cheque for the whole amount to Lent ahead of time? She berated herself for not keeping a closer eye on the other two. Why hadn't she paid attention to counting chickens, birds in the hand, and other useless phrases? Richard would have been appalled had she told him. Overconfidence. And then to ask for four thousand back! She should have left it as it was. But they had insisted on keeping the books straight, being honest.

Perhaps she should have asked Richard's advice all along. Money was something he knew. She considered him, their life, their shared moments, their divergent paths. If he had another woman, he was not seeing much of her unless she played golf.

The doorbell rang. She wasn't in a mood to be interrupted in her thoughts. There were avenues to go down with regard to her marriage and she needed to walk there alone. On the doorstep stood the French Welshman who'd ruined Isabel's trip to Paris by telling her that the author was not the saint she'd always believed him to be. Elsie wasn't about to let him in.

"Is your daughter here?" he asked.

Elsie felt herself grow taller. She looked down at him and said, "I have two daughters neither of whom is here. And I am about to go out. Perhaps you could call at some other time."

"It's about Dorothy's book," he said, smiling at her with a charm to which she was impervious.

"Another time," she replied.

She closed the door knowing that she had behaved badly but smiling anyway. The coffee in the carafe was three hours old but she poured a cup and sat back down at the table. One cookie wouldn't hurt. She could get on with her thinking. About Richard. About the possibility of ending the marriage now while she had the strength and while there was still the possibility of good times. In the near future they could be two deaf, toothless ancients sitting in rocking chairs side by side, hating each other while caregivers looked at them and said, "Married for eighty-three years. What a devoted couple. Sweet."

She heard the phone ring, but before she could get to it the ringing stopped.

A moment later, Richard came into the kitchen and sat down opposite her. He reached across the table and put his hand on top of hers and looked at her in a way that she would always remember. His eyes showed a mixture of love and concern. And even before he spoke, she felt afraid.

"There's been an accident," he said.

Chapter 8

Dear Omar,
Life is so strange. Blows come from where you least expect.
Perhaps wealth and a kind of detachment, your gambling
streak, have shielded you from such things. Though you
come from a country where oracles once spoke and gods
interfered, but that was long ago. Now we pretend not to
believe in any of that. But my great-nephew was struck
down yesterday. Does this prove that Toronto is more dan-
gerous than Kandahar?

All Jake had done was look back. And there were well-
documented cases in which that simple action had been
fatal. In English pantomimes the audience would yell "Look
behind you," to the hero. And the hero, usually played by a
woman with gorgeous long legs, would turn just in time to
ward off danger. But in this scene, when the hero turned
because a lovely young woman called his name, a blue car,
registration HJY 012, had struck him in the side and driven
away. Elvira had been alert enough in that awful moment
to note the number while a passerby called 911 on his cellphone. Dorothy had gathered the young woman up and
followed the shrieking ambulance to the hospital.

Kate was distraught. Delphine was out of her mind.
Dorothy knew that it would be up to her as usual to bring
calm to the situation. He will recover. He's young. It was
easy to tell his mother that. More practically, she would
line up a physiotherapist for when he came home. She
would make sure there was suitable food. She would do
these things quietly, without fuss and without telling any

of them that when Jake had lunch with her last week she had told him that he might help reconcile Elvira with her mother. Talk to her, she had said. Meet her. Take her out after school. Her interference was beginning to look like planned destruction.

You see, Omar, we all have our ways of dealing with this event. Kate will assist Delphine with the worrying and the weeping and wailing. I will be practical and fulfil the needs where I see them. Elsie will spend money and add a touch of luxury. All of us will encourage the boy to be well. And the boy will be well, she wrote. But she was afraid. Her hands were shaking and there was a chilly feeling around her heart.

She'd planned to set up her easel in the garden this week and paint a farewell view of the house from the back but had no energy for it. She'd taken photographs of Matt's mural on the front wall. In the middle of the scene, he'd added a *trompe l'oeil* window with the face of a bear looking out.

She picked up the magazines she'd bought for Jake. A copy of *People* for entertainment and a *Scientific American* for edification. Delphine said he was longing for kumquats. How could a person long for kumquats? When he was feeling better, she would press the boy for more details about the woman he'd met in a village outside Kandahar. He'd been very vague. She was, he said, "oldish, curious, tallish, travelling with another NGO." But he hadn't found out who she was or explained how his aunt's name had come into the conversation. It was, Dorothy decided, another self, the self that wished to be there having an adventure: A projection.

A hot, damp atmosphere that the newspaper meteorologist called 'realfeel' had hit too early in the summer. It was the kind of weather that made people glad they owned a cottage up north even though now streams of polluted air reached as far as Algonquin. She pulled the car over to the side of the road as a siren sounded and a long red van passed by with Hazardous Materials Unit printed on its side. *We are all hazardous and won't be forgiven.*

Elvira was sitting by Jake's hospital bed, holding his hand. Dorothy looked at their faces and pondered on the family line. They were unrelated but their four eyes looked at her with similar looks of unwelcome. Their mouths spoke insincere words of delight at her arrival. Jake was pale and Elvira was blushing.

"I'll just drop these off," Dorothy said.

"Stay, Aunt Dorothy," these twin-like people said in unison.

"I'm just leaving. I have a French class at five." The girl kissed Jake and went out giving a backward look at the patient.

"You got a private room," Dorothy said.

"Lucky, I guess."

Giving him Chance for a second name, and it might as well have been *jeopardy* or *hazard*, his mother had slapped a gauntlet in the face of fate. The boy was lying there with a broken leg and a wound on his face that would leave a scar. Some kind of luck! But she smiled and agreed with him. The room was small and white and a tall birch tree waved its leafy branches outside the window. The hushed sounds of the slow chaos of hospital life invaded from the corridor.

A huge arrangement of lilies and gypsophila and carnations stood on a table by the door.

"From the driver," Jake said. "He went to the police. It was my fault really. I walked into the road."

"But you're fine now, feeling better."

"They're only keeping me here because of a bit of infection. I'll be home on Friday."

"They have to be careful, dear."

"I liked being over there," he said. "I want to go back."

"I sometimes think," Dorothy said, and she had been thinking about it in the night, and for several nights, "that we clutter those places up too much. We go there because it makes us feel good. We want to help. Then we get kidnapped or damaged or killed. And it all adds up to very little."

"You think we should just send money?"

"I'm not sure, Jake."

"It's a hopeless picture, Aunt Dorothy. There are so many poor and starving people over there. And here fat people are eating three Big Macs a day, with fries and ice cream and pie."

"Because it's cheap, honey. By the way, who was the woman you met who knew me?"

He paused, remembering. "Oh yes. Odd thing, she looked a bit like you. I met her in the market and we got to talking. You tend to talk to anyone who's not – well, not them. A Canadian flag on her backpack. I must've mentioned you and Mom."

"What was she doing there?"

"Spying, as far as I could gather. She was a bit mysterious. We talked about Toronto. She grew up..." He tailed off.

Dorothy paid attention to his greenish skin, took hold of his hand. It was hot and there was a feverish look in his eyes. She pressed the bell by his bed.

"It's all very funny," he murmured.

The nurse came in and said, "Visiting hours were over ten minutes ago."

Dorothy stood at the door looking back at the boy. He was turning his head from side to side in a kind of pain. Finally he stayed still long enough for the nurse to poke the little spike of the thermometer into his ear.

Elvira was still in the lobby, talking to Pierre.

"Television," he was saying. "I saw you on TV. What you

said was quite true. I'm an orphan myself. My mother died when I was young."

"I'm sorry."

"I met your mother. In Paris. Worshipping at the shrine of a writer."

"That was my Aunt Isabel."

Dorothy recalled that the man from Special Services had mentioned Pierre's name. She decided to be distant.

"Hello, Dorothy. I was just telling Elvira that she has the same charming look as her aunt."

"She's on her way to her class," Dorothy said. "Are you visiting someone, Pierre?"

"I thought I might look in on the boy."

"Visiting hours are over."

"What are you planning to do for the summer?" the man asked, following them.

"I don't know now," the girl replied.

"Come along, Elvira," Dorothy said.

"I might need an assistant if this book takes off. Sometimes a simple manuscript can sell beyond anyone's wildest dreams. Do you have wild dreams?"

Elvira looked at him as if he were mad. Dorothy knew he had purposely put himself in the child's way. Perhaps he *was* mad.

"Nice to have met you," Elvira said.

He took hold of her elbow. She shook him off. The three of them went out to the parking lot. Dorothy watched Elvira walk to the subway station, then she turned to Pierre the publisher and asked, "How many copies are you printing?"

On Baldwin Street a few days later, Elvira saw Pierre again. She was annoyed that Dorothy had dragged her away from him as if she couldn't take care of herself or as if she could possibly be interested in a man old enough to be her grand-father. He was walking along the opposite sidewalk with his arm around her mother, around Alice, now called Alec. The woman who had told her on that awful day that she had to leave, had no choice, must go, no room in her life for her husband or her daughter; had not meant to tell her like that and would have taken her if she could; had meant to be out of the house by the time she came in; had left a long letter for her to read but she had come home early when she was supposed to have gone to Janie's house after school. *I am fifteen. You can explain.* But mother/Alice/Alec had left that afternoon. And Elvira had never opened the letter.

She tried to keep on walking, not noticing or looking, and bumped into the wall of the Chinese restaurant.

"Elvira!"

Another name called out. Another accident? Another chance of avoidance. She wanted to run away and continue to keep this person at bay. A door locked once should stay locked. They were crossing the road. They were in front of her, Pierre and her mother. Had he, this follower, known that on this morning, at this time, she would be walking here to buy salad and fruit?

There was a moment of standing silence and then Pierre took hold of her arm and said, "You're going to lunch," as if she had no choice when what she wanted to do was remain in her own place, keep to herself all the feelings she had nurtured and that provided her with a sad framework to her life. She found herself, however, moments later, sitting at a wooden table inside a small restaurant.

Elvira hadn't expected to laugh. Laughter had never once figured in the myriad imagined meetings. There had been tears, disdain, haughtiness, a cool approach, the hand held out, the slight kiss, dread and recrimination but no laughter.

It was the wry smile on her mother's face, the look of appeal, the shake of the head and the waiter asking if they wanted anything to drink and the weird pictures of what appeared to be animated vegetables on the walls, and the fact that the man Pierre had taken off as if by magic and the fact that she was there at all and that all she could say was, "I don't eat meat," as if they were the only words that could possibly be said in this situation, that made her put her head back and laugh.

"Neither do I," her mother said.

And the waiter, despising their ignorance, said, "This is a vegetarian restaurant."

Then they both laughed. They might laugh themselves to death in this place or she might get up and yell, *You left me when I needed you.*

"Anything to drink?" the waiter asked.

"Go away," Elvira told him.

"Water and a half litre of your house white, please," the woman opposite her ordered.

So they were to drink wine together. Elvira calmed down. This engineered meeting was in fact taking place; not a dream. The woman opposite reached her hand across the table. Elvira let it lie there. It was a used hand. A hand that played a musical instrument. The woman's face was smooth as if worry had passed her by, but there were lines around her mouth that might be sorrow, disappointment. She began to reach for the hand and then drew back, remembering what Jake had told her just before he walked away. You've got to be kidding, she had shouted at him. You're a liar. They are not sleeping together.

She looked at the woman across the table. Aunt Delphine's lover?

The waiter poured water and said, "I'll be back with your bread."

"Thank you," her mother said, still leaving her hand available to be touched or picked up or maybe bitten.

And how would she play her instrument then!

"How are you?"

What a weird, simple question! Elvira didn't have an answer. All the dammed up words she had silently shouted at this defector over time remained blocked. And then, without being able to stop herself, she began to cry and her first direct words to her mother were, "Jake's accident was your fault."

The waiter, the other customers, everybody in the world, turned to stare as she got up and ran out of the restaurant and her mother followed shouting, "No it fucking wasn't."

Elsie was sitting beside Richard opposite their new lawyer. William Howe, who had dealt with their affairs since they were married, was in a home, his mind now empty of all expertise and knowledge of torts and contracts. The young woman at the other side of the desk introduced herself as Marie Delfont and said she would be happy to take care of the will and any other business they might have.

It was hardly the time to mention divorce, and anyway Elsie hadn't made up her mind. Instinct told her that Richard didn't really have another woman. Golf and opera, those were his delights. She was into some fantasy world of late-in-life escape and told herself to move back into reality. Richard's behaviour since the accident had been kindly and good. He had talked about the shock to Elvira and had called her and told her to come around to see them and to bring her mother too.

Years ago, in his businesslike way, he had written down everything that had to be done with the will, all the provisions. Little was to be changed. A few small immediate bequests and then everything to his wife after the various charities and, on her death, a division of property between their daughters. The only new matter was a codicil leaving a sizable sum to the Canadian Opera Company.

"It's all quite straightforward," he said. And Elsie wondered what cruel impulse had made him tell Isabel that he would cut his daughters out. If Isabel had thought it through, she might have realized that Elsie was likely to outlive her father and then all could be changed in any case.

"Okay with you, sweetheart?"

She looked at him. It was a long time since he'd called her that. Tears came to her eyes. He was planning to move out before she had a chance to do so and this was a cover, a clever trick to lull her into a sense of security. The bastard. What low cunning! Leaving was in the air. Marie Delfont was making notes and, it seemed to Elsie, not paying a lot of attention to these two old people.

"And you had a question?" Richard said.

"A little legal problem with a charity," Elsie answered. And the woman looked up, interested. "But it's all sorted out now."

"I'll call you when it's ready to sign. These are very slight changes, Mr. Edwards. Sharon will see you out."

"What was all that about?" she asked in the elevator. "It's hardly any different."

"Everything must be in order," he replied, his voice barely a whisper. "Order, as I have come to see, is very, very important."

On the way home, he regained his voice and talked about yesterday's *Valkyrie* and tomorrow's *Siegfried*. To her surprise, Elsie had been entranced and at times thrilled by the singing, the music, the drama in the first two parts of *The Ring*. She had enjoyed milling around after the performance in the glorious new glass and wood building, seeing people she knew, listening to their comments. The clutter of bodies on the stage was distracting, Richard said, bad design, but he seemed to know that she would stay with him through to the last note.

~

Dorothy read the obituary notice again. It was one of those that described the man's journey from birth to university and through his long working life, two decades as CEO of Harvey and Burdett, his extensive charity work. Beloved by two wives and four children and many friends. *That means me.* Service on Wednesday. She could go and stand at the back. Others from work would expect to see her there. Her presence would not be an outrage unless – unless he had confessed all his infidelities to his widow. And she could wear her black coat with perhaps a scarlet scarf.

Without a hello or how are you, Delphine walked into the kitchen and said, "This infection is something he caught in Afghanistan."

Dorothy plugged the kettle in, took down the jar of green tea from the shelf, wiped two mugs dry and then said, "How is he today?"

Delphine spoke through tears, "He's very weak."

"What does the doctor say?"

"They're doing all they can."

"Then they are, my dear."

She knew it was too easy to sound reassuring. There was no way to divert Delphine from her grief. She had come to accuse but wouldn't bring herself to say the words. Dorothy could only reach for her hand across the kitchen table and see in her face the girl who had become pregnant too soon, the child who had loved dolls; Kate's girl. It was still a young, pleasing face but this dreadful worry had pencilled in a few more lines and her eyes were swollen.

"You're on your way back to the hospital?"

"Yes."

"He won't want to see you looking like this. Before you go, wash your face, put on a bit of lipstick, spray on some of my nice cologne."

"I don't wear lipstick. And the hospital doesn't like you to wear scents." Delphine smiled very slightly.

"People never used to be allergic to all this stuff," Dorothy said. "It's all in their heads. Have you eaten today?"

She gave Delphine a slice of coffee cake and watched her take a few bites of it. It wasn't the best of foods, but it contained sugar and therefore energy.

"He should have been working at a summer job," Delphine said. "And then going to university in September instead of ever going to that awful place. I'm not going to cry again. I can't. He'll be fine. Won't he?"

The question was a demand and Dorothy almost shouted, "Yes. He will."

Delphine's cellphone rang. She opened it and listened.

"They like my pandas," she said when she put the phone away. "I should be thrilled."

When Delphine had gone. Dorothy thought for a long time about the transitory nature of life and how blows came from where you least expect them and often to quite the wrong people. Leon Ericsson had gone now to his last reward, whatever the hell that meant. Jake was struck down by a foreign virus. Yet Gervais and Robinson and their like were never run down by their own heavy machinery or struck on the head by wrecking balls.

I'm having violent thoughts. Is this the worst of my nature coming out in my last years when I should, I believe, make my way towards the exit being pleasant and loving towards all humankind? Or is it a remnant of that belligerence we

*acquired growing up during a war when killing the enemy
was a heroic deed? Like you, Dr. Zhivago, finding your way
in a country divided when murder for survival was normal.
How do we ever erase the blood from our minds? Maybe we
can't. For I have to say that the image of Gervais the crook
flattened like a cartoon cat gives me pleasure.*

Kate walked up the stairs into a pathetic scene. Jake was
lying in bed, his face to the wall. Delphine, looking tragic,
was holding his hand. It lay on her palm like a leaf. Kate set
down her burden, startling them both. He'd been at home
for a week. His mother seemed to have lost several kilos of
weight. Kate wanted to feed her cake and ice cream and
cheese. But she knew her daughter and in a week or two she
would get back on her life's track.

"I'll get coffee," Delphine said.

The patient turned to see why his hand had been so
abruptly dropped.

"How are you today?" Kate asked.

"A bit better. Would you read to me, Gran? There's a
Koran in the top drawer."

She found the book and began to read from the beginning.

"It's terrible," he said.

"I'll read something else."

"There. The people. The way they live."

Part of his trouble was the darkness of a world he'd seen
at first-hand. He wasn't as ill as he seemed, the doctor said.
There was no need for him to stay in bed. He had to be careful, that was all. But the thought of putting on clothes and
moving around seemed to exhaust him. He had no desire.
He wanted nothing.

She couldn't bring herself to hate Elvira for causing the
accident, or Dorothy for suggesting he go to that wild
country. He'd only been there for a few weeks and yet he

seemed to have a yearning for the place: a place she could only think of as a desert full of murderous men who used dead goats as footballs. Only the nastier stories out of *Arabian Nights* seemed to fit the country. Rich embroidered gowns and silk pointed slippers, magic carpets of exotic design were unreal and had no place there. Jake had gone into danger and might be there now if common sense hadn't intervened. Chance by name and chance by nature. Perhaps her grandson's life was going to be a series of random events. But then whose wasn't?

In the first bad days after the accident, Elvira had come to the hospital in a desperate state, dissolved into guilt, and Kate had been unable then to offer either forgiveness or comfort. But the girl did seem to cheer him up, and she was pretty and smart. As long as Jake didn't fall into the trap of loving her because she had almost got him killed, all would be well.

Kate put the Koran down and took a book from the box she'd brought with her, a copy of *Oryx and Crake*, and began to read from it. After several paragraphs, Jake opened his eyes and said, "That isn't the Koran."

Kate said, "I have some others you might like." She began to unpack the books.

"Don't put those on my legs, Gran."

She looked at him, his young pale face, his sad eyes.

"My mom says Dorothy is an interfering busybody."

"Dorothy read somewhere that knowing the reason for things would lead to happiness. So she tries to find things out any way she can. Besides, we've all come to an age where we wonder whether our lives have made a difference. She wanted to help."

"A lot of people prefer to keep below the radar."

They were silent for a moment. The fan in the corner shifted the air around to make a breeze.

"How are you, Gran? You look great."

"I'm working again. There's nothing like feeling useful."

"That's what I thought I was going to do – be useful."

"You have all your life to be useful. And you have to take time for enjoyment."

"I could take a year off and travel. You know, have time to look around and think. You told me I should do that right after high school."

"Your mother will think I'm an interfering old woman too."

"I think she sees you as the least dangerous of the three."

"Possibly a mistake."

He was looking at her with the late Judge's enquiring stare.

"Tell me something, Gran. Did Aunt D. really cause Graham J.'s death?"

"Ah." The boy had perked up a little. He was interested in gossip, a familiar tonic. Why was that secret still a secret? Sometimes a story is withheld because of timing and the circumstances surrounding it, and then as years go by it remains locked away and gathers more importance than it deserves. "Well," she began, "Dorothy blamed me for part of it."

"I've always imagined the three of you putting his feet in cement and throwing him over the Falls in the dead of night."

"It wasn't quite like that. He suffered from depression and took Valium. Sexually, apparently, he lacked. And besides, I'd just given him my thoughts on his manuscript and he took them too literally. I'd given praise where it was due but said it needed work. I talked about D.H. Lawrence and I think that was about the worst writer I could have mentioned given his state of mind. And then Dorothy..."

"Coffee's here," Delphine said as she came in with three mugs on a tray.

"I'd like a cookie, Mom," Jake said in a spoilt-patient voice.

Delphine left the room and Kate said quickly, "Dorothy made a remark about D.H. knowing a good deal about sex. You have to understand that GJG was a man ready to jump. Despair can be fatal. Always remember that words too can be a deadly weapon." She regretted saying that immediately. It was one of life's untidy lessons that Jake had learned already.

Delphine returned and told them about the new contract with her old company. They needed her and were happy for her to work at home. When she left to go back to her office, Kate said, "Get up, Jake. We're going to the art gallery."

"Why?"

"You need to look at things that are beyond your understanding."

Chapter 9

THE CORTEGE MOVED ALONG Dundas unremarked by pedes-
trians. There was no military band. No groups of apparently
grieving politicians or heads of state stood by. No boots
were hanging backwards in the stirrups of a riderless horse.
There was only a hearse containing the coffin followed by
three black cars driving slowly towards the cemetery.
Looking out of the dim car window, Dorothy saw two elderly men take off their hats in an old-fashioned gesture of
respect and stand at attention as the cars passed. Veterans
perhaps, their own time not far off, thinking that a nod
towards this corpse would ease their own way from this
world to the next.

There had been a well-written notice in the paper but no
one would build a monument to the man or write books
about his influence on industry or on history. He had been
a successful businessman who'd steered carefully between
the rocks of sleaze and corruption.

Elsie and Elvira and Alec with Mike and Isabel were in
the car directly behind the hearse. Isabel had returned from
her trip to give her mother support and love. Hopefully love.
They were a strange family. Semi-detached might be the
word. Dorothy leaned her head back, almost asleep till Kate
tapped her hand and whispered, "Do you think this will
take long?"

"Do you have another engagement!"

"Not exactly."

Delphine told them to be quiet as if they were still in the
funeral home listening to the service. Friends had spoken

words of praise for a man who had mostly deserved them. The gist of it was that what he'd done, he had done well. His charitable efforts had almost matched his capacity to give. He would be much missed by the opera community. One of his golfing buddies had joked about his handicap and then, becoming serious, had said, "He played an honest game."

"I'm surprised he didn't opt to be cremated."

"Not everyone fancies being fried at the end of life."

"He was an efficient, tidy man."

"And five years too old to be the third child."

"What third child?" Delphine asked.

"Just a game we used to play."

Your funeral, Omar, will be a grand affair. You can look forward to that. There'll be long obituaries and your old movies, good and bad, will be shown night after night on TV. Old women who remember you will sigh for their young days when their own lovers seemed romantic too. The man who gives you a room in his posh hotel might be glad you are no longer occupying the space and that he'll be able to rent it out at last. He could of course make it into a shrine and charge pilgrims so much a time to view your bed and perhaps even lie on it for a brief spell, lusting in their hearts.

She'd gone to Leon's memorial service and others from the office had noticed her and smiled the subdued grimace that was right on such occasions. Melissa had come up to her as they were leaving the church and asked how she was enjoying her retirement. Proud of herself, she'd only replied that it was good to have time for one's friends and that she enjoyed using the lovely china and she hoped all was well at work. Then she was introduced to Mrs. Ericsson, a young woman of perhaps thirty, draped in black, holding a handkerchief to her eyes. Melissa murmured, "Deathbed wedding." in her ear. Dorothy had shaken the widow's hand and murmured, "I was a very intimate friend."

My funeral on the other hand, Omar, will be scarcely noticed. My only true friends are Kate and Elsie. Their children are fond of me. And Matt. I shouldn't forget him. Perhaps Pierre. I have other friends with a small f. People I know and talk to from time to time. But they move away or die and it's hard to keep up with them. The obituary might say, She made an effort. She tried. That will be the extent of it. I think what I'd like them to say is, She had a capacity for admiration.

Delphine offered her a mint and she wondered if her breath was sour.

What a waste of real estate, the cemetery! All the stone slabs among trees taking up good property. Did people really need to come and leave flowers on the graves of their dead loved ones? What gods were they trying to appease? Why not build houses here on this great swath of land instead of trying to knock down her little home? But the suggestion would bring cries of sacrilege. *We are still a primitive people, Omar. We like to keep an eye on our dead.*

"And the dead do not care," she said to Kate.

"The living do," Kate replied. "That's what it's all about."

They stood around as Richard in his mahogany box was lowered unevenly into the ground. The clergymen said ritual words. Elsie stood erect, stoic, very smart in her black tailored suit and low-brimmed hat. Alec and Delphine stood together. Elvira's father, Doug, and her stepmother, Janine, were a little apart. Mike held Isabel's arm as if he feared she might jump into the grave. Kate and Dorothy positioned themselves behind Elsie like the bridesmaids they'd been forty-five years ago. They were dressed differently now and not laughing. Elsie bent down to pick up a handful of earth and her hat fell forward over her face. For a moment she teetered on the edge of the awful hole. Alec pulled her back and scattered soil onto the coffin on her mother's behalf.

Richard had decreed that the mourners were not to have a party or to feel obliged to "come back to the house." Delphine had nonetheless arranged to have cocktail food and wine at her place. Elsie was not to be allowed to go straight home and mourn alone.

It was an awkward gathering. Doug kept on looking at Alec. Mike had gone out to the front step to answer a call on his cellphone and Isabel followed him. Janine, long-necked, intelligent, contained, stood by the window staring out. Elvira had retreated to the kitchen. Jake was pouring wine and passing plates. Delphine wasn't a caterer. She had made an effort but the cubes of cheese surrounded by melon balls were damp and hard-edged. Little quiches bought from the supermarket had been left in the oven too long. On any other day, Elsie would have looked askance at the paper napkins, the unpolished forks and the odd assortment of glasses but now she was thanking Delphine in a desperate way as if she'd provided a royal feast.

Three elderly men, Richard's business associates, were standing together talking softly, reminiscing about their years of wheeling and dealing. Dorothy pictured them in their twenties before their arteries and minds had begun to harden. She was surprised that not one of them appeared to be accompanied by a partner. Had their devotion to work, to money, to getting on, rendered them unlovable?

Elsie said, "His sister will be here tomorrow. We'll read the will then. They were in California. She tried to get here by this morning but there was a delay. She knew he wasn't well. We all knew he wasn't well, but we didn't expect him to die, did we? Did any of you think he was going to die?"

Kate took Elsie's hand and led her to the sofa. Then there were tears. The smart jacket was soon crumpled and dotted with bits of Kleenex. Her hat was awry. Alec sat beside her mother in silent solidarity, not touching, not touched.

Dorothy looked out at the garden. The grass was green again and the maple was beginning to shed its leaves. She went to talk to Doug and Janine.

"You've moved to a new house, I gather?"

"A condo, in fact," Janine said. "He wanted us to prepare for our old age."

"You agreed it would be a good idea," her loved one replied.

"He was going to sulk if I didn't agree."

"You're still working at Creeds, Janine?"

"I'm not anywhere near retirement age."

"I just thought you might have moved on. You know. Luxury clothing in these times…"

"What's she saying, Doug? What are you trying to say?"

She had raised her voice and the others looked around.

Dorothy moved away from the woman's defensiveness. She wasn't sure why she'd said that just now. But Janine was irritating. There was a barbed unpleasantness about her, an odour of disappointment. When she married him, Doug had likely promised her that, along with his own devotion and a certain amount of sex, she would acquire, in Elvira, a loving daughter. Janine was one of that sad tribe: a disappointed second wife. Dorothy vowed to be nicer to her at their next encounter.

She heard Jake say to his mother, "I'm a bit tired. I'll lie down for a while if that's okay."

Was the boy relapsing into invalidism? It was over three months since the accident. She watched him climb the stairs slowly and then, thinking himself unobserved, run up the last few steps. Elvira in black top and short skirt was lingering by the food. She picked up a couple of sandwiches and followed Jake. Dorothy watched her go. What was that about? Simply care for the young man she had caused to run out into the road? She looked at the food on the table and decided that when she got home she would make something comforting to eat like scrambled eggs. Meanwhile, she went into Delphine's office to have a moment on her own. There were pictures tacked to the walls, exotic animals and cartoonlike people. It wasn't the right place to spend a moment contemplating the death of a man she had known for nearly five decades. She didn't mean to read the card that was lying open on the desk but her eyes couldn't avoid it. She took in the information: Jake had been right.

Richard's colleagues, men she'd met occasionally at Elsie's charity events in times past, were still standing apart. She went over to make them feel welcome and said, in case they'd forgotten, "I'm Dorothy Graham, Elsie's friend."

"Dorothy! You went to Ottawa and tried to beat up some poor Afghan official."

"We thought he was Hamid Karzai."

"And you took Elsie with you," the tallest one said. "I'm Ed Hauser by the way. Ken Marchant and Gordon Brice."

"Yes. We've met."

"So," Hauser said, "what were you doing there anyway?"

"We really wanted to go to Afghanistan. To find out what happens on the ground."

"But you," he stopped himself from saying, probably, *two elderly women, what earthly use could you be?* "Richard used to talk about you, the three witches. Just joking, you understand. He reckoned you were the bad influence."

"Perhaps I was. Perhaps I am," Dorothy answered. "I hope so."

"This is a sad day," Marchant said. "Richard was..."

There was a sudden dying "Ooooh" from above. Was Richard's soul now released and flying off to heaven? A chill settled over the room. Delphine, not believing in ghosts, ran up the stairs. Kate set off to follow her and then saw her daughter returning quickly, red-faced.

"Elvira hurt herself," she said. "That's all."

"Funerals are dangerous things," Hauser said.

"...a good man," Marchant continued.

"Fine man," his friend echoed. "Yes."

"Did you order bagpipes?" Elsie called out to Delphine. "I don't want bagpipes. Why have you done this? There was no need. He didn't deserve this. He hated that sound. For the last ten years, I didn't love him as I should but he never knew. And besides..."

"Mother!" Alec shouted.

"Hello."

They all turned to look at the man who was standing in the doorway, a tall man with fair hair, wearing a kilt of red and blue and green tartan. "I'm looking for Jake," he said.

Driving home, Dorothy found herself talking aloud to Omar. "Death is exhausting, old friend. A man I've known for over forty years no longer exists. He's taken memories with him and part of us too. He has opened the door to the end of our lives. It's Thanksgiving but not for us. No one is in the mood for turkey."

As she pulled up to the house, she saw someone standing on the doorstep and watched him as he moved around to look in the kitchen window. A spy from Gervais and Co. She got out of the car and shouted, "Hey, you!"

He turned and walked towards her. It was too much. Another face she'd loved in its prime had been rapidly computer-aged like Sharif's at the Royal York. The eyes were young but the skin and hair were those of an elderly man.

"Good evening, Dorothy," the mouth below the grey moustache said.

"You'd better come in," she replied.

Having lunch with Alfred Sparrow at Queen's Quay the following Wednesday was a voyage of discovery, a circumnavigation of the man he'd become. For one thing he was a good deal larger. He'd had to give up beer, but wine was good for him, he said. He was lonely. He'd held on to one chairmanship to give point to his life. He had one child, a daughter, married and living now in Yellowknife. It gave him another reason to come to Canada besides seeking her out. He couldn't believe she was still in the same house. He'd called the number in the phone book and recognized her voice on the machine.

They talked like strangers for a time and in the silences watched the ferry going across to the Island. Sailors in the marina were preparing their yachts for hibernation. Alfred told her his favourite writer was a British fantasist called Terry Pratchett. That was his favourite *living* writer. Of dead ones, he said, there was no one to beat Winston Churchill. Dorothy had expected better, but when he asked her to go with him to the opening at the AGO, she said yes.

A week later, they were standing side by side looking at Monet's garden. He sighed with sensual pleasure and said, "I'd like to go to France again. I've always wanted to go to Giverny. Will you come with me, Dorothy?"

He liked Toronto, he said as they moved towards the *Water Lilies*. His tour business had expanded and he'd finally sold it. He was going to travel while he could still get around. He'd wanted to get in touch with her, but since she'd never answered his letters he figured she must hate him.

"You were so different. You were like a dangerous kind of animal to me. Another species. And the woman who thought she was my wife – we were too young and it turned out we weren't really married at all, but there was a baby. I wrote to tell you. I wish it had been different. I'm sorry."

"You don't have to explain. We're both old and a bit past it."

"But not past love, Dorothy. Not past love."

Oh dear, Omar. Is this a trap? I've been out with Alfred twice now and I like him. One old lover dead and a husband popping up out of nowhere. It can hardly be called rebound. My last leap into bed with Leon happened twenty years ago, and my moments with Matt were more desperation than affection. But in a curious way, death refreshes our emotions, makes them new again. No use expecting advice from you. I can hear you saying, 'Life is short as has been demonstrated to you twice lately. Go for it, Dorothy.' What I should be going for, my dear, is the laundry. I let things slide and then remember I haven't changed the bed for two weeks and the towels are limp. When I'm in the new place, I'll have to take my dirty things down to the basement in the elevator and be aggravated when all the machines are already full and I don't have the right change. Back to the old days at university.

Alfred had, between telling her about himself, listened intently as she described her return home, her quick marriage to the Russian, her life at work. As they'd finished the last of the wine, they'd smiled at each other across the table. When he reached for her hand, her hand, of its own accord, had moved to meet his. She saw again the young driver describing an invisible countryside as rain splashed onto the windows of the bus.

She looked at her watch. She'd promised to drive Kate to the optometrist to have her eyes checked and was going to be late. So much for daydreaming! She picked up the newspaper to read while she waited and ran out of the house, realising as she did so that at least she could still run.

∼

Alistair had been staying with them for two weeks and Delphine didn't like to ask when he was leaving. In the evenings, he went out with Elvira and Jake and they often returned after midnight. She waited up for them and worried whenever Jake's skin took on a feverish look.

Alec had moved into a motel and Delphine, against all her maternal instincts, wanted Alec back. These hungry young people could lead their lives elsewhere. Instead of sharing the house with a lover, she had become a den mother to three twenty-something-year-olds who weren't behaving very well.

She brought up a picture on her screen of a row of animated babushka dolls, talking as they climbed back in order of size into the largest one. She was proud of the image. If they liked it, RussiaToursInc would pay very well. Getting the dialogue right was paramount.

Just then she heard the stairs creak, soft footsteps, loud voices. Alistair and Jake were in the kitchen getting breakfast. But it wasn't a Scottish accent she could hear.

"I'm not sure," Jake was saying.

"You're supposed to say, I love you too," Elvira replied.

"I'm only thinking it might be a time before I can go back to work."

"I earn twenty-six thousand dollars a year."

"And we could play house?"

Delphine got up and went to the doorway. Jake was thin and he was pale. She looked at his unshaven cheek. The prognosis was good and in a month or two he would be quite himself again, the doctor said. But there was something missing and she thought it was the desire for happiness. The will for happiness. That obscure drive that kept the knight going on through the impassable thorns and gave hope to the maiden waiting day after day alone in her tower: The impulse that drove people to renovate their basements and decorate their nurseries and plant their gardens.

"I think sometimes it would be better to be brought up in a place like Groman Towers. Then everywhere you lived after that would be an improvement. Unless you ended up on the street," he said.

Jake would work. He would look out for the good of the world. But was that enough for a life, a satisfied life?

"I love you," Elvira repeated, as if by repeating it she could elicit a better response.

Would he, though, ever want to go dancing? Would he ever, this new serious Jake, frivolously take a day off work in January and drive down to the Falls to see them in their winter glory?

"Would you like some coffee, Mom?" he said, seeing her there.

"I'd better get dressed," Elvira said and went back upstairs.

"Please," Delphine said. She hadn't seen her son entirely naked for many years and was sad that his ribs showed through his skin. Elvira had a lovely young body, not attacked by gravity. She was moved by their youth, surprised by their boldness. "Be careful," she said. "Don't catch cold." But it wasn't what she meant.

"I can take care of myself," he replied. Anything else he might have said was drowned out by the coffee grinder.

Alistair came into the kitchen fully dressed carrying a pile of clothes.

"I'm off to New York tomorrow," he said. "It's been

great staying here. I didn't mean to stay so long. I really only came to ask..."

Delphine was glad that he stopped there. The young man recognized Jake's frailty and had not tried to persuade him to go back to Afghanistan. Elvira came downstairs wearing a ragged denim skirt and a shirt that barely covered her breasts. She gave Alistair a hug and said, "I might see you there. You could show me the city, Ali. I've got to go now. Bye, Aunt Delph."

"If I could do my laundry," the Scot said.

Chapter 10

Dear Omar,
Few things in life turn out the way you expect. I can't even
remember when I last wrote. My memory is slipping and
things are happening quickly, almost too quickly for me to
keep up. Accidents, funerals, weddings. And now I really
have to move. Money talks more loudly than it has any right
to do and the crook Gervais is going to knock down my
house, my shell. I'm planning anyway to rent a cheap place
so I can travel a little and hand out a few nice gifts, one to
Elvira who is about to make a terrible mistake.

Until the child had some kind of epiphany or another
shock, she might go on making mistakes. Dorothy simply
hoped that she'd be happy until the inevitable day when she
discovered that life is not, in either the best or the worst of
times, a fairy tale. She had survived the Wicked Stepmother
chapter of her story and taken a seven-league step into the
forest of Romance.

Meanwhile, a group of artists was lobbying to preserve
Matt's mural on the wall of her house by taking it down
brick by brick and moving it to a site as yet undecided.
Either way, her home was to be dismantled. She walked
about touching the shelves, the ornaments, looking out at
the day. It was a yellowish October morning; a slight breeze
was swirling leaves around. A higher window, a narrower
view, were to be hers for the rest of her life. She'd looked
down this cul-de-sac with its broken line of maples for forty-
five years. Some of the trees had died. Long ago there'd been
street parties, fireworks displays, people who watched out

for their neighbours. That population had left. Transients came and went now because the houses, destined for destruction, were not worth buying. She could hear the wreckers taking down the house to the left. The one on the right was already gone.

Kate was walking up the path, coming to help her pack her ornaments as she had promised. *I'll help with your precious things.* How precious were these damn things now that Gervais had won and the house was no longer her home? Dorothy picked up a plate from the counter and threw it against the wall.

"Come in. Come in," she yelled to Kate as she hurled a saucer. "We're going to have some fun. I never liked this china."

"It could go to the thrift shop," Kate cried. "Someone would be glad of it." But she couldn't help, just for the joy of it, throwing a cup at the wall and watching it fall in pieces to the floor. And then a saucer, and a plate.

As she threw another plate at the wall, Dorothy shouted, "One for the crook Gervais."

Kate called out, "Robert Charbonneau. This is for you."

"That was my retirement gift," Dorothy said ten minutes later when were no more whole pieces left of the set. She was looking at the cupboard beside the sink.

"No!" Kate said. "You need something to eat from."

"Move," Dorothy shouted. She heaved at the sides of the cupboard and, as two shelves came forward, ran to one side. They fell down with a great crash of pottery and glass, scattering pieces all over the counter and the floor.

"You could've killed us!"

"I don't see, "Dorothy said, as she moved shards around with her feet like a kid walking through fallen leaves, "why the wreckers should have all the fun."

∽

From: Xkate@redwood.ca
To: Elsed@global.com
We must keep an eye on Dorothy. I think the move is driving her crazy. Do you think I should stay with her for a few days?

Kate felt sorry as soon as she'd pressed send. After all, she'd joined in the party and revelled in it. She and Dorothy had drunk juice from the carton and laughed as they shovelled the debris into a garbage can. *Destruction is good for you.* New slogan for self-help books. Rip. Tear. Throw. Shriek. Dorothy's whole house would soon be rubble; she was entitled to a few acts of random violence.

Random violence. The words sank into Kate's mind. Objects thrown. Without reason. There it was. The answer. She hit herself on the head with both hands. Eureka! The poltergeist, the 'noisy and mischievous spirit,' living in the apartment was herself. She had not physically thrown the Mickey Mouse clock and the pictures around, but the energy that had built up inside her fuelled by her own anger and frustration had caused the things to move. And this afternoon, as she had helped Dorothy hurl china at the wall, she had exorcised the imp and at the same time forgiven Robert. She felt, in fact, sorry for him and yet glad that he had left. She had a life now and could afford to be generous. Carrying a return ticket, she would go and see him through the operation and a few days convalescence. Her two friends might cry out in dismay, but she would tell them she was off to visit Brian and Megan and their kids for two weeks. *I am their grandmother too.*

As for Dorothy, she'd rejected Elsie's offer of space in her home, as Elsie had known and probably hoped she would.

But the words were kind and Dorothy needed all the kindness she could get at the moment. The apartment she'd chosen was not at all the best value for her money. It was as if she wanted to be a martyr and say, this is what I've come to. Small and dark, it was part of a large house but at least it was in a safe area and there were trees on the property. Maybe she didn't expect to be there for very long. Dorothy kept some things to herself, as they all did.

To forestall the email message, Kate keyed in the number of Elsie's land line.

∿

Elsie heard the phone ring and sat up sharply forgetting where she was. She banged her head and lay down again. Whoever it was could wait. She was on the floor looking at the pipe under the sink. She had never quite understood the way water and garbage could flow as they did up and down that u-shape. And now the garburator, unhappy at being fed a goat dinner for six, had disgorged the lot and somehow broken down. Its vomit was all over the cupboard covering detergent, soap, Pledge and bottles at the back that had been there for years.

She howled. She was a widow now and surely deserved better treatment than this, at least for a few more months. That very morning, she'd made up her mind that trying to provide dinners at home was foolish. Instead she would simply go about giving talks on the need for help, for money, for time. It was what she was good at. And she knew better, she really had known better, than to put all that meat into the maws of the machine, but it had been a gesture. *Farewell, goat.* Last week, she'd made another gesture when she'd bagged all Richard's clothes, even the odd things she'd found at the back of his closet, and left them outside for Big

Brothers and Sisters to collect. *Goodbye, Richard.*

It was time now to say, *Hello Elsie*, if only she could stand up. She had to roll over onto her side and then get to her knees, grab the edge of the counter and raise her body upright. Simple if her joints would co-operate. She decided to stay where she was a moment longer. The floor was a good place to think. Before this eruption, she'd been in the process of making a list: Things that mattered and things that didn't. Health, she supposed, should come first. Taking care of Richard's investments so that she could pass the money on to the girls was high up there. If she cut back on charity projects, she could spend more time on the family and her two old friends. But right now, she had to rise. *Make an effort, girl. Why don't you go to the gym? Because I don't like looking at all those elderly men and women puffing and panting, knowing they will die soon anyway.*

She rolled onto her left side and knelt and cried out in pain. How long before that damn knee needed to be replaced? And how high on the list was that? She slowly hauled herself to her feet and went to take stock of herself in the hall mirror. Her hair was awry and her eyes appeared to be madly crossed. She was the madwoman of Shallott. No, that was a lady. The madwoman was from elsewhere. *I am Elsie of Elsewhere.* Time to calm down, have a good wash and then call a plumber.

A foolish rush to fill her time, to be busy, had led to this mess. From now on, she resolved, I will be unavailable on certain days. Wednesday and Thursday perhaps. I will take time out for reflection. I will make Alice come out to lunch with me and I will buy her something suitable to wear at the wedding.

The doorbell rang. She wished, she hoped, it would be her Alice: The beautiful child who had been distant and was now nearby. She thought of Richard. Was he perhaps a homosexual? That would account for...

"Mother! Are you in there?"

She opened the door to her other daughter.

"Come in, Isabel. I just have to wash my hands."

When Elsie returned to the living room, Isabel was turning the pages of the wedding issue of *Gourmet* magazine.

"See this cake, Mom?"

The cake was three tiers high, the list of ingredients was long and the preparation time was given as an optimistic three hours.

"I could do it in an afternoon. Elvira's friend Jen has offered to ice it."

"It will turn out lopsided."

"What's that smell? What are you making for dinner?"

Elsie considered the second question. She thought about it for a long moment. It was a question that presupposed her devotion and her willingness to cook for her middle-aged child and her partner. She felt a flicker of resentment that could easily be fanned into a flame.

"Mom?"

"I have to call the plumber. There's a bit of a mess in the kitchen under the sink. You'll find paper towels in the cleaning cupboard. Just go mop it up a bit."

Moments later she heard Isabel cry out, "What have you done!"

Elsie poured two glasses of non-alcoholic wine and told Isabel to forget it for now.

"It won't clear itself up, Mother."

"Ignore it. I'll call MaryMaid." She fended off Isabel's look that read, how can you expect someone else to do that? and asked her about the prize.

"I couldn't believe it. My idea was really, really far out. But apparently the big donor wants it this way. Homelike, unthreatening. The waits might still be long but the atmosphere will be pleasant. And I get to go to Vancouver again."

"Here's to an enlightened billionaire. And here's to you. Congratulations, dear."

"Thanks. Mom?"

Ah here it came. There was enough in the tone of that one syllable to build a suite in the retirement home, clear out and sell the house she'd lived in for thirty years, settle for a narrowing down, a limitation, walls closing around her, getting tighter and tighter. She was indignant. It was far too soon.

"No," she said. "I am not ready."

"I want to talk to you about the wedding."

"Well, it's too sudden. The child is out of her mind but I'm her grandmother and you're her aunt and we have to do it up right. And there's Alice to consider."

The doorbell rang. The plumber? So quickly? But it was Mike, nice, dependable Mike. Elsie told him to go into the living room while she fetched him a beer. When she went back, Mike was looking over Isabel's shoulder at a picture in *Gourmet*.

"This is a white cake," she was saying. "Light and elegant. Do you think they want light and elegant?"

"Why don't you ask them?" He looked at the picture, three tiers of confection in ascending order of size, a tower of cake topped by two sugar dolls. "Can you really do this?"

"Anybody can follow a recipe."

"Anybody who knows what baking powder is and why sifted flour and how to separate eggs."

"I'll have to buy the right size of pans. Large, medium, small. They'll all have to be the same depth, you see. I could do it on Saturday. Then Elvira's friend has a week to ice it."

"You're a kind auntie."

"I've decided to be that."

"If you have to make an investment like that, buy those

pans I mean, it would be economically smart to make two wedding cakes."

It was weird, Elsie thought, the many different ways in which people responded to the loss of a loved one. She left Mike and Isabel on their own and went to put on her rubber gloves. *You make the mess, you clear it up.* She'd always told her children that.

&

Alec said, "I'm not waiting for them to blink, Delph. I've stood outside my mother's house and waited for the door to open. I did my best at the funeral. But they hold back from me as if I smell. I feel despised."

Delphine looked at Alec wondering how far a family could fall into the pit of dysfunction simply because each one of them felt misunderstood. "You're imposing feelings on them that might not be true. And if you don't knock or ring the bell how can your mother know you're there!"

"Elvira hasn't talked to me about the wedding. What's my role in that? The stepmother seems to be arranging it all. And she blames me for Jake's accident! How does she figure that?"

Alec sitting there was still the Alice who had laughed with her about so many things before the 'fall,' before Jake. Delphine didn't mention that Elvira's father was happily paying for the event and therefore had some rights. But before she could speak softly and kindly, a resistant voice took over and began to shout.

"For Chrissake, you're not a dummy, Alec. You're not crippled. You can move. You have some money. You've been hanging around here like a creeping limpet and you stay up too late and drink too much and you've made me drink too much and I can't get on with my work and you don't buy

groceries and if you want to talk to your family go and talk
to them. Your mother's just lost the man she was married
to for forty-five years. Your daughter's about to do something incredibly stupid and where are you? Sitting here
whining. She might not listen. None of them might listen
but you could just damn well try and talk to them, especially
to Elvira. You've been here four months now and you have
not made one shred of effort. Are you waiting for gifts?
Flowers? 'Come back dear Alice, all is forgiven?'"

Alec looked stunned for a moment and then she yelled,
"Yes!"

She got up and took her sax and slammed the door as she
left. Then she came back and said, "Limpets don't creep."

⌒

*What would you do if you had life to live over, Omar? Was
there one particular woman you would have liked to spend
your life with? Would you have refused to make below-
average films? Gone to meetings for Gamblers Anonymous?
If I had life over, I'd take it more slowly. I would, for instance,
sit and stare at a horse chestnut tree in bloom until I could
see nothing but the tree and the world became pure tree-ness.
I would 'realize' things more. And...*

"I would have more sex," she said out loud. And then
she shouted it, "I would have more sex!"

"What did you say?" Elsie had walked in to the house.
"You shouldn't leave the door unlocked, Dorothy." She was
carrying two paper cups of coffee and a bag of muffins. "I
know you haven't any cups. What are you going to do in
your apartment without china? I'll have to have a house-
warming shower for you."

"I'll buy new. I'll go to the thrift shop." Dorothy could

see from her friend's face that it might be a day for tears. "Come and sit down."

Elsie sat on the red chair in the living room, her hands folded like a nun at prayer, while Dorothy fetched paper towels to use as plates.

"I understand now," Elsie said.

Dorothy waited.

"We are all, really, always, alone. All our lives. No one understands us completely, and we understand no one else."

Richard had only been dead for a few weeks but Elsie seemed to be discounting all the years they'd lived together. She sipped at her coffee and pulled a face. "This is yours. Sugar!"

They exchanged cups and Elsie went on, "You were the smart one, Dorothy. You didn't keep those men around. You got rid of them."

"It wasn't that I didn't like them. I loved them all in their season. And one of them seems to..." She stopped, not ready yet to disclose the return of Alfred the Almost-bigamist.

"Were you sane? Was I? What were we all thinking? If I'd known what I know now, I'd have left him long ago. I would have kept on with my career. I would have been running a company of my own by the time I was forty."

"Did he really have another woman?"

"Not exactly."

Dorothy could tell that for the moment that was all the information she was going to get about Richard's perceived faults or infidelities. She wasn't about to suggest that he was gay or that, on the plus side, he was wealthy.

"Anyway, I found his opera tickets. Would you like to come to something called *Swoon* next month? It's supposed to be funny." She began to cry. At first it was just a snuffle and then she wept.

After Elsie had gone, Dorothy took some old newspaper and wrapped up the owl and the picture of Jake as a baby and put them in a box. What unhappy person was going to turn up next? When the phone rang, she expected tragedy but it was Matt in a cheerful mood. He'd gathered commissions for four more walls downtown. Admittedly all the houses were due for demolition, but it was exposure. He wanted her help.

She was about to say no, she was tired, her head ached, but if he hadn't painted the mural on the outside of the house, it might already have been torn down. He had given her a few weeks grace. The figures in the picture were not recognizable and he had at least stayed with three or four positions and had not explored the whole pantheon. Nor had they. Not with her bad knee and his bad back. But now the council had its reason to force her to leave. The wall had become notorious. A journalist had taken pictures and written it up in Tantalus. People stopped by in their cars to take photos with digital cameras and images of her house had spread out through space. Unlike her, it would have life after death. And now that he'd gotten what he wanted, was the crook Gervais, who admitted he had sent her the roses, going to come and help her write the change of address cards, call the phone company, talk to her new landlord about the blinds in the bathroom?

Another prying idiot was looking at the wall, actually coming to the door. But it was only Delphine carrying delphiniums. These particular flowers were her resistance to the idea that her mother had named her after the Delphi of oracles and gloomy seers. Her mother had loved the classics and read the *Odyssey* aloud to her children when they might have preferred *Curious George*. We have various ways of blighting kids' minds, Dorothy thought. Delphine followed her into the kitchen.

"Hell! Have they started to demolish while you're still in it?"

"That cupboard was ready to come apart."

"And what's going to happen to Matt's wall?"

"I never thought my house would be turned into a pornographic artifact."

"It's kind of attractive."

"It's going to be moved."

"He must be pleased."

"A cat with two tails. Anyway, I want to see Jake. I've got to get this begging letter out to the masses. And a form letter for people to sign to send to the government. They go on about freedom and the people having independence. Sure they're independent! Free to live without electricity, good water, proper food, jobs. They're independent as hell! It makes me sick."

"How are you – really?"

"A bit of indigestion. This diet the doctor put me on doesn't work. It might if I stuck to it. I'm fine. I'll be fine for the wedding. They really are going to get married? I thought marriage was over."

"Elvira's a romantic. And Elsie's involved. It's helping her cope with Richard's death."

"A sudden man, Richard. A sudden end. The best kind."

She looked at the flowers as if perhaps they were a harbinger.

"They must have been expensive," she said. "This time of year."

"Nothing is ever out of season now, Aunt Dorothy."

"You're right. There's no excitement about the first strawberries. Not like it used to be."

Dorothy accepted the bouquet for what it was.

"Jake is better?"

"Much better, thank you."

"He's a fine boy. I'm very fond of him." *I'm an old woman who says fond when she means love.*

"It's all right," Delphine said. And Dorothy understood not so much that she was forgiven but that she was no longer blamed. Forgiveness would follow in time.

"Was he disappointed? I mean did he mind dreadfully? Did you?"

"Too many questions in a row, Auntie. Elvira felt guilty about the accident and her way of making herself feel better was to have sex with him. I'm not saying Jake was unhappy about that! And now, well, I suppose it was a bit of a shock but he's got used to the idea. As for me, I'm not ready to be desperate for grandchildren. And she's a nice kid but."

"Not good enough for your boy?"

Delphine laughed. "At the moment, she's wondering if she can persuade Alec to wear a dress when Alistair's parents arrive. You know what Brits can be like."

"I think Alec should give Elvira away. She and her father, dressed alike, should walk her up the aisle between them. I'll tell her that."

"Don't you dare, Aunt Dorothy!"

"It would make a lovely photo."

"I've got to get to the airport. How am I going to recognize these people?"

"They'll probably be wearing plaid hats."

"It's a direct flight from Glasgow. All the passengers will be wearing plaid hats."

When Delphine had gone, Dorothy called Kate but there was no reply. She wanted to talk about Elsie's odd statement. Friends should always be at home when you want to talk to them. That was the point of Omar. He was always there. She left a message on Kate's machine saying: *Call me.*

So Delphine was off to the airport for the first time since she had seen her beloved child off to war. There was no disguising the fact that it was a war. They talked of peacekeeping and of rebuilding but every picture showed shattered homes, ruined streets and injured human beings.

Can we give way to despair, Omar? Do we have the right? I suppose it was desperation that made us organize the dinner. You won't be hearing from me much more, my love. The doctor says I have carpal tunnel syndrome in my right hand and tapping at the keyboard is painful. I've always been a little ambidextrous and can use a brush with my other hand so I'll paint instead. In case you're wondering, I have no idea of moving in with Alfred Sparrow. But I will see him now and then. Do I regret all the years we might have spent together? Yes, Omar. Yes I do. That's the truth. A long blue streak of regret runs through my soul when I think about it so I'll try not to. But, you know something, even as I'm writing this, I'm making up my mind to go to France with him.

Little Elvira would likely never look as glamorous as this again. The beige silk gown, tight at the waist and flowing down to the floor gave her a Tennysonian look. Her father's arm was shaking as he walked his daughter down the aisle. Her mother was in the far corner playing an offbeat variation of 'Here comes the bride' on her alto sax. Her stepmother had made the bouquet of yellow and white roses. Everybody loved the princess.

The princess was possibly wishing she were a virgin, a Victorian maiden approaching her new husband with feelings of dread and desire, walking into the unknown, shivering with pleasurable terror. The aisle of the chapel was short and all the people on either side must know that she was not pure, not simple. Therefore, this had to be about love. Still she seemed unsure. Alistair in his kilt and jacket and Jake in a dark suit were standing side by side at the altar. Both of them turned towards her.

Guilt moved her first towards Jake, but then she turned to her bridegroom and smiled at him because there was no going back now.

In the front row, his parents and his uncle did not look happy. There had been a suddenness, a lack of reflection about this arrangement. And had their son stolen his friend's love? What kind of girl was she if she would so easily give up one man for another? Was fickleness ingrained in her nature? They were not prepared to love her yet, pretty though she was. They would need proof of her character. It could take time.

"I wish she wasn't doing this," Elsie murmured.

"It's too late for just impediments," Dorothy whispered. "I wish I'd known what I know now."

"Sssssh!"

Elsie's granddaughter had chosen a future in a country she knew very little about on the promise of a castle that might exist only in the air.

Let the child have her day, for better, for worse.

They'd gone for tradition and the usual words were spoken, except for "obey." At least there appeared to be plenty of 'worldly goods' to endow upon the girl. As she was listening to the lovely words, Dorothy realized that her marriage to Dmitri Ostrevsky had been false. She was the bigamist herself after all. But time had swallowed her unwitting sin and, for better or worse, she was still technically married to Alfred Sparrow.

So soon after Richard's death, it hadn't seemed proper to rent a hall and gather a hundred and twenty people together to celebrate the union. But those who said there was no such thing as a small wedding had been wrong. The young couple had kept the number down to forty-five close friends and rel-

atives. The reception was held in a private room at the
Georgian Hotel. The tables were decorated with red and
gold. The Scottish uncle, jolly now, was toasting the happy
couple and saying, "I've been married for three decades and
every day has seemed like a year." He was swaying slightly
and began to sing, "'Ye banks and braes o bonnie Doon,
How can ye bloom sae fresh and fair.'" He sang on, becoming teary-eyed and getting angry looks from the groom's
contingent. "'Departed never to return.'" Alistair went to
him and gently made him sit down before he could start on
the next verse.

Pierre was sitting at the family table, talking to Alistair's
parents as if he'd known them forever. He had moved in,
was included in the wedding photographs and had perhaps
found what he'd been seeking for a long time: a family, a
home, a companion. He and Kate were going to find a big-
ger apartment and run the publishing company together.
He'd come to Toronto in search of Isabel and found an older
woman. And Kate was happy.

The DJ played the "Wedding Waltz". Dorothy could
hardly bear it. What young person knew how to dance in
three-quarter time as she and Graham J had done? One two
three four, he would whisper in her ear. One two three four.
For a brief time, they had loved. They had loved passion-
ately. And for years after he'd gone she couldn't hear a
quickstep or a foxtrot without wishing him back. She would
never tell anyone the words she had said to him that night.
She kept the secret even from herself much of the time. *He
would've done it anyway,* was her self-justifying phrase. It
was after a long exasperating night of trying to cheer him
up that she'd said, "All right. Go drown yourself then, if
that's what you want."

Matt was sitting beside her. He'd given the young couple
a bleak painting of Lake Ontario in winter as a wedding gift.

It would, he said, make Elvira feel at home in Scotland.

"I'll come and paint your new place for you, Dodo."

"I will kill you if you call me that. Anyway, I think there are rules," she said. "Only certain colours are allowed." And it came to her that she was no longer exactly free.

"Thanks to you, Dorothy, I'm getting recognition. I'm in demand."

"It wasn't me; it was my wall. I'm glad for you." She looked at his face. This late success had cheered him. He was renewed, a phoenix rising from the dusty remains of her house.

"How long have they known each other?" The question seemed to run around the room, following the young couple as they turned and turned, her dress flaring out, his kilt swinging; lovely in their youthfulness.

"Everybody!" the DJ commanded.

Jake moved onto the floor with his mother. Doug led Janine who looked on this day pleased and at home. Elsie was escorted by the uncle. Several couples now were moving in the romantic around. Isabel and Mike. Alistair's parents. As the music reached in to her and she saw Kate and Pierre getting up to join in the dance, Dorothy wanted to cry. She was alone and old and dispossessed.

And then Alec who had previously been Alice came to her and said, "May I have the pleasure?"

As the younger woman led her around the floor, Dorothy remembered the way of it, where to put her feet, how to turn without getting dizzy. She could have believed Graham was there again. With no warning, the music changed and the bodies separated and began a kind of waving, back and forth insect-mating ritual that seemed to have no romance, no connection to love.

"I'd like to sit down now," she said. "Thank you, Alec. Your daughter looks lovely."

"If I'd..."

"No," Dorothy said. "They do what they do, whatever. It might be just fine. He seems to be worthy. She needs an adventure."

"It rains in Scotland." Tears were rolling down Alec's face. Elvira came to the table and sat down beside her. They hugged each other. Dorothy took Alistair to the window to point out the landmarks of the city.

When the music stopped, Isabel's cake, unsteady beneath the weight of Jen's icing, was cut and handed around.

"She's an odd girl. Fanciful, Elsie, your granddaughter."

"She's grown up a fair bit since she nearly killed poor Jake."

"Not on purpose," Jake's grandmother said.

"Accidents," Dorothy put in, and stopped. There was no good way to continue with that.

Here they were, the three of them, like the good or bad godmothers at the feast, looking on, eating their sweet treat, considering the bridegroom.

"Nice legs," Kate said.

"I like to see a man in knee socks," Dorothy agreed.

"What do we know about him except that he's hand-some?" Elsie said. "I can't help worrying."

"If we'd known what any of them were like, would we have ever married?" Kate asked. "My Robert? Graham and your other two, Dorothy? Richard? I've certainly regretted it."

"Come on," Dorothy said. "There were good years. There was dancing. There was sex. There was laughter. There was talk. Someone listening some of the time."

They pondered this and then Elsie whispered, "Richard liked wearing women's underwear."

"You're kidding," Dorothy said.

"I suppose it's not a terrible crime. It was the shock of finding the stockings, panties, a garter belt for god's sake.

A blue garter belt. No goddam taste even. I'm just glad I was sorting out his clothes by myself. What if Isabel or Alice had been there?"

"They might have laughed," Kate said, laughing.

"I think they should keep a decent image of their father. I'll never tell them."

"You're a good woman, Elsie."

"Richard's other woman was himself." Elsie stuck her chin out and smiled a heart-breaking smile. "Come on, girls, we should mingle."

Dorothy felt disinclined to move. The cake was rich and not going down easily. She felt uncomfortable, fearing an onset of the pain that now and then attacked her. She watched her two brave friends move away. Elsie with her head held high, wearing exactly the right grandmother-of-the-bride outfit in shades of blue. Kate in a green linen dress and jacket, grandmother of the jilted lover. Both of them were coping with the last stage of life in different ways. Elsie had discovered that Richard was a man with a little secret. They all had secrets – men. You just never knew what the secret might be. Or if in the end it mattered. And Kate was moving into uncharted territory but had given up on her dream Islands since she'd discovered that cruise ships stopped there.

Isabel came to sit with her. "Are you all right, Aunt Dorothy?"

"As right as I'll ever be."

"I saw you three standing here, picking the whole thing over."

"We were talking about marriage as a concept."

"Mike and I are going to marry after Christmas."

"Really?"

"I don't like the sound of that."

"I'm sure you've thought it through, dear."

Dorothy let herself into her new home, too wired to make a cup of tea or even pour herself a drink. The funeral, the wedding. The whole of the last few months had been like a circus parade going by, the animals, the acrobats, the high-wire acts, the fire-eaters. An invisible ringmaster had arranged it all according to his whim. And now that stranger, her husband, kept calling to ask when she would set out for France with him.

She sat down at the computer, still in her wedding outfit. The wedding, unlike the funeral, was the end of a period. A watershed. Between them, the three friends only had four grandchildren. Two of Kate's were far away. Elvira had now married and was about to leave the country, and Jake was learning to speak Pashtun. They had constructed an inverse pyramid leaving fewer people behind.

She herself was a motherless child and a childless woman. She hadn't felt the real sting of it often during her life, only now and then. But it was all right, it had been all right, because she had friends and had always felt the necessity of going on from day to day and now she had her book to look forward to. Pierre had apologized for the delay but promised that when he returned from visiting his sister in Montreal, he would bring her the first copies of *That Said* Meanwhile, she and Kate had to arrange some project to involve Elsie, who needed taking out of herself.

Dear Omar,

Thank you for listening to me. Not that you really have. But I think you would have, had I ever had a chance to talk to you. I chose you for my one-sided correspondence because of your looks, your apparent sympathy and your worldliness. My brother-in-law turned out to have an odd hobby by the way. It makes me wonder if you too – but it's none of my business. At any rate, he kindly left me a little money. If I come to Paris, I'd have a chance to visit you, but I don't think I could stand the letdown if you turned out to be ill-mannered or treated me in an offhand way. And I won't go to Egypt where, possibly, there is a plaque on the wall of the house in Cairo where you grew up. I've had enough of deserts. The desert nearly killed Kate's grandson.

I see from the newspaper that you plan to make another movie with Peter O'Toole. I could have written to him, I suppose, but he is thin and edgy and his accent is too British. The journalist wrote that you received three thousand proposals of marriage in one week. I wonder which week that was. Did the prospective brides all turn up in person? It must have felt like a swarm of locusts.

So you have your plan, you two old men. I hope the movie is a smash hit, though even before you've made it the critics sound doubtful. And my plan for the future, in case you're interested, is as follows: I'm going to tidy up the WANT files and hand over the work to Elvira's friend Jennifer. Maybe after the book comes out, I will take a trip. Alone? Perhaps not.

One thing about life, as you know from the movie that made you famous – there is always love, even in times of great destruction. Goodbye, my dear.

Affectionately, Dorothy

Chapter 11

A GLASS OF SPARKLING WINE was put into her hand and, as she floated into the room, the side panels of her filmy blue dress flared out behind her. Copies of her book were piled high on the table beside the podium. Dorothy knew she was dreaming. It was a dream within a dream. She squeezed the arm of the person who handed her the glass to get a sense of reality and the person said, "Don't do that," in Kate's voice.

Pierre, who was fading in and out like a man in an old movie, got up and announced, "It's my great pleasure to introduce the author tonight."

So it's night, Dorothy thought.

"I little suspected when I met Isabel Edwards in Paris that I would become intimately involved with this extended family." He smiled at Kate. "Two weddings and a funeral and one fine book later, here we are to congratulate Dorothy Graham on her writing and on her wisdom."

I am a wise woman after all.

He pointed at her and Dorothy obediently went to stand behind the lectern. Applause shook the room. She flicked through the pages of her life trying to decide which letter would most please her audience. Names and paragraphs leapt out at her as if to say, "Pick me." *Dear Dr. Morgentaler,* she had written, thirty years before, *I am sorry you are being persecuted for your work on behalf of women and I want you to know that my friends and I...* Perhaps not that just now. *To the late Lester B. Pearson, In the section of heaven reserved for blessed peacemakers, you are probably arguing about what is happening here below...*

Marlene was murmuring in her ear, " Me me me! 'It took more than one man to change my name'..."

Dorothy looked up and set the book aside and began, '"Dear Mr. Sharif, It's your birthday today, so I thought I would write.'"

There was a murmur from those who'd read the manuscript and knew he was not included.

"We have known each other for a very long time," she said.

In his own sexy voice, he replied, *And both of us have caused a certain amount of chaos.*

She acknowledged that and went on, " That's true, Omar, we have had our effect on the world."

She looked at the faces in front of her. Women mostly and a few men. Leaning against the wall at the back, smiling at her, was a familiar young man in a new uniform. As she stared at them the faces multiplied, row upon row, until there were thousands and the walls of the room expanded to accommodate all those who had come to listen to her: To Dorothy Graham, nee Bowles, later Sparrow, briefly Ostrevsky and still, as it turned out, Sparrow.

"I had a long working life. Some days interesting, some boring. Same somehow with my sex life. And perhaps with yours." She ignored the crude laughter and heard herself say boldly as she thought of the crocodile hunter and the racing car driver, "And I am now doing what I like best."

Acknowledgements

I AM DEEPLY GRATEFUL to Edna Alford for her insightful reading of the manuscript and for her dedicated editorial care. My thanks also to everyone involved at Coteau Books for their thoughtful attention to the novel.

I would like, too, to thank Ron and Pat Smith for their helpful comments on an earlier draft.

The first letter to Omar was included in *The Magician's Beautiful Assistant* (short story collection), Hedgerow Press, 2005.

The full account of Isabel's trip to Paris was published as *The Woman Who Drowned in Lake Geneva*, in The Malahat Review (#141 2002). That story was also included in *The Magician's Beautiful Assistant*, Hedgerow Press, 2005.

About the Author

Photo by Tony Bounsall

RACHEL WYATT is a prolific and award-winning author of novels, short fiction, stage and radio plays and non-fiction works. Her six novels include *The String Box, Foreign Bodies,* and *Time's Reach.* Her stage plays, including *Crackpot* and *Knock, Knock* have been produced across Canada and in the US and the UK. She has also had over 100 plays produced by CBC and BBC radio, and monologues and scenes from her works have been included in many anthologies, most recently in the *Oxford Book of Stories by Canadian Women.*

Rachel Wyatt immigrated to Canada with her family in 1957. She was Director of the Writing Program at the Banff Centre for the Arts during the 1990s and has appeared at writers' conferences across Canada and internationally. She has won the CBC Literary Competition Drama Award and was awarded the Order of Canada in 2002 and the Queen's Jubilee Medal in 2003.

Mixed Sources

Cert no. SW-COC-001271
© 1996 FSC

FSC